ALSO BY BRITTAINY CHERRY

THE ELEMENTS SERIES
The Air He Breathes
The Fire Between High & Lo
The Silent Waters
The Gravity of Us

THE Gravity OF Us

THE ELEMENTS SERIES

THE
Gravity
OF
Us

BRITTAINY CHERRY

sourcebooks
casablanca

Published by Sourcebooks Casablanca, an imprint of Sourcebooks
P.O. Box 4410, Naperville, Illinois 60567-4410
(630) 961-3900
sourcebooks.com

Originally self-published in 2017 by Brittainy Cherry.

Cataloging-in-Publication Data is on file with the Library of Congress.

Printed and bound in the United States of America.
PAH 10 9 8 7 6 5 4 3 2 1

To love,
and all the heartache that weighs it down.

To love,
and all the heartbeats that lift it up.

Dear Reader

May you feel
the magic
of this love
story.

Maktub,

♥ BC
xo

PROLOGUE
Lucy

2015

Before Mama passed away years ago, she left three gifts for my sisters and me. On my sister Mari's front porch sat the wooden rocking chair Mama gave her. Mari received the rocking chair because Mama worried that her mind was always on the go. Mari was the middle child and had a way of constantly feeling as if she was missing out on something in life, which led to her oftentimes living in limbo. "If you don't stop overthinking things, you're going to put your brain into overdrive, baby girl. It's okay to go slower sometimes," Mama would say to her. The rocking chair was a reminder for Mari to slow down and take a few moments to embrace life, to not let it pass her by.

Our oldest sister, Lyric, received a small music box with a dancing ballerina. When we were children, Lyric dreamed of being a dancer, but over the years, she packed that dream away. After growing up with Mama, who was a lifelong wild child, Lyric began to resent the idea of a career based on passion. Mama lived her life in the most passionate way, and at times, that meant we didn't know where our next meal would be coming from. When the rent was due, we'd be packed up and off on our next adventure.

Lyric and Mama fought all the time. I believed my sister felt responsible for us all, feeling as if she had to mother her own mother. Mari and I were young and free, and we loved the adventures, but Lyric hated them. She hated not having a solid place to call home, hated the fact that Mama had no structure in her life. She hated that her freedom was her cage. When the opportunity came for Lyric to leave, she left our side and went off to become a fancy lawyer. I never knew what happened to the small music box, but I hoped Lyric still held on to it. *Always dance, Lyric*, Mama used to say to my sister. *Always dance.*

My gift from Mama was her heart.

It was a tiny heart-shaped gem she'd worn around her neck since she was a teenager, and I felt honored to receive it from her. "It's the heart of our family," she told me. "From one wild one to another, may you never forget to love fully, my Lucille. I'll need you to keep our family together and be there for your sisters during the hard times, okay? You'll be their strength. I know you will because you already love so loudly. Even the darkest souls can find some kind of light from your smile. You'll protect this family, Lucy, I know you will, and that's why I'm not afraid to say goodbye."

The necklace hadn't left my neck since Mama passed away years ago, but that summer afternoon, I held it tighter in my hand as I stared at Mari's rocking chair. After Mama's death, Mari was shaken to her core, and every belief she'd been taught about spirituality and freedom felt like a lie.

"She was too young," Mari told me the day Mama passed away.

She believed we were supposed to have time that was closer to forever. "It's not fair," she cried.

I was only eighteen when she passed, and Mari was twenty. At the time, it felt like the sun had been stolen away from us, and we didn't have a clue how to move forward.

"Maktub," I whispered, holding her close. The word was tattooed on both of our wrists, meaning "it is written." Everything in life happened for a reason, happened exactly how it was meant to, no matter how painful it seemed. Some love stories were meant to be forever and others just for a season. What Mari had forgotten was that the love story between a mother and daughter was always there, even when the seasons changed.

Death wasn't something that could alter that kind of love, but after Mama passed away, Mari let go of her free-spirited nature, met a boy, and planted her roots in Wauwatosa, Wisconsin—all in the name of love.

Love.

The emotion that made people both soar and crash. The feeling that lit humans up and burned their hearts. The beginning and ending of every journey.

When I moved in with Mari and her husband, Parker, I knew it wouldn't be a permanent situation, but I was completely thrown off when I caught him leaving that afternoon. The late summer air was sharp with the scent of autumn's chill waiting in the shadows. Parker hadn't heard me walk up behind him—he was too busy tossing a few pieces of luggage into his gray sedan.

Between his tight lips sat two toothpicks, and his navy blue designer suit lay perfectly flat against his skin with his folded handkerchief in the left breast pocket of his blazer. When the day came for him to die, I was certain he'd want to be buried with all his hand-kerchiefs. It was an odd obsession of his, along with his collection of socks. I'd never seen someone iron so many handkerchiefs and socks before I met Parker Lee. He told me it was a common practice, but his definition of *common* differed from mine.

For example, having pizza five days a week was a common practice to me, while Parker saw it as unnecessary carbohydrates. That should've been a big warning sign when I first met him. He had many red flags along the way. A man who didn't like pizza, tacos, or pajamas on Sunday afternoons wasn't someone who was meant to cross my path.

He bent forward into his trunk and started shifting his suitcases around to make more room.

"What are you doing?" I asked.

My voice threw him off-kilter, and he jumped a few inches into the air, banging his head against the hood. "*Shit!*" He stood up and rubbed the back of his head. "Jesus, Lucy. I didn't see you there." His hands ran through his dirty-blond hair before he stuffed them into his slacks. "I thought you were at work."

"The boys' dad came home early," I said, referring to my nanny job as my eyes stared at the trunk of his car. "Do you have a work conference or something? You should've called me. I could've come back to—"

"Does that mean you're losing pay for today?" he asked, cutting me off and avoiding my question. "How are you going to help with everything? With the bills? Why didn't you pick up more hours at the coffee shop?" Sweat dripped from his forehead as the summer sun beat down on our skin.

"I quit the coffee shop weeks ago, Parker. I wasn't exactly bringing home the bacon. Plus, I figured if you were working, I could be helping more here."

"Jesus, Lucy. That's so like you. How could you be so irresponsible? Especially with everything going on." He started pacing, tossing his hands around in anger, pissing and moaning, confusing me more and more each second.

"What exactly *is* going on?" I stepped toward him. "Where are you going, Parker?"

He stood still, and his eyes grew heavy. Something shifted inside him. His state of annoyance transformed to reveal his hidden remorse. "I'm sorry."

"Sorry?" My chest tightened. "For what?" I didn't know why, but my chest began to cave in as an avalanche of emotions overtook my mind. I was already predicting the doom of his next chosen words. My heart was set to break.

"I can't do it anymore, Lucy. I just can't do it."

The way the words burned from his lips made my skin crawl. He said it as if he felt guilty, but the bags in his car showed that even with that guilt, he'd decided. In his mind, he was far gone.

"She's getting better," I said, my voice shaky with unease and fear.

"It's too much. I can't… She's…" He sighed and brushed the back of his palm against his temple. "I can't stay and watch her die."

"Then stay and see her live."

"I can't sleep. I haven't eaten in days. My boss is getting on my case because I'm falling behind, and I can't lose that job, especially with the medical expenses. I worked too hard to get everything I have, and I can't lose it because of this. I can't sacrifice anymore. I'm tired, Lucy."

I'm tired, Lucy.

How dare he use those words? How dare he claim to be exhausted as if he were the one going through the hardest fight of his life? "We're all tired, Parker. We're all dealing with this. I moved in with you two so I could look after her, to make it easier for you, and now you're just giving up on her? On your marriage?" No words from him. My heart… it cracked. "Does she know? Did you tell her you're leaving?"

"No." He shook his head sheepishly. "She doesn't know. I figured this would be easiest. I don't want her to worry."

I huffed, shocked by the lies he was throwing my way, even more stunned by how he somehow believed those words to be true.

"I'm sorry. I left some money on the table in the foyer. I'll check in with you to make sure she's okay, to make sure she's comfortable. I can even wire you more money if you need it."

"I don't want your money," I said, my voice unsympathetic to his pained expression. "We don't need anything from you."

He parted his lips to speak but shut them quickly, unable to form any sentences that could make the situation any easier. I watched every step he took to reach his driver's side door, and when he did, I called his name. He didn't turn to look at me, but his ears perked up, waiting.

"If you leave my sister right now, you don't get to come back. You don't get to call when you're drunk or check in when you're sad. When she beats this cancer—which she *will*—you don't get to step back in and pretend you love her. Do you understand?"

"I do."

Those two words were the same he'd used to promise himself to Mari in sickness and in health. Those two words were now forever drenched in agony and filthy lies.

He stepped into his car before driving off without once hitting his brakes. I stayed in the driveway for a few moments, unsure of how to walk inside and tell my sister that her husband had abandoned her during her storm.

My heart cracked again.

My heart broke for my sister, the innocent one in a world full of ruthlessness. She'd given up her free-spirit life to live a more structured one, and both worlds had turned against her.

I took a deep breath and placed the palm of my hand around my heart-shaped necklace.

Maktub.

Instead of running like Parker, I went to see Mari. She was lying in her bed resting. I smiled her way, and she smiled back at me. She was so skinny, her body pushing each day to fight against expiration. Her head was wrapped in a scarf, her once-long brunette hair now nothing more than a memory. It made her sad at times, staring into the mirror, but she didn't see what I saw. She was so beautiful, even in sickness. Her true glow couldn't be stolen away by such changes to her body, because her beauty stemmed from her soul, where only goodness and light resided.

She'd be okay. I knew she would, because she was a fighter.

Hair grew back, bones regained strength, and my sister's heart was still beating, which was reason enough to celebrate each day.

"Hey, Pea," I whispered, hurrying over to the bed and crawling into it to lie beside her. I lay on my side, and she turned on hers to face me.

Even in her weakness, she found a way to smile each day. "Hey, Pod."

"There's something I need to tell you."

She shut her eyes. "He's gone."

"You knew?"

"I saw him packing when he thought I was sleeping." Tears started rolling from the corners of her eyes, which she kept closed. For a while, we just lay there. Her sadness became my tears, and her tears articulated my sadness.

"Do you think he'll miss me when I die?" she asked me. Whenever she brought up death, I wanted to curse the universe for hurting my best friend, my family.

"Don't say that," I scolded.

"But do you think he will?" She opened her eyes, reached across to me, and held my hands in hers. "Remember when we were kids and I had that awful dream about Mama dying? I spent the whole day crying, and then she gave us all a talk about death? About how it isn't the end of the journey?"

I nodded. "Yes, she told us we'd see her in everything—the sunbeams, the shadows, the flowers, the rain. She said death doesn't kill us; it only awakens us to more."

"Do you ever see her?" she whispered.

"Yes, in everything. In absolutely everything."

A small whimper fell from her lips, and she nodded. "Me too, but mostly I see her in you."

Those words were the kindest I'd ever had delivered to me. I missed Mama every second of every day, and to have Mari say she saw her within me meant more than she'd ever know. I moved in closer to her and wrapped her in a hug. "He'll miss you. He'll miss you while you're alive and healthy, and he'll miss you when you're a part of the trees. He'll miss you tomorrow, and he'll miss you when you become the wind brushing against his shoulder. The world's going to miss you, Mari, even though you'll still be here for many years to come. The second you're better, we're going to open our flower shop, okay? You and me, we're going to do it."

All our lives, my sister and I had been in love with nature. We always had a dream to open a floral shop and even went so far as to attend the Milwaukee School of Flower Design. We each earned degrees in business so we'd have all the knowledge available to us. If it weren't for the cancer, we would've had our shop. So once the cancer was gone, I planned to do everything in my power to bring that shop to life.

"Okay, Mari? We're going to do that," I said once more, hoping to sound more convincing, hoping to bring her ease.

"Okay," she said, but her voice dripped with doubt. Her brown doe eyes, which were shaped like Mama's, were filled with the deepest look of sorrow. "Can you get the jar? And the bag of coins?"

I sighed but agreed. I hurried to the living room, where we'd left the jar and the bag of change sitting the night before. The mason jar was wrapped with pink and black ribbon, and it was almost full of coins. We had started the jar when Mari was diagnosed seven months ago. The jar had the letters *NT* written on the side, which stood for *negative thoughts*. Whenever one of us had a bad thought race through our minds, we'd place a coin in the jar. Every negative thought was leading to a beautiful outcome—Europe. Once Mari was better, we'd use the money to go toward us backpacking across Europe, a dream we'd always wanted to bring to life.

For every present negative thought, the coins were a reminder of better tomorrows.

We had eight jars filled to the top already.

I sat back down on Mari's bed, and she pushed herself up a bit, then grabbed the bag of change.

"Pod," she whispered.

"Yes, Pea?"

Tears raced down her cheeks faster and faster as her small frame was overtaken by emotion. "We're going to need more change."

She poured all the coins into the jar, and when she finished, I wrapped her up in my arms where she continued to fall apart. They had been married and healthy for five years, and it only took seven months of sickness to make Parker vanish, leaving my poor sister brokenhearted.

"Lucy?" I heard as I sat on the front porch. I'd been sitting in the rocking chair for the past hour as Mari rested, trying my best to understand how everything that unfolded was destined to happen. When I looked up, I saw Richard, my boyfriend, hurrying my way as he leaped off his bicycle and then leaned it against the porch. "What's going on? I got your text message." Richard's shirt was covered in paint as always, a result of him being the creative artist he was. "I'm sorry I didn't answer your calls. My phone was on mute while I drank my sorrows away about being denied an invite to yet another art gallery." He walked up to me and kissed my forehead. "What's going on?" he asked again.

"Parker left."

It only took two words for Richard's mouth to drop. I filled him in on everything, and the more I said, the more he gasped. "Are you kidding? Is Mari okay?"

I shook my head. Of course she wasn't.

"We should get inside," he said, reaching for my hand, but I declined.

"I have to call Lyric. I've been trying to for hours, but she hasn't answered. I'm just going to keep trying for a while. Do you think you can go check on Mari and see if she needs anything?"

He nodded. "Of course."

I reached out and wiped some yellow paint from his cheek before leaning in to kiss him. "I'm sorry about the gallery."

Richard grimaced and shrugged. "It's okay. As long as you're okay with dating a turd who's not good enough for his work to be showcased, then I'm okay with it."

I'd been with Richard for three years now, and I couldn't imagine being with anyone other than him. I just hated how the world hadn't given him a chance to shine yet; he was worthy of success.

But until it came, I'd stand by his side, being his biggest cheerleader.

As he went inside, I dialed Lyric's number one more time.

"Hello?"

"Lyric, finally." I sighed, sitting up straighter as I heard my sister's voice for the first time in a long time. "I've been trying to reach you all day."

"Well, not everyone can be Mrs. Doubtfire and work part-time at a coffee shop, Lucy," she said, her sarcasm loud and clear.

"I actually only nanny now. I quit the coffee shop."

"*Shocking,*" she replied. "Listen, do you need something, or were you just bored and decided to call me repeatedly?"

Her tone was the same one I'd known for most of my life—complete disappointment in my entire existence. Lyric had a way of putting up with Mari's quirks, especially since Mari had finally settled down with Parker. Lyric was, after all, the one who introduced the couple to each other. When it came to my relationship with my eldest sister, it was the complete opposite. I often thought she hated me because I reminded her too much of our mother.

As time went by, I realized she hated me because I was nothing more than myself.

"Yeah, no. It's Mari."

"Is she okay?" she asked, her voice drenched with fake concern. I could hear her still typing away on her computer, working late into the night. "She's not…?"

"Dead?" I huffed. "No, she's not, but Parker left today."

"Left? What do you mean?"

"He just left. He packed his bags, said he couldn't deal with watching her die, and drove away. He left her alone."

"Oh my God. That's intense."

"Yeah, I agree."

There was a long moment of silence and me listening to her type before she spoke again. "Well, did you piss him off or something?"

I stopped rocking in the chair. "What?"

"Come on, Lucy. Since you moved in to help, I'm sure you haven't been the easiest person to live with. You're a lot to handle." She somehow managed to do what she always did when I was involved in any situation—she made me the villain. She said it was my fault a coward walked out on his wife.

I swallowed hard and ignored her comment. "I just wanted you to know, that's all."

"Is Parker okay?"

What? "I think what you meant to say was 'Is Mari okay? and no, she's not. She's dealing with cancer, her husband just left her, and she hardly has a penny to her name, let alone the strength to keep going."

"Ah, there it is," Lyric murmured.

"There what is?"

"You're calling me for money. How much do you need?"

My stomach knotted at her words, and a taste of disgust spread on my tongue. She thought I'd called her because I wanted money. "I called you because your sister is hurting and feels alone, and I thought you might want to come see her and make sure she's okay. I don't want your money, Lyric. I want you to start acting like a freaking sister."

Another moment of silence passed, along with more typing.

"Look, I'm swamped at work. I have these cases coming up for the firm, and I can't be pulled away from them right now. There's no way I'd be able to stop by her place until maybe next week or the week after."

Lyric lived downtown—a short twenty-minute drive away—but still, she was convinced it was too far away.

"Never mind, okay? Just pretend I never called." My eyes watered, shocked by the coldness of someone I'd once looked up to in my life. DNA told me she was my sister, but the words she spoke conveyed that she was nothing more than a stranger.

"Stop it, Lucy. Stop with the passive-aggressive approach. I'll drop a check in the mail tomorrow, all right?"

"Don't, seriously. We don't need your money, and we don't need your support. I don't even know why I called you. Just mark it down as a low point of mine. Goodbye, Lyric. Good luck with your cases."

"Yeah, okay. And, Lucy?"

"Yeah?"

"You might want to get that coffee job back as soon as possible."

After a while, I stood up from the rocking chair and walked to the guest room, where I'd been staying. I shut the bedroom door, held my hand around my necklace, and shut my eyes. "Air above me, earth below me, fire within me, water surround me..." I took deep breaths and kept repeating the words Mama had taught me. Whenever she'd lose her balance in life and feel far from grounded, she'd repeat that chant, finding her inner strength.

Even though I repeated the words, I felt like a failure.

My shoulders drooped, and my tears began to fall as I spoke to the only woman who had ever truly understood me. "Mama, I'm scared, and I hate it. I hate that I'm afraid, because that means I'm somewhat thinking what Parker was thinking. A part of me feels like she won't make it, and I just feel terrified each day."

There was something so heartbreaking about watching your best friend fall apart. Even though I knew death was simply the next chapter in her beautiful memoir, it didn't make it any easier for me to grasp. In the back of my mind, I knew each hug could be the last, knew each word could be goodbye.

"I feel guilty, because for every good thought I have, five negative ones pass through. I have fifteen coin jars filled in my closet that Mari doesn't even know exist. I'm tired, Mama. I'm exhausted, and then I feel guilty for almost falling apart. I have to stay strong, because she doesn't need anyone falling apart around her. I know you taught us girls not to hate, but I just hate Parker. God forbid, but if these are Mari's last days, I hate that he tainted them. Her final days shouldn't be filled with the memory of her husband walking out on her."

It wasn't fair that Parker could pack his bags and just escape to a new life without my sister. He might find love again someday, but what about Mari? He'd be the love of her life, and that hurt me more than she'd ever know. I knew my sister like the back of my hand, knew how gentle her heart was. She felt every hurt ten times more than most people. Her heart resided on her sleeve, and she allowed everyone to listen to its beautiful heartbeat—even those who were undeserving of hearing the sound. She prayed they loved her heart's sound too. She always wanted to feel loved, and I hated that Parker made her feel like a failure. She'd leave the world feeling as if she had somehow failed her marriage, all in the name of love.

Love.

The emotion that made people both soar and crash. The feeling that lit humans up and burned their hearts. The beginning and ending of every journey.

As the days, months, and years passed by, Mari and I heard less and less from both Parker and Lyric. The pity check-ins grew less frequent, and the guilt-driven checks stopped coming through the mail. When the divorce papers landed in the mailbox, Mari cried for weeks. I stood strong for her in the light, and teared up for her heart in the shadows.

It wasn't fair how the world took Mari's health and then had the nerve to come back to make sure her heart was shattered into a trillion pieces too. With every inhale, she cursed her body for betraying her and ruining the life she'd built. With every exhale, she prayed for her husband to return home.

I never told her, but with every inhale, I begged for her healing, and with every exhale, I prayed for her husband to never come back.

CHAPTER 1

Graham

2017

Two days before, I'd bought flowers for someone who wasn't my wife. Since the purchase, I hadn't left my office. Papers were scattered all around—note cards, Post-it notes, crumpled pieces of paper with pointless scribbles and words crossed out. On my desk sat five bottles of whisky and an unopened box of cigars.

My eyes burned from exhaustion, but I couldn't shut them as I stared blankly in front of me at my computer screen, typing words I'd later delete.

I never bought my wife flowers.

I never gave her chocolates on Valentine's, I found stuffed animals ridiculous, and I didn't have a clue what her favorite color was.

She didn't have a clue what mine was either, but I knew her favorite politician. I knew her views on global warming, she knew my views on religion, and we both knew our views on children: we never wanted them.

Those things were what we agreed mattered the most; those things were our glue. We were both driven by career and had little time for each other, let alone family.

I wasn't romantic, and Jane didn't mind because she wasn't either. We weren't often seen holding hands or exchanging kisses in public. We weren't into snuggling or social media expressions of love, but that didn't mean our love wasn't real. We cared in our own way. We were a logical couple who understood what it meant to be in love, to be committed to each other, yet we never truly dived into the romantic aspects of a relationship.

Our love was driven by a mutual respect, by structure. Each big decision we made was always thoroughly thought out and often involved diagrams and charts. The day I asked her to be my wife, we made fifteen pie and flow charts to make sure we were making the right decision.

Romantic?

Maybe not.

Logical?

Absolutely.

Which was why her current invasion of my deadline was concerning. She never interrupted me while I was working, and for her to barge in while I was on a deadline was beyond bizarre.

I had ninety-five thousand more to go.

Ninety-five thousand words to go before the manuscript went to the editor in two weeks. Ninety-five thousand words equated to an average of six thousand seven hundred eighty-six words a day. That meant the next two weeks of my life would be spent in front of my computer, hardly pulling myself away for a breath of fresh air.

My fingers were on speed, typing and typing as fast as they could.

The purplish bags under my eyes displayed my exhaustion, and my back ached from not leaving my chair for hours. Yet when I sat in front of my computer with my drugged-up fingers and zombie eyes, I felt more like myself than any other time in my life.

"Graham," Jane said, breaking me from my world of horror and bringing me into hers. "We should get going."

She stood in the doorway of my office. Her hair was curly, which was bizarre seeing as how her hair was always straight. Each day, she awoke hours before me to tame the curly blond mop on her head. I could count on my right hand the number of times I'd seen her with her natural curls. Along with the wild hair, her makeup was smudged, left on from the night before.

I'd only seen my wife cry two times since we'd been together: one time when she learned she was pregnant seven months ago, and another when some bad news came in four days ago.

"Shouldn't you straighten your hair?" I asked.

"I'm not straightening my hair today."

"You always straighten your hair."

"I haven't straightened my hair in four days." She frowned, but I didn't make a comment about her disappointment. I didn't want to deal with her emotions that afternoon. For the past four days, she'd been a wreck, the opposite of the woman I married, and I wasn't one to deal with people's emotions.

What Jane needed to do was pull herself together.

I went back to staring at my computer screen, and my fingers started moving quickly once more.

"Graham," she grumbled, waddling over to me with her very pregnant stomach. "We have to get going."

"I have to finish my manuscript."

"You haven't stopped writing for the past four days. You hardly make it to bed before three in the morning, and then you're up by six. You need a break. Plus, we can't be late."

I cleared my throat and kept typing. "I decided I'm going to have to miss out on this silly engagement. Sorry, Jane."

Out of the corner of my eye, I saw her jaw slacken. "Silly engagement? Graham…it's your father's funeral."

"You say that as if it should mean something to me."

"It does mean something to you."

"Don't tell me what does and doesn't mean something to me. It's belittling."

"You're tired," she said.

There you go again, telling me about myself. "I'll sleep when I'm eighty, or when I'm my father. I'm sure he's sleeping well tonight."

She cringed. I didn't care.

"You've been drinking?" she asked, concerned.

"In all the years of us being together, when have you ever known me to drink?"

She studied the bottles of alcohol surrounding me and let out a small breath. "I know, sorry. It's just…you added more bottles to your desk."

"It's a tribute to my dear father. May he rot in hell."

"Don't speak so ill of the dead," Jane said before hiccupping and placing her hands on her stomach. "God, I hate that feeling." She took my hands away from my keyboard and placed them on her stomach. "It's like she's kicking me in every internal organ I have. I cannot stand it."

"How motherly of you," I mocked, my hands still on her.

"I never wanted children." She breathed out, hiccupping once more. "*Ever.*"

"Yet here we are," I replied. I wasn't certain Jane had fully come to terms with the fact that in two short months, she'd be giving birth to an actual human being who would need her love and attention twenty-four hours a day.

If there was anyone who gave love less than I did, it was my wife.

"God," she murmured, closing her eyes. "It just feels weird today."

"Maybe we should go to the hospital," I offered.

"Nice try. You're going to your father's funeral."

Damn.

"We still need to find a nanny," she said. "The firm gave me a few weeks off for maternity leave, but I won't need all the time if we find a decent nanny. I'd love a little old Mexican lady, preferably one with a green card."

My eyebrows furrowed, disturbed. "You do know saying that is not only disgusting and racist, but saying it to your half-Mexican husband is also pretty distasteful, right?"

"You're hardly Mexican, Graham. You don't even speak a lick of Spanish."

"Which makes me non-Mexican. Duly noted, thank you," I said coldly. At times, my wife was the person I hated the most. While we agreed on many things, sometimes the words that left her mouth made me rethink every flowchart we'd ever made.

How could someone so beautiful be so ugly at times?

Kick.

Kick.

My chest tightened, my hands still resting around Jane's stomach.

Those kicks terrified me. If there was anything I knew for certain, it was that I was not father material. My family history led me to believe anything that came from my line of ancestry couldn't be good.

I just prayed to God that the baby wouldn't inherit any of my traits—or worse, my father's.

Jane leaned against my desk, shifting my perfectly neat paperwork as my fingers lay still against her stomach. "It's time to hop in the shower and get dressed. I hung your suit in the bathroom."

"I told you, I cannot make this engagement. I have a deadline to meet."

"While you have a deadline to meet, your father has already met his deadline, and now it's time to send off his manuscript."

"His manuscript being his casket?"

Jane's brows furrowed. "No. Don't be silly. His body is the manuscript; his casket is the book cover."

"A freaking expensive book cover too. I can't believe he picked one that is lined with gold." I paused and bit my lip. "On second thought, I easily believe that. You know my father."

"So many people will be there today. His readers, his colleagues."

Hundreds would show up to celebrate the life of Kent Russell. "It's going to be a circus," I groaned. "They'll mourn for him, in complete and utter sadness, and they'll sit in disbelief. They'll start pouring in with their stories, with their pain. 'Not Kent, it can't be. He's the reason I even gave this writing thing a chance. Five years sober because of that man. I cannot believe he's gone. Kent Theodore Russell, a man, a father, a hero. Nobel Prize winner. Dead.' The world will mourn."

"And you?" Jane asked. "What will you do?"

"Me?" I leaned back in my chair and crossed my arms. "I'll finish my manuscript."

"Are you sad he's gone?" Jane asked, rubbing her stomach.

Her question swam in my mind for a beat before I answered. "No."

I wanted to miss him.

I wanted to love him.

I wanted to hate him.

I wanted to forget him.

But instead, I felt nothing. It had taken me years to teach myself to feel nothing toward my father, to erase all the pain he'd inflicted on me, on the ones I loved the most. The only way I knew how to shut off the hurt was to lock it away and forget everything he'd ever done to me, to forget everything I'd ever wished him to be.

Once I locked the hurt away, I almost forgot how to feel completely.

Jane didn't mind my locked-away soul, because she didn't feel much either.

"You answered too quickly," she told me.

"The fastest answer is always the truest."

"I miss him," she said, her voice lowering, communicating her pain over the loss of my father. In many ways, Kent Russell was a best friend to millions through his storybooks, his inspirational speeches, and the persona and brand he sold to the world. I would've missed him too if I didn't know the man he truly was in the privacy of his home.

"You miss him because you never actually knew him. Stop moping over a man who's not worth your time."

"No," she said sharply, her voice heightened with pain. Her eyes started to water over as they'd been doing for the past few days. "You don't get to do that, Graham. You don't get to undermine my hurt. Your father was a good man to me. He was good to me when you were cold, and he stood up for you every time I wanted to leave, so you don't get to tell me to stop moping. You don't get to define the kind of sadness I feel," she said, full-blown emotion taking over her body as she shook with a flood of tears falling from her eyes.

I tilted my head toward her, confused by her sudden outburst, but then my eyes fell to her stomach.

Hormonal mess.

"Whoa," I muttered, a bit stunned.

She sat up straight. "What was that?" she asked, a bit frightened.

"I think you just had an emotional breakdown over the death of my father."

She took a breath and groaned. "Oh my God, what's wrong with me? These hormones are making me a mess. I hate everything about being pregnant. I swear I'm getting my tubes tied after this." She stood up, trying to pull herself together, and wiped away her tears as she took more deep breaths. "Can you at least do me one favor today?"

"What's that?"

"Can you pretend you're sad at the funeral? People will talk if they see you smiling."

I gave her a tight fake frown.

She rolled her eyes. "Good, now repeat after me: my father was truly loved, and he will be missed dearly."

"My father was truly a dick, and he won't be missed at all."

She patted my chest. "Close enough. Now go get dressed."

Standing up, I grumbled the whole way.

"Oh! Did you order the flowers for the service?" Jane hollered my way as I slid my white T-shirt over my head and tossed it onto the bathroom floor.

"All five thousand dollars' worth of useless plants for a funeral that will be over in a few hours."

"People will love them," she told me.

"People are stupid," I replied, stepping into the burning water falling from the showerhead. In the water, I tried my best to think of what type of eulogy I'd deliver for the man who was a hero to many but a devil to me. I tried to dig up memories of love, moments of care, seconds of pride he'd delivered me, but I came up blank. Nothing. No real feelings could be found.

The heart inside my chest—the one he'd helped harden—remained completely numb.

CHAPTER 2
Lucy

Here lies Mari Joy Palmer, a giver of love, peace, and happiness. It's a shame the way she left the world. It was sudden, unspeakable, and more painful than I'd ever thought it would be." I stared down at Mari's motionless body and wiped the back of my neck with a small towel. The early morning sun beamed through the windows as I tried my best to catch my breath.

"Death by hot yoga." Mari sighed, inhaling deeply and exhaling unevenly.

I laughed. "You're going to have to get up, Mari. They have to set up for the next class." I held my hand out toward my sister, who was lying in a puddle of sweat. "Let's go."

"Go on without me," she said theatrically, waving her invisible flag. "I surrender."

"Oh no, you don't. Come on." I grabbed her arms and pulled her to a standing position, with her resisting the whole way up. "You went through chemotherapy, Mari. You can handle hot yoga."

"I don't get it," she whined. "I thought yoga was supposed to make you feel grounded and bring about peace, not buckets of sweat and disgusting hair."

I smirked, looking at her shoulder-length hair, which was frizzy and knotted on top of her head. She'd been in remission for almost two years now, and we'd been living our lives to the fullest ever since then, including opening the flower shop.

After quick showers at the yoga studio, we headed outside, and when the summer sun kissed our skin and blinded us, Mari groaned. "Why the heck did we decide to ride our bikes here today? And why is six a.m. hot yoga even a thing we'd consider?"

"Because we care about our health and well-being and want to be in the best shape of our lives," I mocked. "Plus, the car's in the shop."

She rolled her eyes. "Is this the point where we bike to a café and get doughnuts and croissants before work?"

"Yup!" I said, unlocking my bike from the pole and hopping onto it.

"And by doughnuts and croissants, do you mean…"

"Green kale drinks? Yes, yes, I do."

She groaned again, this time louder. "I liked you better when you didn't give a crap about your health and just ate a steady diet of candy and tacos."

I smiled and started pedaling. "Race you!"

I beat her to Green Dreams—obviously—and when she made it inside, she draped her body across the front counter. "Seriously, Lucy, regular yoga, yes, but hot yoga?" She paused, taking a few deep breaths. "Hot yoga can go straight back to hell where it came from to die a long painful death."

A worker walked over to us with a bright smile. "Hey, ladies! What can I get for you?"

"Tequila, please," Mari said, finally raising her head from the countertop. "You can put it in a to-go cup if you want. Then I can drink it on the way to work."

The waitress stared at my sister blankly, and I smirked. "We'll take two green machine juices and two egg and potato breakfast wraps."

"Sounds good. Would you like whole wheat, spinach, or flaxseed wraps?" she asked.

"Oh, stuffed crust pizza will do just fine," Mari replied. "With a side of chips and queso."

"Flaxseed." I laughed. "We'll have the flaxseed."

When our food came out, we grabbed a table, and Mari dived in as if she hadn't eaten in years. "So," she started, her cheeks puffed out like a chipmunk. "How's Richard?"

"He's good," I said, nodding. "Busy but good. Our apartment currently looks like a tornado blew through it with his latest work, but he's good. Since he found out he's having a showcase at the museum in a few months, he's been in panic mode, trying to create something inspiring. He's not sleeping, but that's Richard."

"Men are weird, and I can't believe you're actually living with one."

"I know." I laughed. It had taken me years to finally move in with Richard, mainly because I didn't feel comfortable leaving Mari's side when she got sick. We'd been living together for the past four months, and I loved it. I loved him. "Remember what Mama used to say about men moving in with women?"

"Yes. The second they get comfortable enough to take their shoes off in your house and go into your fridge without asking, it's time for them to go."

"A smart woman."

Mari nodded. "I should've kept living by her rules after she passed away. Maybe then I could've avoided Parker." Her eyes grew heavy for a few seconds before she blinked away her pain and smiled. She hardly talked about Parker since he'd left her over two years ago, but whenever she did, it was as if a cloud of sadness hovered above her. She fought the cloud, though, and never let it release rain for her to wallow in. She did her best to be happy, and for the most part, she was, though there were seconds of pain sometimes.

Seconds when she remembered, seconds when she blamed herself, seconds when she felt lonely. Seconds when she allowed her heart to break before she swiftly started piecing it back together.

With every second of hurt, Mari made it her duty to find a minute of happiness.

"Well, you're living by her rules now, which is better than never, right?" I said, trying to help her get rid of the cloud above her.

"Right!" she cheered, her eyes finding their joy again.

It was odd how feelings worked, how a person could be sad one second and happy another. What amazed me the most was how a person could be both things all within the same second. I believed Mari had a pinch of both emotions in that moment, a little bit of sadness intermingled with her joy.

I thought that was a beautiful way to live.

"So shall we get to work?" I asked, standing up from my chair.

Mari moaned, annoyed, but agreed as she dragged herself back out to her bicycle and started pedaling to our shop.

Monet's Gardens was my and my sister's dream come to life. The shop was fashioned after the paintings of my favorite artist, Claude Monet. When Mari and I finally made it to Europe, I planned to spend a lot of time standing in Monet's gardens in Giverny.

Prints of his artwork were scattered around the shop, and at times, we'd shape floral arrangements to match the paintings. After we signed our lives away with bank loans, Mari and I worked our butts off to open the shop, and it came together swimmingly over time. We almost didn't even get the shop, but Mari came through with a final loan she tried for. Even though it was a lot of work and took up so much time I never even considered having a social life, I couldn't really complain about spending my days surrounded by flowers.

The building was small but big enough to have dozens of different types of flowers, like parrot tulips, lilies, poppies, and, of course, roses. We catered to all kinds of functions too; my favorites were weddings, and the worst were funerals.

Today was one of the worst, and it was my turn to drive the delivery truck to drop off the order.

"Are you sure you don't want me to do the Garrett wedding and you do the Russell funeral?" I asked, getting all the white gladiolus bulbs and white roses organized to move into the truck. The person who'd passed away must've been very loved, based on the number of arrangements ordered. There were dozens of white roses for the casket spray, five different cross easels with sashes that said FATHER across them, and dozens of random bouquets to be placed around the church.

It amazed me how beautiful flowers for such a sad occasion could be.

"No, I'm sure. I can help you load up the van though," Mari said, lifting up one of the arrangements and heading back to the alleyway where our delivery van was parked.

"If you do the funeral today, I'll stop dragging you to hot yoga each morning."

She snickered. "If I had a penny for every time I'd heard that, I'd already be in Europe."

"No, I swear! No more sweating at six in the morning."

"That's a lie."

I nodded. "Yeah, that's a lie."

"And no more putting off our trip to Europe. We are officially going next summer, right?" she asked, her eyes narrowed.

I groaned. Ever since she got sick two years ago, I'd been putting off taking our trip. My brain knew that she was better, she was healthy and strong, but a small part of my heart feared traveling so far from home with the possibility of something going wrong with her health in a different country.

I swallowed hard and agreed. She smiled wide, pleased, and walked into the back room.

"Which church am I even going to today?" I wondered out loud, jumping onto the computer to pull up the file. I paused and narrowed my eyes as I read the words: *UW-Milwaukee Panther Arena.*

"Mari," I hollered. "This says it's at the arena downtown. Is that right?"

She hurried back into the room and peered at the computer, then shrugged. "Wow. That explains all the flowers." She ran her hands through her hair, and I smiled. Every time she did that, my heart overflowed with joy. Her growing hair was a reminder of her growing life, of how lucky we were to be in the place we were. I was so happy the flowers in the truck weren't for her.

"Yeah, but who has a funeral at an arena?" I asked, confused.

"Must be someone important."

I shrugged, not thinking too much of it.

I arrived at the arena two hours before the ceremony to get everything set up, and the outside of the building was already surrounded with numerous people. I swore there had to be hundreds crowding the downtown streets of Milwaukee, and police officers paced the area.

Individuals were writing notes and posting them on the front steps; some cried while others were engaged in deep conversations.

As I drove the van around to the back to unload the flowers, I was denied access to the actual building by one of the arena workers. He pushed the door open and used his body to block my entrance. "Excuse me, you can't come in here," the man told me. "VIP access only." He had a large headset around his neck, and the way he slightly closed the door behind him to avoid me peering inside made me suspicious.

"Oh no, I'm just dropping off the flowers for the service," I started to explain, and he rolled his eyes.

"More flowers?" he groaned, and then he pointed to another door. "The flower drop-off is around the corner, third door. You can't miss it," he said flatly.

"Okay. Hey, whose funeral is this exactly?" I asked. I stood on my tiptoes and tried to get a peek of what was happening inside.

He shot me a dirty look filled with annoyance. "Around the corner," he barked before slamming the door shut.

I yanked on the door once and frowned.

Locked.

One day, I'd stop being so nosey, but obviously that day wasn't today.

I smiled to myself and mumbled, "Nice meeting you too."

When I drove the van around the corner, I realized we weren't the only floral shop who'd been contacted for this event. Three vans were in line before me, and they weren't even able to go inside the building; there were employees collecting the flower arrangements at the door. Before I could even put the car in park, workers were at the back, pounding on the back doors for me to open it up. Once I did, they started grabbing the flowers without much care, and I cringed at the way one of the women handled the white rose wreath. She tossed it over her arm, destroying the green bells of Ireland.

"Careful!" I hollered, but everyone seemed to not be listening.

When finished, they slammed my doors shut, signed my paperwork, and handed me an envelope. "What's this for?"

"Didn't they tell you already?" The woman sighed heavily, then placed her hands on her hips. "The flowers are just for show, and the son of Mr. Russell instructed that they be returned to the florists who delivered them after the service. Inside is your ticket for the event, along with a pass to get backstage afterward to collect your flowers. Otherwise, they will be tossed."

"Tossed?" I exclaimed. "How wasteful."

The woman arched an eyebrow. "Yes, because there was no possible chance the flowers wouldn't have died all on their own," she stated sarcastically. "At least now you can resell them."

Resell funeral flowers? Because that wasn't morbid.

Before I could reply, she waved me off without a goodbye.

I opened the envelope and found my ticket and a card that read, *After the service, please present this card to pick up the floral arrangements. Otherwise, they will be disposed of.*

My eyes read the ticket repeatedly.

A ticket.

For a funeral.

Never in my life had I witnessed such an odd event. When I rounded the corner to the main street, I noticed even more people had gathered around and were posting letters to the walls of the building.

My curiosity hit a new high, and after circling around a few times in search of parking, I pulled into a parking structure. I parked the van and climbed out to go see what everyone was doing there and whose funeral was taking place. As I stepped onto the packed sidewalk, I noticed a woman kneeling down, scribbling on a piece of paper.

"Excuse me," I said, tapping her on the shoulder. She looked up with a bright smile on her face. "I'm sorry to bother you, but…whose funeral is this exactly?"

She stood up, still grinning. "Kent Russell, the author."

"Oh, no way."

"Yeah. Everyone's writing their own eulogies about how he saved their lives and taping them to the side of the building to honor his memory, but between you and me, I'm most excited to see G.M. Russell. It's a shame it had to be for an event such as this one though."

"G.M. Russell? Wait, as in the greatest thriller and horror author of all time?!" I gushed, realization finally setting in. "Oh my gosh! I love G.M. Russell!"

"Wow. Took you long enough to connect those dots. At first I thought your blond hair was dyed that color, but now I see that you are actually a true-blue blond," she joked. "It's such a big event, because you know how G. M. is when it comes to public appearances—he hardly makes them. At book events, he doesn't engage with the readers except for his big fake grin, and he doesn't ever allow photographs, but today we'll be able to take pictures of him. This. Is. Big!"

"Fans were invited to attend the funeral?"

"Yeah, Kent put it in his will. All the money is being donated to a children's hospital. I got solid seats. My best friend Heather was supposed to come with me, but she went into labor. Freaking kids ruin everything."

I laughed.

"Do you want my extra ticket?" she asked. "It's super close up front. Plus, I'd rather sit beside another G. M. fan than a Papa Russell fan. You'd be shocked by how many people are here for him." She paused, cocked an eyebrow, and went digging through her purse. "On second thought, maybe not, seeing as how he was the one who croaked and all. Here you go. They're opening the doors now." She handed me her spare ticket. "Oh, and my name's Tori."

"Lucy," I said with a smile. I hesitated for a moment, thinking how weird and out of the ordinary attending a stranger's funeral in an arena was, but then again...G.M. Russell was inside that building, along with my flowers, which were going to be tossed in a few hours.

We made it to our seats, and Tori couldn't stop snapping photographs. "These are amazing seats, aren't they? I can't believe I snatched this ticket up for only two thousand!"

"Two thousand?!" I gasped.

"I know, right? Such a steal, and all I had to do was sell my kidney on Craigslist to some dude named Kenny."

She turned to the older gentleman sitting on her left. He had to be in his late seventies and was handsome. He wore an open trench coat and, underneath it, a brown suede suit with a blue and white polka-dot bow tie. When he looked our way, he had the most genuine smile.

"Hey, sorry, just curious. How much did you pay for your seat?"

"Oh, I didn't pay," he said with the kindest grin in the world. "Graham was a former student of mine. I was invited."

Tori's arms flew out in a state of complete and utter shock. "Wait, wait, wait, time-out. You're Professor Oliver?!"

He smirked and nodded. "Guilty as charged."

"You're, like, the Yoda to our Luke Skywalker. You're the wizard behind Oz. You're the freaking shit, Professor Oliver! I've read every article Graham ever wrote, and I must say, it's just so great to meet the person he spoke so highly of—well, highly in G.M. Russell terms, which isn't really highly, if you know what I mean." She chuckled to herself. "Can I shake your hand?"

Tori continued talking through almost the whole service but stopped the moment Graham was called up to the stage to deliver the eulogy. Before his lips parted, he unbuttoned his suit jacket, took it off, unhooked his cuffs, and rolled up his sleeves in such a manly-man style. I swore he rolled each sleeve up in slow motion as he rubbed his lips together and let out a small breath.

Wow.

He was so handsome and effortlessly so too.

He was more handsome in person than I thought he'd be. His whole persona was dark, enchanting, yet extremely uninviting. His short midnight-black hair was slicked back with loose tiny waves, and his sharp square jaw was covered with a few days' growth of beard. His copper-colored skin was smooth and flawless, not a blemish of imperfection anywhere to be found, except for a small scar that ran across his neck, but that didn't make him imperfect.

If I'd learned anything about scars from Graham's novels, it was that they too could be beautiful.

He hadn't smiled once, but that wasn't shocking—after all, it was his father's funeral—but when he spoke, his voice came out smooth, like whisky on the rocks. Just like everyone else in the arena, I couldn't tear my eyes from him.

"My father, Kent Russell, saved my life. He challenged me daily not only to be a better storyteller but to become a better person."

The next five minutes of his speech led to hundreds of people crying, holding their breaths, and wishing that they too were kin to

Kent. I hadn't ever read any of Kent's tales, but Graham made me curious to pick up one of his books. He finished his speech, looked up at the
ceiling, and gave a tight grin. "So I'll end this in the words of my father:
'Be inspiration. Be true. Be adventurous.' We only have one life to live,
and to honor my father, I plan to live each day as if it's my final chapter."

"Oh my gosh," Tori whispered, wiping tears from her eyes. "Do
you see it?" she asked, gesturing her head toward her lap.

"See what?" I whispered.

"How massive my invisible boner currently is. I didn't know it was
possible to be turned on by a eulogy."

I laughed. "Neither did I."

After everything finished, Tori exchanged numbers with me and
invited me to her book club. After our goodbyes, I made it to the back
room to collect my floral arrangements. As I searched for my roses, I
couldn't help but think how uncomfortable I felt at the lavishness of
Kent's funeral. It almost seemed a bit…circus-like.

I wasn't one who understood funerals, at least not the typical
mainstream ones. In my family, our final goodbyes normally involved
planting a tree in our loved one's memory, honoring their life by bringing more beauty to the world.

As a worker walked by with one of my floral arrangements, I
gasped and called after her. "Excuse me!" The headphones in her
ears kept her from hearing me though, so I hurried, pushing my way
through a crowd, trying to keep up with her. She walked up to a door,
held it open, and tossed the flowers outside before shutting the door
and walking off, dancing to the sound of her music.

"Those were three-hundred-dollar flowers!" I groaned out loud,
hurrying through the door. As it slammed, I raced over to the roses ,
which had been tossed into a trash bin in a gated area.

The night's air brushed against my skin, and I was bathed in the light of the moon shining down as I gathered the roses. When I finished, I took a deep inhale. There was something so peaceful about the night, how everything slowed a bit, how the busyness of the day disappeared until morning.

When I went to open the door to head back inside, I panicked.

I yanked on the handle repeatedly.

Locked.

Oh crap.

My hands formed fists, and I started banging against the door, trying my best to get back inside. "Hello?!" I hollered for what felt like ten minutes straight before I gave up.

Thirty minutes later, I had sat down on the concrete and was staring at the stars when I heard the door behind me open. I twisted myself around and gasped lightly.

It's you.

Graham Russell.

Standing right behind me.

"Don't do that," he snapped, noting my stare glued to him. "Stop noticing me."

"Wait, wait! It—" I stood up, and right before I could tell him to hold the door, I listened to it slam shut. "Locks."

He cocked an eyebrow, processing my words. He yanked on the door, then sighed heavily. "You have got to be kidding me." He yanked again and again, but the door was locked. "It's locked."

I nodded. "Yup."

He patted his slacks pockets and groaned. "And my phone is in my suit jacket, which is hanging on the back of a chair inside."

"Sorry, I would offer you my phone, but it's dead."

"Of course it is," he said moodily. "Because the day just couldn't get any worse."

He pounded on the door for several minutes without any results, then started cursing the universe for an extremely sucky life. He walked over to the other side of the gated area and placed his hands behind his neck. He looked completely exhausted over the day's events.

"I'm so sorry," I whispered, my voice timid and low. What else could I say? "I'm so sorry for your loss."

He shrugged, uninterested. "People die. It's a pretty common aspect of life."

"Yes, but that doesn't make it any easier, and for that, I'm sorry."

He didn't reply, but he didn't have to. I was still just amazed to be standing so close to him.

I cleared my throat and spoke again, because being silent wasn't something I knew how to do. "That was a beautiful speech."

He turned his head in my direction and gave me a cold, hard stare before turning back around.

I continued. "You really showcased what a kind, gentle man your father was and how he changed your life and the lives of others. Your speech tonight…it was just such…" I paused, searching my mind for the right words to describe his eulogy.

"Bullshit," he stated.

I stood up straighter. "What?"

"The eulogy was bullshit. I grabbed it from outside. A stranger wrote it and posted it on the building, someone who'd probably never spent ten minutes in the same room as my father, because if they had, they would've known how shitty a person Kent Russell was."

"Wait, so you plagiarized a eulogy for your father's funeral?"

"When you say it like that, it sounds awful," he replied dryly.

"It probably sounds that way because it kind of is."

"My father was a cruel man who manipulated situations and people to get the best bang for his buck. He laughed at the fact that you people paid money for his pile of shit inspirational books and lived your lives based on the garbage he wrote about. I mean, his book *Thirty Days to a Sober Life*? He wrote that book drunk off his ass. I literally had to lift him up out of his own vomit and filth more times than I'm willing to admit. *Fifty Ways to Fall in Love*? He screwed prostitutes and fired personal assistants for not sleeping with him. He was trash, a joke of a human, and I'm certain he didn't save anyone's life, as many have so dramatically stated to me this evening. He used you all to buy himself a boat and a handful of one-night stands."

My mouth dropped open, stunned. "Wow." I laughed, kicking around a small stone with my shoe. "Tell me how you really feel."

He took my challenge and turned slowly around to face me, stepping closer, making my heart race. No man should've been as handsomely dark as he was. Graham was a professional at grimacing. I wondered if he knew how to smile at all. "You want to know how I really feel?"

No.

Yes.

Um, maybe?

He didn't give me a chance to answer before he continued to speak. "I think it's absurd to sell tickets to a funeral service. I find it ridiculous to profit from a man's death, turning his final farewell into a three-ring circus. I think it's terrifying that individuals paid extra to have access to a VIP gathering afterward, but then again, people paid to sit on the same couch Jeffrey Dahmer sat on. I shouldn't be surprised by humans at all, but still, each day, they tend to shock me with their lack of intelligence."

"Wow." I smoothed out my white dress and swayed back and forth. "You really didn't like him, did you?"

His stare dropped to the ground before he looked back up at me. "Not in the least."

I looked out into the darkness of the night, staring up at the stars. "It's funny, isn't it? How one person's angel could be another's biggest demon."

He wasn't interested in my thoughts though. He moved back to the door and started banging again.

"Maktub." I smiled.

"What?"

"Maktub. It means *it is written*. That everything happens for a reason." Without much thought, I extended my hand out toward Graham. "I'm Lucy, by the way. Short for Lucille."

He narrowed his eyes, not amused. "Okay."

I giggled and stepped in closer, still holding my hand out. "I know sometimes authors can miss out on social cues, but this is the moment when you're supposed to shake my hand."

"I don't know you."

"Surprisingly, that's exactly when you're supposed to shake a person's hand."

"Graham Russell," he said, not taking my hand. "I'm Graham Russell."

I lowered my hand, a sheepish grin on my lips. "Oh, I know who you are. Not to sound cliché, but I'm your biggest fan. I've read every word you've ever written."

"That's impossible. There are words I've written that have never been published."

"Perhaps, but if you did, I swear I'd read them."

"You've read *The Harvest*?"

I wiggled my nose. "Yes."

He smiled. No, it was just a twitch in his lip. *My mistake.*

"It's as bad as I think it is, isn't it?" he asked.

"No, I just… It's different from the others." I chewed my bottom lip. "It's different, but I can't put my finger on why."

"I wrote that one after my grandmother passed away." He shifted his feet around. "It's complete shit and should've never been published."

"No," I said eagerly. "It still stole my breath away, just in a different kind of way, and trust me, I'd tell you if I thought it was complete trash. I've never been a good liar." My eyebrows wiggled and my nose scrunched up as I moved on my tiptoes—the same way Mama used to—and went back to staring up at the stars. "Have you thought of planting a tree?"

"What?"

"A tree, in honor of your father. After someone close to me passed away, she was cremated, and my sister and I planted a tree with her ashes. On her birthday, we take her favorite cake, sit beneath the tree, and eat the cake in her honor. It's a full circle of life. She came in as energy of the world and went back into it as the same."

"You're really feeding into those millennial stereotypes, aren't you?"

"It's actually a great way to preserve the beauty of the environment."

"Lucille—"

"You can call me Lucy."

"How old are you?"

"Twenty-six."

"Lucy is a name for a child. If you ever truly want to make it in the world, you should go by Lucille."

"Noted. If you ever want to be the life of the party, you should consider the nickname Graham Cracker."

"Are you always this ridiculous?"

"Only at funerals where people have to buy tickets."

"What was the selling price?"

"They ranged from two hundred to two thousand dollars."

He gasped. "Are you kidding me? People paid two thousand dollars to look at a dead body?!"

I ran my hands through my hair. "Plus tax."

"I'm worried about the future generations."

"Don't worry. The generation before you worried about you too, and it's obvious you're a bright, charming personality," I mocked.

He almost smiled, I thought.

And it was almost beautiful.

"You know what? I should have known you didn't write that eulogy based on how it ended. That was a huge clue that it wasn't written by you."

He cocked an eyebrow. "I actually did write that eulogy."

I laughed. "No, you didn't."

He didn't laugh. "You're right, I didn't. How did you know?"

"Well…you write horror and thriller stories. I've read every single one since I was eighteen, and they never, ever end happily."

"That's not true," he argued.

I nodded. "It is. The monsters always win. I started reading your books after I lost one of my best friends, and the darkness of them kind of brought me a bit of relief. Knowing there were other kinds of hurts out in the world helped me with my own pain. Oddly enough, your books brought me peace."

"I'm sure one ended happily."

"Not a single one." I shrugged. "It's okay. They are all still mas-
terpieces, just not as positive as the eulogy was tonight." I paused and
giggled again. "A positive eulogy. That was probably the most awkward
sentence I've ever said."

We were silent again, and Graham went back to the banging of the
sealed door every few minutes. After each failed attempt, he'd heavily
sigh with disappointment.

"I'm sorry about your father," I told him once more, watching how
tense he seemed. It'd been a long day for him, and I hated how clear it
was that he wanted to be alone and I was the one standing in his way.
He was literally caged with a stranger on the day of his father's funeral.

"It's okay. People die."

"Oh no, I'm not sorry about his death. I'm one of those who
believe that death is just the beginning of another adventure. What
I mean is I'm sorry that for you, he wasn't the man he was to the rest
of the world."

He took a moment, appearing to consider saying something, but
then he chose silence.

"You don't express your feelings very often, do you?" I asked.

"And you express yours too often," he replied.

"Did you write one at all?"

"A eulogy? No. Did you post one outside? Was it yours I read?"

I laughed. "No, but I did write one during the service." I went
digging into my purse and pulled out my small piece of paper. "It's
not as beautiful as yours was—*yours* being a stretch of a word—but
it's words."

He held his hand out toward me, and I placed the paper in his
hold, our fingers lightly brushing against one another.

Fangirl freak-out in three, two…

"'Air above me, earth below me, fire within me, water surround me.'" He read my words out loud and then whistled low. "Oh," he said, nodding slowly. "You're a hippie weirdo."

"Yes, I'm a hippie weirdo."

The corner of his mouth twitched, as if he was forcing himself not to smile.

"My mother used to say it to my sisters and me all the time."

"So your mom's a hippie weirdo too."

A slight pain hit my heart, but I kept smiling. I found a spot on the ground and sat once again. "Yeah, she was."

"Was," he murmured, his brows knitting together. "I'm sorry."

"It's okay. Someone once told me people die, that it's a pretty common aspect of life."

"Yes, but…" he started, but his words faded away. Our eyes locked, and for a moment, the coldness they held was gone, and the look he gave me was filled with sorrow and pain. It was a look he'd spent his whole day hiding from the world, a look he'd probably spent his whole life hiding from himself. "I did write a eulogy," he whispered, sitting down on the ground beside me. He bent his knees, and his hands pushed up the sleeves of his shirt.

"Yeah?"

"Yes."

"Do you want to share it?" I asked.

"No."

"Okay."

"Yes," he muttered softly.

"Okay."

"It's not much at all," he warned, reaching into his back pocket and pulling out a small, folded piece of paper.

I nudged him in the leg. "Graham, you're sitting outside an arena trapped with a hippie weirdo you'll probably never see again. You shouldn't be nervous about sharing it."

"Okay." He cleared his throat, his nerves more intense than they should've been. "I hated my father, and a few nights ago, he passed away. He was my biggest demon, my greatest monster, and my living nightmare. Still, with him gone, everything around me has somehow slowed, and I miss the memories that never existed."

Wow.

His words were few, yet they weighed so much. "That's it?" I asked, goose bumps forming on my arms.

He nodded. "That's it."

"Graham Cracker?" I said softly, turning my body toward him, moving a few inches closer.

"Yes, Lucille?" he replied, turning more toward me.

"Every word you've ever written becomes my new favorite story."

As his lips parted to speak again, the door swung open, breaking us from our stare. I turned to see a security guard holler behind him.

"Found him! This door locks once closed. I'm guessing he got stuck."

"Oh my God, it's about freaking time!" a woman's voice said. The moment she stepped outside to meet us, my eyes narrowed with confusion.

"Jane."

"Lyric?"

Graham and I spoke in unison, staring at my older sister, who I hadn't seen in years—my older sister who was pregnant and wide-eyed as she stared my way.

"Who's Jane?" I asked.

"Who's Lyric?" Graham countered.

Her eyes filled with emotion, and she placed her hands over her chest. "What the hell are you doing here, Lucy?" she asked, her voice shaking.

"I brought flowers for the service," I told her.

"You ordered from Monet's Gardens?" Lyric asked Graham.

I was somewhat surprised she knew the name of my shop.

"I ordered from several shops. What does it matter? Wait, how do you two know each other?" Graham asked, still confused.

"Well," I said, my body shaking as I stared at Lyric's stomach and then into her eyes, which matched Mama's. Her eyes filled with tears as if she'd been caught in the biggest lie, and my lips parted to speak the biggest truth. "She's my sister."

CHAPTER 3
Graham

Y our sister?" I asked, repeating Lucy's words as I stared blankly at my wife, who wasn't speaking up at all. "Since when do you have a sister?"

"And since when are you married and pregnant?" Lucy questioned.

"It's a long story," she said softly, placing her hand against her stomach and cringing a bit. "Graham, it's time to go. My ankles are swollen, and I'm exhausted."

Jane's eyes—*Lyric's eyes*—darted to Lucy, whose eyes were still wide with confusion. Their eyes matched in color, but that was the only resemblance they shared. One pair of chocolate eyes was ice-cold as always, while the other was soft and filled with warmth.

I couldn't take my stare off Lucy as I searched my mind, trying to understand how someone like her could've been related to someone like my wife.

If Jane had an opposite, it would be Lucy.

"*Graham*," Jane barked, breaking my stare from the woman with warm eyes.

I turned her way and arched an eyebrow.

She crossed her arms over her stomach and huffed loudly. "It has been a long day, and it's time to go."

She turned away and started to walk off when Lucy spoke, staring at her sister.

"You kept the biggest parts of you secret from your family. Do you really hate us that much?" Lucy asked, her voice shaking.

Jane's body froze for a moment, and she stood up straight yet didn't turn around. "You are not my family."

With that, she left.

I stood there for a few seconds, uncertain if my feet would allow me to move. As for Lucy, I witnessed her heart break right in front of me. Completely and unapologetically, she began to fall apart. A wave of emotion filled those gentle eyes, and she didn't even try to keep the tears from falling down her cheeks. She allowed her feelings to overtake her fully, not resisting the tears and body shakes. I could almost see it—how she placed the entire world on her shoulders and how the world was slowly weighing her down. Her body bent, making her appear much smaller than she was as the hurt coursed through her. I'd never seen someone feel so freely when it came to emotions, not since…

Stop.

My mind was traveling back to my past, to memories I had buried deep within me. I broke my stare away from her, rolled down my sleeves, and tried to block out the noise of the pain she was feeling.

As I moved toward the door—which the security guard was still holding open—I glanced back at the woman who was falling apart and cleared my throat.

"Lucille," I called, straightening my tie. "A bit of advice."

"Yes?" She wrapped her arms around her body, and when she looked at me, her smile was gone, replaced by a heavy frown.

"*Feel* less." I breathed out. "Don't allow others to drive your emotions in such a way. Shut it off."

"Shut off my feelings?"

I nodded.

"I can't," she argued, still crying. Her hands fell over her heart, and she shook her head back and forth. "This is who I am. I am the girl who feels everything."

I could tell that was true.

She was the girl who felt everything, and I was the man who felt nothing at all.

"Then the world will do its best to make you nothing," I told her. "The more feelings you give, the more they'll take from you. Trust me. Pull yourself together."

"But…she's my sister, and—"

"She's not your sister."

"What?"

I brushed my hand against the back of my neck before placing my hands into my pockets. "She just said you're not her family, which means she doesn't give a damn about you."

"No." She shook her head, holding the heart-shaped necklace in her hand. "You don't understand. My relationship with my sister is—"

"Nonexistent. If you loved someone, wouldn't you speak their name? I've never once heard of you."

She remained silent, but her emotions slowed down a tad as she wiped away her tears. She shut her eyes, took a deep breath, and began to softly speak to herself. "Air above me, earth below me, fire within me, water surround me, spirit becomes me."

She kept repeating the words, and I narrowed my eyes, confused about who Lucy truly was as a person. She was all over the place: flighty, random, passionate, and emotionally overcharged. It was as if she was fully aware of her faults, and she allowed them to exist regardless. Somehow, those faults made her whole.

"Doesn't it tire you?" I asked. "To feel so much?"

"Doesn't it tire you not to feel at all?"

In that moment, I realized I'd come face-to-face with my polar opposite, and I didn't have a clue what else to say to a stranger as strange as her.

"Goodbye, Lucille," I said.

"Goodbye, Graham Cracker," she replied.

"I didn't lie," Jane swore as we drove back to our home.

I hadn't called her a liar, hadn't asked her any questions whatsoever about Lucy or the fact that I hadn't known she existed up until that evening. I hadn't even shown Jane any kind of anger regarding the issue, and still, she kept telling me how she hadn't lied.

Jane.

Lyric?

I didn't have a clue who the woman sitting beside me was, but in reality, had I really known who she was before the sister revelation that evening?

"Your name is Jane," I said, my hands gripped the steering wheel.

She nodded.

"And your name is Lyric?"

"Yes." She shook her head. "No. Well, it was, but I changed it years ago, before I even met you. When I started applying to colleges, I knew no place would take me seriously with a name like Lyric. What kind of law firm would hire someone named Lyric Daisy Palmer?"

"Daisy," I huffed out. "You've never told me your middle name before."

"You never asked."

"Oh."

She raised an eyebrow. "You're not mad?"

"No."

"Wow." She took a deep breath. "Okay then. If it were the other way around, I would be so—"

"It's not the other way around," I cut in, not feeling like speaking after the longest day of my life.

She shifted around in her seat but remained quiet.

The rest of the way home, we sat in silence, my head swirling with questions, a big part of me not wanting to know the answers. Jane had a past she didn't speak about, and I had a past of the same kind. There were parts of all lives that were better left in the shadows, and I figured Jane's family was a prime example. There was no reason to go over the details. Yesterday, she hadn't had a sister, and today, she did.

Though I doubted Lucy would be coming over for Thanksgiving anytime soon.

I headed straight into our bedroom and started unbuttoning my shirt. It only took her a couple seconds to follow me into the room with a look of nerves plastered on her face, but she didn't speak a word. We both started undressing, and she moved over to me, quiet, and turned her back to me, silently asking for me to unzip her black gown.

I did as she requested, and she slid the dress off her body before tossing on one of my T-shirts, which she always used as her night-gowns. Her growing stomach stretched them out, but I didn't mind.

Minutes later, we stood in the bathroom, both brushing our teeth, no words exchanged. We brushed, we spat, we rinsed. It was our normal routine. Silence was always our friend, and that night hadn't changed anything.

When we climbed into bed, we both shut off the lamps sitting on our nightstands, and we didn't mutter a word, not even to say good night.

As my eyes closed, I tried my best to shut my brain off, but some-thing from that day split my memories open. So instead of asking Jane about her past, I crawled out of bed and went to my office to lose myself in my novel. I still needed about ninety-five thousand words, so I decided to fall into fiction in order to forget about reality for a while. When my fingers were working, my brain wasn't focused on anything but the words. Words freed me from the confusion my wife had dumped in my lap. Words freed me from remembering my father. Words freed me from falling too deep into my mind, where I stored all the pain from my past.

Without writing, my world would be filled with loss.

Without words, I'd be shattered.

"Come to bed, Graham," Jane said, standing in my doorway. It was the second time in one day that she'd interrupted me while I was writing. I hoped it wasn't becoming a common thing.

"I have to finish up my chapter."

"You'll be up for hours, just like the last few days."

"It doesn't matter."

"I have two," she said, crossing her arms. "I have two sisters."

I grimaced and went back to typing. "Let's not do this, Jane."

"Did you kiss her?"

My fingers froze, and my brows lowered as I turned to face her. "What?"

She ran her fingers through her hair, and tears were streaming down her face. She was crying—again. Too many tears from my wife in one day. "I said, 'Did you kiss her?'"

"What are you talking about?"

"My question is pretty simple. Just answer it."

"We're not doing this."

"You did, didn't you?" she cried, any kind of rational mindset she'd previously had now long gone. Somewhere between us shutting off our lights and me heading to my office, my wife had turned into an emotional wreck, and now her mind was making up stories crafted completely of fiction. "You kissed her. You kissed my sister!"

My eyes narrowed. "Not now, Jane."

"Not now?"

"Please don't have a hormonal breakdown right now. It's been a long day."

"Just tell me if you kissed my sister," she repeated, sounding like a broken record. "Say it. Tell me."

"I didn't even know you *had* a sister."

"That doesn't change the fact that you kissed her."

"Go lie down, Jane. You're going to raise your blood pressure."

"You cheated on me. I always knew this would happen. I always knew you'd cheat on me."

"You're paranoid."

"Just tell me, Graham."

I threaded my fingers through my hair, uncertain of what to do other than telling the truth. "Jesus! I didn't kiss her."

"You did," she cried, wiping away the tears from her eyes. "I know you did, because I know her. I know my sister. She probably knew you were my husband and did it to get back at me. She destroys everything she touches."

"I didn't kiss her."

"She's this—this plague of sickness that no one sees. I see it though. She's so much like my mother, she ruins everything. Why can't anyone else see what she's doing? I can't believe you'd do that to me—to us. I'm pregnant, Graham!"

"*I didn't kiss her!*" I shouted, my throat burning as the words somersaulted from my tongue. I didn't want to know anything more about Jane's past. I hadn't asked her to tell me about her sisters, I hadn't dug, I hadn't badgered her, but still, we somehow ended up in an argument about a woman I hardly knew. "I have no clue who your sister is, and I don't care to know anything more about her. I don't know what the hell is eating you up in your head, but stop taking it out on me. I didn't lie to you. I didn't cheat on you. I didn't do anything wrong tonight, so stop attacking me on today of all days."

"Stop acting like you care about today," she whispered, her back turned to me. "You didn't even care about your father."

My mind flashed.

Still, with him gone, everything around me has somehow slowed, and I miss the memories that never existed.

"Now's a good time to stop talking," I warned.

She wouldn't.

"It's true, you know. He meant nothing to you. He was a good man, and he meant nothing to you."

I remained quiet.

"Why won't you ask me about my sisters?" she asked. "Why don't you care?"

"We all have a past we don't speak about."

"I didn't lie," she said once again, but I had never called her a liar. It was as if she was trying to convince herself she hadn't lied, when in fact, that was exactly what she'd done. The thing was, I didn't care, because if I'd learned anything from humans, it was that they all lied. I didn't trust a soul.

Once a person broke trust, once a lie was brought to the surface, everything they ever said, true or false, felt as if it was at least partially covered in betrayal.

"Fine. Okay, let's do this. Let's just put it all out there on the table. Everything. I have two sisters, Mari and Lucy."

I cringed. "Stop, please."

"We don't talk. I'm the oldest, and Lucy is the youngest. She's an emotional wreck." It was an ironic statement, seeing as how Jane was currently in the middle of her own breakdown. "And she's the spitting image of my mother, who passed away years ago. My father walked out on us when I was nine, and I couldn't even blame him. My mother was unstable."

I slammed my hands down on my desk and flipped around to face her. "What do you want from me, Jane? You want me to say I'm pissed at you for not telling me? Fine, I'm pissed. You want me to be understanding? Fine, I understand. You want me to say you're right for ditching those people? Great, you're right for ditching them. Now can I please get back to work?"

"Tell me about yourself, Graham. Tell me about your past—you know, the one you never talk about."

"Leave it alone, Jane." I was so good at keeping my feelings at bay.

I was so good at not getting emotionally involved, but she was pushing me, testing me. I wished she would stop, because when the feelings unleashed from the darkness of my soul, it wasn't sadness or misery that came shooting out.

It was anger.

Anger was creeping up, and she was mentally slamming a sledge-hammer against me.

She was forcing me to turn back into the monster she hadn't known she lay beside each night.

"Come on, Graham. Tell me about your childhood. What about your mom? You had to have one of those, right? What happened to her?"

"Stop," I said, shutting my eyes tight, my hands forming fists, but she wouldn't let it go.

"Did she not love you enough? Did she cheat on your father? Did she die?"

I walked out of the room, because I felt it climbing to the surface. I felt my anger getting too big, too much, too overbearing. I tried my best to escape from her, but she followed me through the house.

"Okay, you don't want to talk about your mom. How about we talk about your dad? Tell me why you despise your father so much. What did he do? Did it bother you that he was busy working all the time?"

"You don't want to do this," I warned once more, but she was too far gone. She wanted to play nasty, but she was playing with the wrong person.

"Did he take away your favorite toy? Did he not let you get a pet as a child? Did he forget your birthday?"

My eyes grew heavy, and she noticed it as my stare met hers.

"Oh," she whispered. "He missed a lot of birthdays."

"*I kissed her!*" I finally snapped, turning to face my wife, whose jaw was hanging open. "Is that what you want? Is that the lie you want me to tell?!" I hissed. "I swear you're acting like an idiot."

She slammed her hands against me.

Hard.

Each time she hit me, another emotion started coming to the surface. Each time she slammed, a feeling hit my gut.

This time it was regret.

"I'm sorry," I said on an exhale. "I'm sorry."

"You didn't kiss her?" she asked as her voice shook.

"Of course not."

"It's been a long day and—ow," she whispered as she bent over in pain. "Ouch!"

"What is it?" When my eyes met hers, my chest caved in. Her hands clutched her stomach, and her legs were soaking wet and shaking as she stood in my stretched-out T-shirt. "Jane?" I whispered, nervous and confused. "What just happened?"

"I think my water broke."

CHAPTER 4
Graham

I t's too early, it's too early, it's too early," Jane kept whispering to herself as I drove her to the hospital. Her hands rested on her stomach as the contractions kept coming.

"You're fine. Everything's okay," I reassured her out loud, but in my mind, I was terrified. *It's too early, it's too early, it's too early...*

Once we made it to the hospital, we were rushed into a room where we were surrounded by nurses and doctors asking questions as they tried to figure out what had happened. Whenever I asked a question, they'd smile and tell me I'd have to wait to speak with the attending neonatologist. Time passed slowly, and each minute felt like an hour. I knew it was too early for the child—she was only at thirty-one weeks. When the neonatologist finally made his way to our room, he had Jane's chart in his grip and a small smile on his face as he pulled up a chair to the side of her bed.

"Hey there, I'm Doctor Lawrence, and I'll be the one you get sick of soon enough." He started flipping through his folder and brushed one of his hands against his hairy chin. "It looks to me like your baby's giving you quite the fight right now, Jane. Being that it's still so early in the pregnancy, we are concerned about the safety of performing a delivery with there still being a good twelve weeks left until you're due."

"Nine," I corrected. "There are only nine weeks left."

Dr. Lawrence's bushy eyebrows lowered as he went flipping through his paperwork. "No, definitely twelve, which brings about some pretty complex issues. I know you've probably been going over all these questions with the nurses already, but it's important to know what's going on with you and the child. So first, have you been under any kind of stress lately?"

"I'm a lawyer, so that's the definition of my life," she replied.

"Any kind of alcohol or drugs?"

"No and no."

"Smoking?"

She hesitated.

I raised an eyebrow. "Come on, Jane. Seriously?"

"It's only been a few times a day," she argued, stunning me. She turned to the doctor and tried to explain. "I've been under a lot of stress at work. When I found out I was pregnant, I tried to quit, but a few cigarettes a day was better than my half a pack."

"You told me you quit," I said through gritted teeth.

"I tried."

"That's not the same as quitting!"

"You don't get to yell at me!" she bellowed, shaking. "I made a mistake, I'm in a lot of pain, and you yelling at me isn't going to help anything. Jesus, Graham, sometimes I wish you could be more kind like your father."

I felt her words deep in my soul, but I did my best not to react.

Dr. Lawrence grimaced before finding that small smile again.

"Okay, smoking can lead to many different complications when it comes to childbirth, and although it's impossible to know the exact cause of it, it's good that we have this information. Seeing as how you're so early and are having contractions, we are going to give you a toco-lytic drug to try to stop the premature labor. The baby still has a lot of growing to do, so we'll have to do our best to keep her inside for a bit more. We'll keep you here and monitored for the next forty-eight hours."

"Forty-eight hours? But what about my job?"

"I'll write you a very good doctor's note." Dr. Lawrence winked and stood up to leave. "The nurses will be back in a second to check on you and start the medicine."

As he left, I stood quickly and followed him out of the room. "Dr. Lawrence."

He turned back to me and stepped my way. "Yes?"

I crossed my arms and narrowed my eyes. "We got into a fight, right before her water broke. I yelled and…" I paused and ran a hand through my hair before crossing my arms once more. "I just wanted to know if that was the cause. Did I do this?"

Dr. Lawrence smiled out of the left side of his mouth and shook his head. "These things happen. There's no way to know the cause, and beating yourself up isn't going to do anyone any good. All we can do right now is live in the moment and make sure to do what's best for your wife and child."

I nodded and thanked him.

I tried my best to believe his words, but in the back of my mind, I felt as if it was all my fault.

After forty-eight hours and the baby's heart rate dropping, the doctors informed us that we had no other choice but to deliver the baby via C-section. It was all a blur once it happened, and my heart was lodged in my throat the whole time. I stood in the operating room, uncertain of what to feel once the baby was delivered.

When the doctors finished with the C-section and the umbilical cord was cut, everyone hurried around, shouting at one another.

She wasn't crying.

Why wasn't she crying?

"Two pounds, three ounces," a nurse stated.

"We're gonna need CPAP," another one said.

"CPAP?" I asked as they hurried past me.

"Continuous positive airway pressure, to help her breathe."

"She's not breathing?" I asked another.

"She is. It's just very weak. We're going to transfer her to the NICU, and we'll have someone contact you once she's stable."

Before I could ask anything else, they were rushing the child away.

A few people stayed to take care of Jane, and once she was moved to a hospital room, she spent a few hours resting. When she finally awoke, the doctor filled us in on the health of our daughter. They told us of her struggles, of how they were doing their best to care for her in the NICU and how her life was still at risk.

"If anything happens to her, know that it was your fault," Jane told me once the doctor left the room. She turned her head away from me, toward the windows. "If she dies, it isn't my fault. It's yours."

"I understand what you're saying, Mr. White, but—" Jane stood in the NICU with her back to me as she spoke on her cell phone. "I know, sir,

I completely understand. It's just, my child's been in the NICU, and…"
She paused, shifted her feet around, and nodded. "Okay. I understand.
Thank you, Mr. White."

She hung up the phone and shook her head back and forth, wiping
at her eyes before she turned back toward me.

"Everything all right?" I asked.

"Just work stuff."

I just nodded once.

We stood still, staring down at our daughter, who was struggling
with her breathing.

"I can't do this," Jane whispered, her body starting to shake. "I can't
just stay here doing nothing. I feel so useless."

The night before, we thought we'd lost our little girl, and in that
moment, I felt everything inside me begin to fall apart. Jane wasn't
handling it well at all, and she hadn't gotten a minute of sleep.

"It's fine," I said, but I didn't believe it.

She shook her head. "I didn't sign up for this. I didn't sign up for
any of this. I never wanted kids. I just wanted to be a lawyer. I had
everything I wanted. And now…" Jane kept fidgeting. "She's going to
die, Graham," she whispered, her arms crossed. "Her heart isn't strong
enough. Her lungs aren't developed. She's hardly even here. She's only
existing because of all this"—she waved at the machines attached to
our daughter's tiny body—"this *crap*, and we're just supposed to sit
here and watch her die?! It's cruel."

I didn't reply.

"I can't do this. It's been almost two months in this place, Graham.
Isn't she supposed to start getting better?"

Her words annoyed me, and her belief that our daughter was
already too far gone sickened me. "Maybe you should just go home

and shower," I offered. "Take a break. Maybe go to work to help clear your mind."

She shifted in her shoes and grimaced. "Yeah, you're right. I have a lot to catch up on at work. I'll be back in a few hours, okay? Then we can switch, and you can take a break to shower."

I nodded.

She walked over to our daughter and looked down at her. "I haven't told anyone her name yet. It seems silly, right? To tell people her name when she's going to die."

"Don't say that," I snapped at her. "There's still hope."

"Hope?" Jane's eyes filled with confusion. "Since when are you a hopeful man?"

I didn't have an answer, because she was right. I didn't believe in signs or hope or anything of that nature. I hadn't known God's name until the day my daughter was born, and I felt too foolish to even offer him a prayer.

I was a realist.

I believed in what I saw, not what I hoped might be, but still, there was a part of me that looked at that small figure and wished I knew how to pray.

It was a selfish need, but I needed my daughter to be okay. I needed her to pull through, because I wasn't certain I'd make it through losing her. The moment she was born, my chest ached. My heart somewhat awakened after years of being asleep, and when it awakened, it felt nothing but pain. Pain of knowing my daughter could die. Pain of not knowing how many days, hours, or minutes were left with her. Therefore, I needed her to survive so the aching of my soul would disappear.

It was much easier to exist when it was shut off.

How had she done that? How had she turned it back on merely by being born?

I hadn't even spoken her name...

What kind of monsters were we?

"Just go, Jane," I said, my voice cold. "I'll stay here."

She left without another word, and I sat in the chair beside our daughter, whose name I too was too nervous to speak out loud.

I waited hours before trying to call Jane. I knew at times she'd get so wrapped up in her work, she'd forget to step away from her office, the same way I did when I was wrapped in my writing.

There wasn't an answer on her cell phone. I called again for the next five hours with no reply, so I went ahead and called her office's front desk. When I spoke to Rosie, the receptionist, I felt gutted.

"Hi, Mr. Russell. I'm sorry, but...um...she was actually let go earlier this morning. She's missed so much, and Mr. White let her go. I figured you would know." Her voice lowered. "How is everything going? With the baby?"

I hung up.

Confused.

Angered.

Tired.

I tried Jane's cell phone again, and it went straight to voicemail.

"Do you need a break?" one of the nurses asked me, coming to check on my daughter's feeding tube. "You look exhausted. You can go home and rest for a bit. We'll call you if—"

"I'm fine," I said, cutting her off.

She started to speak again, but my stern look made her shut her lips. She finished checking all the stats, and then she gave me a small smile on her way out.

I sat with my daughter, listening to the beeping machines working, waiting for my wife to come back to us. As hours went by, I allowed myself to go home for a shower and to grab my laptop so I could write at the hospital.

I made it quick, jumping into the steaming water, letting it hit me and burn my skin. Then I got dressed and hurried to my office to grab my computer and some paperwork. That was when I noticed it—the folded piece of paper sitting on my keyboard.

Graham,

I should've stopped reading there. I knew nothing good could come from her next words. I knew nothing good ever came from an unexpected letter written in black ink.

> *I can't do this. I can't stay and watch her die. I lost*
> *my job today, the thing I worked hardest for, and*
> *I feel as if I lost a part of my heart. I can't sit and*
> *watch another part of me fade away too. It's all too*
> *much. I'm sorry.*
>
> *—Jane*

I stared at the paper, rereading her words multiple times before folding the paper and placing it in my back pocket.

I felt her words deep in my soul, but I did my best not to react.

CHAPTER 5
Lucy

I completely blanked," the stranger told me, his voice shaky. "I mean, we were both swamped with exams, and I'm just trying to keep my head above water, and I totally forgot about our anniversary. It was a given that she hadn't when she showed up with my gifts and dressed for the dinner date I forgot to book."

I gave the guy a smile and nodded as he told me the full saga of why his girlfriend was currently pissed off at him.

"And it doesn't help that I missed her birthday too, seeing as how I'd just gotten rejected from med school the week before. That put me in a big funk, but, man. Okay, yeah, sorry. I'll just get these flowers."

"Will that be all?" I asked, ringing up the dozen red roses the guy had picked out as an attempt to apologize to his girlfriend for forgetting the only two dates he really had to remember.

"Yeah, do you think it's enough?" he asked nervously. "I just really messed up, and I'm not sure how to even start apologizing."

"Flowers are a good start," I told him. "And words help too. Then I think your actions will speak the loudest."

He thanked me as he paid and walked out of the shop.

"I give them two weeks before they break up," Mari said with a smirk on her lips as she trimmed a few tulips.

"Ms. Optimist." I laughed. "He's trying."

"He's asking a stranger for advice on his relationship. He's failing," she replied, shaking her head. "I just don't get it. Why do guys find the need to apologize *after* they screw up? If they could just *not* screw up, there wouldn't be anything to apologize for. It's not that hard to just…be good."

I gave her a tight smile, watching her cut the flower stems aggressively while her eyes filled with emotion. She wouldn't admit to the fact that she was currently taking her pain out on the beautiful plants, but it was clear that she was.

"Are you…okay?" I asked as she picked up a handful of daisies and shoved them into the vase.

"I'm fine. I just don't understand how that guy could be so insensitive, you know? Why in the world would he ask you for advice?!"

"Mari."

"What?"

"Your nose is flaring, and you're waving scissors around like a madwoman because a guy bought his girlfriend flowers for forgetting their anniversary. Are you really upset about that, or does it have something to do with today's date? Seeing as how it would've been your—"

"Seven-year anniversary?" She chopped up two roses into tiny pieces. "Oh? Is that today? I hardly noticed."

"Mari, back away from the scissors."

She looked up at me and then down at the roses. "Oh no. Am I having one of those mental breakdown moments?" she asked as I walked over and slowly removed the scissors from her grip.

"No, you're having one of those human moments. It's fine,

really. You're allowed to be angry and sad for as long as you need to. Remember? Maktub. It just becomes an issue when we start destroying our own things over asshole men, especially flowers."

"Ugh, you're right. I'm sorry." She groaned, placing her head in the palms of her hands. "Why do I still care? It's been years."

"Time doesn't just shut off your feelings, Mari. It's fine, but it's also fine that I booked you and me a date for tonight."

"Seriously?"

I nodded. "It involves margaritas and tacos."

She perked up a bit. "And queso dip?"

"Oh yeah. All the queso dip."

She stood up and wrapped me in a tight hug. "Thank you, Pod, for always being there for me even when I don't say I need you."

"Always, Pea. Let me go grab a broom to clean up your anger management mess." I hurried into the back room and heard the bell ring at the front of the store, announcing a customer's arrival.

"Hi, uh, I'm looking for Lucille?" a deep voice said, making my ears perk up.

"Oh, she just went in the back," Mari replied. "She'll be out in a—"

I hurried out to the front of the shop and stood there, staring at Graham. He looked different without his suit and tie but still somewhat the same. He wore dark blue jeans and a black T-shirt that hugged his body, and that same cold stare lived in his eyes.

"Hi," I said breathlessly, crossing my arms and walking farther into the room. "How can I help you?"

He was fidgeting with his hands, and whenever we made eye contact, he looked away. "I was just wondering, have you seen Jane lately?" He cringed a bit and cleared his throat. "I mean, Lyric. I mean, your sister. Have you seen your sister lately?"

"You're Graham Cracker?" Mari said, standing up from her chair.

"Graham," he said sternly. "My name is Graham."

"I haven't seen her since the funeral," I told him.

He nodded, a spark of disappointment making his shoulders round forward. "All right. Well, if you do…" He sighed. "Never mind."

He turned to leave, and I called after him.

"Is everything okay? With Lyric?" I paused. "Jane." My chest tightened as the worst possibilities shot through my mind. "Is she okay? Is it the baby? Is everything all right?"

"Yes and no. She delivered the baby almost two months ago, a girl. She was premature and has been at St. Joseph's ever since."

"Oh my gosh," Mari muttered, placing her hand over her heart. "Are they doing better?"

"We…" He started to answer, but the way his words faded showed his doubt, the same way his heavy eyes displayed his fears. "That's not why I'm here. I'm here because Jane is missing."

"Huh?" My mind was racing with all the information he was giving me. "Missing?"

"She left yesterday around twelve in the afternoon, and I haven't heard from her since. She was fired from her job, and I don't know where she is or if she's okay. I just thought perhaps you'd heard from her."

"I haven't." I turned to Mari. "Have you heard from Lyric?"

She shook her head.

"It's fine. Sorry I stopped by. I didn't mean to bother you."

"You're not a—" Before I could finish my sentence, he was out the door. "Bother," I murmured.

"I'm gonna try to call her," Mari said, racing to her cell phone, her heart probably racing at the same speed as mine. "Where are you going?" she asked as I headed for the front door.

I didn't have time to reply as I left in the same hurry Graham had.

"Graham!" I called, just seconds before he stepped into his black Audi. He looked up at me, almost as if he was confused by my entire existence.

"What?"

"I... What... You can't just barge into my shop, drop all this information, and then rush off. What can I do? How can I help?"

His brows lowered, and he shook his head. "You can't." Then he climbed into his car and drove off, leaving me baffled.

My sister was missing, and I had a niece fighting for her life, and there was nothing I could do to help?

I found that hard to believe.

"I'm going to go to the hospital," I told Mari as I stepped back inside the building. "To check in on everything."

"I'll come too," she offered, but I told her it was best if she kept the shop up and running. There was too much to do, and if both of us left, we would fall too far behind on everything.

"Also, keep trying to get a hold of Lyric. If she's going to answer for one of us, it would be you."

"Okay. Promise to call me if anything goes wrong and you need me," she told me.

"Promise."

When I walked into the NICU, I noticed Graham's back first. He was sitting in a chair, hunched over, his eyes glued to the small crib that held his daughter. "Graham," I whispered, making him look up.

When he turned to see me, he looked hopeful, almost as if he thought I was Jane. The flash of hope disappeared as he stood up and stepped closer to his daughter.

"You didn't have to come here," he told me.

"I know. I just thought I should make sure everything was okay."

"I don't need the company," he said as I stepped in closer. The closer I got, the more he tensed up.

"It's okay if you're sad or scared," I whispered, staring at the little girl's tiny lungs working so hard to breathe. "You don't have to be strong at all times," I said.

"Will my weakness save her?" he snapped.

"No, but—"

"Then I won't waste my time."

I shifted around in my shoes. "Have you heard from my sister?"

"No."

"She'll be back," I said, hoping I wasn't a liar.

"She left me a note that said otherwise."

"Seriously? That's…" My words faded away before I could say it was shocking. In a way, it wasn't. My oldest sister had always been a bit of a runner, like our father. I shifted the conversation. "What's her name?" I asked, looking down at the tiny girl.

"There's no point in telling people if she's going to…" His voice cracked. His hands formed fists, and he shut his eyes. When he reopened them, something about his cold stare shifted. For a split second, he allowed himself to feel as he watched his child trying her best to live. He lowered his head and whispered, "If she's going to die."

"She's still here, Graham," I promised, nodding her way. "She's still here, and she's beautiful."

"But for how long? I'm just being a realist."

"Well, lucky for you, I'm a hope-ist."

His hands were clenched so hard, forcing his skin to turn red. "I don't want you here," he told me, turning my way.

For a moment, I considered how disrespectful I was, staying when I wasn't welcome.

But then I noticed his shaking.

It was a small tremble in his body as he stared at his daughter, as he stared at the unknown. It was right then that I knew I couldn't leave him.

I reached out and unwrapped his fists, taking his hand into my hold. I knew the child was fighting a hard battle, and I could tell Graham was also at war. As I held his hand, I noticed a small breath release from between his lips.

He swallowed hard and dropped my hand a few seconds later, but it seemed to be enough to make him stop shaking. "Talon," he whispered, his voice low and frightened, almost as if he thought telling me her name meant kissing his child with a death wish.

"Talon," I repeated softly, a small smile spreading across my lips. "Welcome to the world, Talon."

Then, for the first time in my presence, Talon Russell opened her eyes.

CHAPTER 6
Graham

"Are you sure you're okay?" Lucy asked, unaware she'd overstayed her welcome at the hospital. She'd been to the hospital every day for the past two weeks, checking in on Talon, checking in on me. As each day passed, I grew more and more irritated by her persistence in showing up. I didn't want her there, and it was clear that my stopping at the floral shop in search of Jane had been a bad idea.

The worst part of it all? Lucy never shut up.

She wasn't one to ever stop talking. It was as if every thought she ever had needed to pass through her lips. What was worse was how each word was filled with positive hippie mumbo jumbo. The only things missing from her speeches were a joint, rock crystals, and a yoga mat.

"I can stay if you need me to," she offered once more.

Talon was getting her feeding tube taken out, and the doctors felt confident she'd be able to start eating on her own, which was a step in the right direction after months of uncertainty.

"Really, Graham. It's no problem for me to stay a few more hours."

"No. Go."

She nodded and finally stood up. "Okay. I'll come back tomorrow."

"Don't."

"Graham, you don't have to do this alone," she insisted. "I can stay here and help if—"

"Don't you see?" I snapped. "You're not wanted. Go bother someone else with your pity."

Her lips parted, and she took a few steps backward. "I don't pity you."

"Then you must pity yourself for not having a life of your own," I muttered, not making eye contact with her yet still seeing the pained look on her face out of the corner of my eye.

"There are moments when I see you, you know—when I see how hurt you are, when I see your pain and worry—but then you go ahead and cancel it out with your rudeness."

"Stop acting like you know me," I told her.

"Stop acting like you're heartless," she replied. She went digging into her purse and pulled out a pen and paper, then scribbled down her phone number. "Here, take this in case you need me or you change your mind. I used to be a nanny, and I could give you a hand if you need it."

"Why don't you get it? I don't need anything from you."

"You think this is about you?" She snickered, shaking her head as she wrapped her fingers around her heart-shaped necklace. "It seems your egotistic ways are getting in the way of you realizing the truth of the matter. I'm not here for you. I hardly know you. The last thing my mother asked from me was to look after my sisters, and seeing as how Lyric is missing in action, I find it important for me to look after her daughter."

"Talon is not your responsibility," I argued.

"Maybe not," she said. "But like it or not, she is my family, so please don't let your pride and misplaced anger keep you from reaching out if you need me."

"I won't need you. I don't need anyone," I barked at her, feeling annoyed by her giving personality. How ridiculous it was for her to give so much of herself so freely.

Her eyes narrowed, and she tilted her head, studying me. I hated the way she stared at me. I hated how when our eyes locked, she stared as if she saw a part of my soul that I hadn't even discovered. "Who hurt you?" she whispered.

"What?"

She stepped in closer to me, unfolded my clenched hand, and placed her number in my grasp. "Who hurt you so bad and made you so cold?"

When she left, my eyes followed her, but she didn't look back once.

Three weeks passed before the doctors and nurses informed me it was time for Talon and me to go home. It took me over two hours to make sure the car seat was installed properly, along with having five different nurses check to make sure it was securely fastened.

I'd never driven so slowly in my life, and every time I turned to check on Talon, she was sleeping peacefully.

I'm going to fuck this up.

I knew I would. I knew nothing about being a father. I knew nothing about taking care of a child. Jane would've been great at it. Sure, she never wanted children, but she was a perfectionist. She would've taught herself to become the best mother in the world. She would've been the better option when it came to one of us caring for Talon.

My having her felt like a cruel mistake.

"Shh," I tried to soothe her as I carried the car seat into the house. She'd started crying the moment I took her out of the car, and my gut was tightened with nerves.

Is she hungry? Does she need a diaper change? Is she too hot? Too cold? Did she just miss an inhale? Are her lungs strong enough? Will she even make it through the night?

Once Talon was in her crib, I sat on the floor beside it. Anytime she moved, I was up on my feet, checking on her. Anytime she didn't shift, I was up on my feet, checking on her.

I'm going to fuck this up.

The doctors were wrong. I knew they were. They shouldn't have sent her home yet. She wasn't ready. I wasn't ready. She was too small, and my hands were too big.

I'd hurt her.

I'd make a mistake that would cost Talon her life.

I can't do this.

Pulling out my cell phone, I made a call to the number I'd been calling for weeks. "Jane, it's me, Graham. I just wanted to let you know…Talon's home. She's okay. She's not going to die, Jane, and I just wanted to let you know that. You can come home now." My grip on the phone was tight, my voice stern. "Come home. Please. I can't…I can't do this without you. I can't do this alone."

It was the same message I'd left her multiple times since the moment the doctors told me Talon was going to be discharged. But still, Jane never came back.

That night was the hardest night of my life.

Every time Talon started screaming, I couldn't get her to stop. Every time I picked her up, I was terrified I'd break her. Every time I fed her and she wouldn't eat, I worried about her health. The pressure was too much. How could someone so small rely on me as her life support?

How was a monster supposed to raise a child?

Lucy's question from the last time I saw her played over and over again in my head.

Who hurt me so bad and made me so cold?

The *who* part was easy.

It was the reason that was blurred.

CHAPTER 7
Eleventh Birthday

The boy stood still in the darkened hallway, unsure if his father wanted him to be noticed. He'd been home alone for some time that night and felt safer when he was the only one there. The young boy was certain his father would come home intoxicated, because that was what the past had taught him. What he wasn't certain of was which drunken version would walk through the front door this time.

Sometimes his father was playful, other times extremely cruel.

His father would come home so cruel that the boy would oftentimes close his eyes at night and convince himself that he'd made up the actions of the drunken man, telling himself his father would never be so cold. He'd tell himself no person could hate his own flesh and blood so much—even with the aid of alcohol.

Yet the truth of the matter was sometimes the ones we loved most were the monsters that tucked us in at night.

"Come here, son," the grown man called, making the boy stand up taller. He hurried himself into the living room, where he spotted his father sitting with a woman. The father grinned as the woman's hands rested in his hold. "This," he said, his eyes light, practically shining, "is Rebecca."

The woman was beautiful, with chocolate hair that fell against her shoulders and a slender nose that fit perfectly between her brown doe eyes. Her lips were full and painted red, and when she smiled, she kind of reminded the boy of his mother.

"Hello, there," Rebecca said softly, her voice brimming with kindness and gentleness. She extended her hand toward the boy. "It's wonderful to finally meet you."

The boy stayed at a distance, uncertain of what he should say or feel.

"Well," his father scolded. "Shake her hand. Say hello, son."

"Hello," the boy said in a whisper, as if he was worried he was walking into his father's trap.

"Rebecca is going to be my new wife, your new mother."

"I have a mother," the boy barked, his voice louder than he meant it to be. He cleared his throat and returned to his whispering sounds. "I have a mom."

"No," his father corrected. "She left us."

"She left you," the boy argued. "Because you're a drunk!" He knew he shouldn't have said it, but he also knew how much his heart hurt thinking that his mother would walk out on him, leaving him with the monster. His mother loved him—he was certain of that. One day, she just got too scared, and that fear had driven her away.

He often wondered if she realized she'd left him behind.

He often prayed she'd come back someday.

His father sat up straighter, and his hands formed fists. As he was about to snap at his loudmouthed son, Rebecca placed her hand on his shoulder, soothing him. "It's okay. This is a new situation for all of us," she said, moving her hands to rub his back. "I'm not here to replace *your mom. I know she meant a lot to you, and I'd never want to take her place. But I am hoping that someday, you'll somehow find a place for me in your heart too, because that's the thing about hearts—when you think they're completely full, you somehow find room to add a little more love."*

The boy remained silent, unsure what he should say. He could still see the anger in his father's eyes, but something about Rebecca's touch kept him calm. She seemed to be the beauty that somehow tamed the beast.

For that reason alone, the boy secretly hoped she'd stay the night and perhaps the morning too.

"Now, on to the fun things," Rebecca said, standing up and walking over to the dining room table. She came back with a cupcake in her hand, and it bore a yellow-and-green-striped candle. "Rumor has it that it's your eleventh birthday. Is that true?"

The boy nodded warily.

How had she known?

His own father hadn't even mentioned it all day.

"Then you must make a wish." Rebecca smiled big, like his mother used to do. She reached into her purse, pulled out a lighter, and flicked on the flame. The boy watched as the candlewick began to burn, the wax slowly dripping down the sides of the candle, melting into the frosting. "Go ahead. Blow out the candle, and make your wish."

He did as she said, and she smiled even wider than before.

The young boy made a mistake that night, and he didn't even notice. It happened so quickly, between the moment he opened his mouth to blow out the candle and the moment when the flame dissipated.

In that split second, in that tiny space of time, he accidentally opened his heart and let her in.

The last woman to remember his birthday was his mother, and how he loved her so.

Rebecca reminded him so much of his mother, from her kind smile and gentle approach, her painted lips and doe eyes, to her willingness to love.

Rebecca wasn't wrong about hearts and love. Hearts were always welcoming to new love, but when that love settled in, heartbreak sometimes began to creep in the shadows as well.

In the shadows, heartbreak poisoned the love, twisting it into something darker, heavier, uglier. Heartbreak took love and mutilated it, humiliated it, scarred it. Heartbreak slowly began to freeze heartbeats that had once been so welcoming to love.

"Happy birthday," Rebecca said, taking a swipe of frosting from his cupcake with her finger and placing it in her mouth. "I hope all your wishes come true."

CHAPTER 8
Lucy

It was the middle of the night when my cell phone started ringing. I rolled over in my bed in search of Richard, but he wasn't there. I glanced toward the hallway, where a light shone and light jazz music was playing, which meant he was up working on his artwork. My phone kept ringing, and I rubbed my eyes as I went to answer. "Hello?" I yawned, trying my best to keep my eyes open. The shades were drawn in my room, and no sunlight was peeking in, clearly indicating that it was far from morning.

"Lucille, it's Graham. Did I wake you?" he asked, his voice shaky.

I heard a crying baby in the background as I sat up in my bed and yawned once more. "No, I'm always awake at three in the morning." I chuckled. "What is it? What's wrong?"

"Talon came home today."

"That's great."

"No," he replied, his voice cracking. "She won't stop crying. She won't eat. When she's asleep, I think she's dead, so I check her heart-beat, which in turns wakes her and leads to the crying again. When

I put her in the crib, she screams even louder than when she's in my arms. I need…I—"

"What's your address?"

"You don't have—"

"Graham, address, now."

He complied and gave me directions to his house in River Hills, which told me at least one thing: he lived a comfortable life.

I got dressed fast, tossed my messy curly hair into an even messier bun, and hurried into the living room, where I saw Richard sitting. He was staring intensely at one of his charcoal drawings.

"Still working?" I asked.

His eyes darted to me, and he raised a brow. "Where are you going?" His face was different, his full beard shaven, leaving only his mustache.

"You have no beard," I commented. "And…a mustache."

"Yeah, I needed inspiration, and I knew shaving my face would bring about some kind of expression. You like it?"

"It's…" I wiggled my nose. "Artistic?"

"Which is exactly what this artist strives for. So wait, where are you going?"

"Graham just called me. He brought Talon home from the hospital and is having a lot of trouble with her."

"It's…" Richard glanced at his watch with narrowed eyes. He'd lost his glasses somewhere in the mess of his creation, I was certain. "Three in the morning."

"I know." I walked over to him and kissed him on the top of his head. "Which is exactly why you should get some sleep."

He waved me off. "People who get showcases at museums don't sleep, Lucy. They create."

I laughed, walking to the front door. "Well, try to create with your eyes shut for a bit. I'll be back soon."

As I pulled into Graham's driveway, I was stunned by the size of his house. Of course, all the mansions in River Hills were stunning, but his was hauntingly breathtaking. Graham's property was much like his personality—secluded from the rest of the world. The front of the house was surrounded by trees, while the backyard had a bit of open land to it. There were pebbled pathways that marked the areas that were supposed to be made into gardens, but the wild grass just grew high in those areas. It would've been great for a beautiful garden. I could envision the types of unique flowers and vines that could exist in the space. Behind the patch of field were more trees that traveled far back.

The sun hadn't risen yet, and his house was dark but still so beautiful. In front of his porch sat two huge lion statues, and on his rooftop were three gargoyles.

I walked up to his door carrying two cups of coffee, and right as I was about to ring the doorbell, Graham was already there, rushing me inside.

"She won't stop screaming," he said, not greeting me, just hurrying me into the house with the crying baby. The house was pitch-black, except for a lamp that sat on the living room table. The draping on all the windows was heavy red velvet, making the home feel even darker. He led me to Talon's room where the tiny girl was lying in her crib, her face flushed as she hollered.

"She doesn't have a temperature, and I laid her on her back, because you know..." He shrugged. "I read up a lot about SIDS, and I know she's not able to roll, but what if she does by mistake? And she's not eating much. I'm not sure what to do, so I was going to try kangaroo care."

I almost laughed at his nerves, except there was the issue that Talon was in distress. I looked around the room, noting that the little girl's bedroom was two times the size of my own. Scattered across the floor were dozens of parenting books opened to certain pages, with other pages folded down so he could return to them at a later time.

"What's kangaroo care?" I asked.

When I looked up from the books, I noticed a shirtless Graham standing before me. My eyes danced across his toned chest and caramel skin before I forced myself to stop gawking at him. For an author, he was unnervingly good-looking and fit. A tattoo traveled up his left arm, wrapping around to the back of his shoulder blade, and his arms appeared as if his biceps had their own biceps, who had then given birth to their own biceps.

For a moment, I considered if he truly was an author and not Dwayne Johnson.

After he took off Talon's onesie, leaving her in only a diaper, he reached into the crib, lifted the crying baby into his muscular arms, and started swaying back and forth as her ear lay against his chest, over his heart.

"It's when the parent and the child have skin-to-skin contact to form a bond. It works best for mothers, I believe, though the nurses told me I should try it, which seems pointless," he grumbled as the crying continued. He held her as if she was a football and swayed frantically, almost as if he was falling apart from not being able to calm her.

"Maybe we should try feeding her again," I offered. "Do you want me to make a bottle?"

"No." He shook his head. "You wouldn't know how warm it would have to be."

I smiled, unbothered by his lack of faith in me. "That's fine. Here, hand her over, and you can go make the bottle."

His brows furrowed, and doubt crept into his frown, deepening it.

I sat down in the gray gliding chair in the corner and held my arms out. "I promise to not let her go."

"You have to protect her head," he told me as he slowly—*very slowly*—placed Talon in my arms. "And don't move until I'm back."

I laughed. "You have my word, Graham."

Before he left the room, he glanced back at me, as if he expected the baby to be on the floor or something ridiculous. I couldn't fault him for his fears though; it seemed Graham had a hard time when it came to trust, especially after my sister walked out on him.

"Hello, beautiful," I said to Talon, gliding her in the chair, holding her close to me. She was beautiful, a work of art almost. A few weeks ago, she had been a tiny peanut, and since the last time I saw her, she had gained five pounds. She was a survivor, a beacon of hope. The more I glided in the chair, the more she seemed to calm down. By the time Graham returned to the room, she was sleeping peacefully in my arms.

He cocked an eyebrow. "How did you do that?"

I shrugged. "I guess she just really loves this chair."

He grimaced and reached for Talon, taking her from my hold and placing her sleeping self into the crib. "Leave."

"What?" I asked, confused. "I'm sorry, did I do something wrong? I thought you wanted—"

"You can go now, Lucille. Your services are no longer needed."

"My services?" I remarked, stunned by his coldness. "I just came to help. You called me."

"Now I'm uncalling you. Goodbye."

He hurried me to the front door and ushered me out without

another word. Not even a thank-you was mentioned before he slammed the door in my face.

"Don't forget to drink the coffee I brought you that's sitting on the counter!" I hollered, banging on his door. "It's black. Ya know, like your soul."

"He called you over at three in the morning?" Mari asked, unlocking the shop the next morning. We were closed on Sundays, but we went in to prep for the following week ahead. "Granted, I was happy when you didn't come to wake me at five in the morning for hot yoga, but I was wondering where you were. How's the baby?"

"Good. She's doing well." I smiled as I thought about her. "She's perfect."

"And he's…handling it all by himself?"

"The best he can," I said, walking inside. "He's struggling, I think. Him calling me was a big deal, I could tell."

"That's so weird that he'd call you. He hardly knows you."

"I don't think he has family of his own. I think his father was the last family he had. Plus, I gave him my number in case he needed the help."

"And then he kicked you out?"

"Yup."

Mari rolled her eyes. "That totally seems like a stable living arrangement for a child. I could tell when he came into the shop that he had an edge to him."

"He's definitely rough around the edges, but I think he really wants to do right by Talon. He was forced into a situation and thought he'd have a partner to help him, but now he's doing it all on his own."

"I couldn't imagine," my sister said. "I can't believe Lyric just left him. You'd think she'd be more thoughtful after she saw what went on with Parker and me."

"She abandoned her newborn baby in the hospital, Mari. Any thoughtfulness we thought Lyric possessed went straight out the window and is now void." It was wild how you could know a person your whole life and then realize you knew nothing about them at all.

Time was a curse, the way it slowly morphed relationships into foreign affairs.

Mari shook her head. "What a mess. But on a brighter note, I have a surprise for you."

"Is it a green smoothie?"

She cocked an eyebrow. "I said a surprise, not a disgusting ground-up plant. We are officially hiring an additional florist! I'm interviewing a few people over these next few weeks."

Since opening our floral shop, we'd always talked about hiring on more staff, but we hadn't had enough profit to actually do it. So the fact that we were now at that stage where we could afford to bring on more staff was exciting. There was nothing more exhilarating than watching your dream grow.

As I went to reply, the bell over the front door rang, making us both look up. "Sorry, we're not actually open tod—" I couldn't even finish my sentence when I saw who was standing there with a bouquet of roses.

"Parker," Mari said as she breathed out, her strength dissipating as his name rolled off her tongue. Her body physically reacted to him as her shoulders drooped and her knees buckled. "Wh-what are you do-doing here?" Her voice trembled, and I wished it hadn't. It gave away the effect he had on her—the effect he obviously wanted to have.

"I…um…" He chuckled nervously and looked down at the flowers. "I guess it's a little stupid to bring flowers to a flower shop, huh?"

"What are you doing here, Parker?" I said, my voice much sterner than my sister's. I crossed my arms and didn't look away from him for a second.

"It's good to see you too, Lucy," he remarked. "I was hoping to speak to my wife for a minute."

"You don't have a wife anymore," I told him. Every step he took toward Mari, I interfered. "You lost her when you packed your bags and left all those years ago."

"Okay, okay, fair enough. I deserve that," he replied.

Mari murmured something under her breath, making Parker arch an eyebrow.

"What did you say?"

"I said, 'You don't deserve shit'!" Mari barked out, her voice still shaky but louder now. Mari wasn't one to ever curse, so when the last word flew off her tongue, I knew he had her really shaken up.

"Mari," Parker started. She turned her back to him, but he kept talking. "It would've been seven years a few weeks ago."

She didn't turn to face him, but I saw her body react.

Stay strong, sister.

"I know I screwed up. I know it seems like a real shitty thing to do to show up here after all this time with some crap flowers, but I miss you."

Her body reacted more.

"I miss us. I'm an idiot, okay? I made a lot of shitty mistakes. I'm not asking you to take me back today, Mari. I'm not asking you to fall in love with me. I'm just a boy, standing in front of a girl, asking her to get coffee with me."

"Oh my gosh," I groaned.

"What?" Parker asked, offended by my annoyance.

"You stole that line from *Notting Hill*!"

"Not exactly! Julia Roberts asked Hugh Grant to love her. I just asked for a cup of coffee," Parker explained.

I couldn't roll my eyes hard enough. "Whatever. Leave."

"No offense, Lucy, but I didn't come here for you. I came for Mari, and she hasn't told me to—"

"Leave," Mari said, her voice rediscovering its strength as she turned back to face him. She stood tall, like a strong oak tree.

"Mari…" He stepped closer to her, and she held up a hand to halt him.

"I said go, Parker. I have nothing to say, and I want nothing to do with you. Now just leave."

He hesitated for a second before he placed the flowers down on the counter and left.

The moment the door shut, Mari released the breath she'd been holding, and I hurried to the back room.

"What are you doing?" she called after me.

"Getting the sage stick," I hollered back. When we were kids, Mama kept a sage stick in our house that she'd burn whenever there was an argument of any kind. She always said fights brought bad energy to a space, and it was best to clear it out right away. "There's nothing good about Parker's energy, and I refuse to let his negativity seep into our lives again. Not today, Satan." I lit the sage and walked through the shop, waving it.

"Speaking of Satan," Mari mentioned, picking up my cell phone when it started ringing.

I reached over for it, and Graham's name flashed across the screen.

Warily, I answered, passing the sage stick to my sister. "Hello?"

"The chair doesn't work."

"What?"

"I said the chair doesn't work. You told me she liked the gliding chair, and that's how you got her to sleep, but it's not working. I've been trying all morning, and she won't sleep. She's hardly eating and…" His words dropped off for a moment before he softly spoke again. "Come back."

"Excuse me?" I leaned against the counter, flabbergasted. "You shoved me out of your house."

"I know."

"That's all you can say? That you know?"

"Listen, if you don't want to come help, fine. I don't need you."

"Yes, you do. That's why you're calling." I bit my bottom lip and closed my eyes. "I'll be there in twenty minutes."

"Okay."

Again, not a thank-you.

"Lucille?"

"Yes?"

"Make it fifteen."

CHAPTER 9
Graham

Lucy pulled up to my house in her beat-up burgundy car, and I opened the door before she even climbed out of her vehicle. I held Talon in my arms, rocking her as she cried from discomfort.

"That was twenty-five minutes," I scolded her.

She just smiled. She was always smiling.

She had a smile that reminded me of my past, a beautiful smile filled with hope.

Hope was the weak man's remedy for life's issues.

I only knew that was true from the past I'd lived.

"I like to call it fashionably late."

The closer she got, the tenser I became. "Why do you smell like weed?"

She laughed. "It's not weed; it's sage. I was burning it."

"Why were you burning sage?"

A sly grin found her, and she shrugged. "To fight off negative energy like yours."

"Oh right, hippie weirdo. I bet you travel with crystals and stones with you too."

With no effort at all, she reached into her over-the-shoulder purse and pulled out a handful of crystals.

Because *of course* she did.

"Here." She reached out, took Talon from my hands, and began rocking her. "You need rest. I'll watch her."

The guilt I had from the fact that Talon so effortlessly seemed to calm down when she was in Lucy's arms was strong.

"I can't sleep," I told her.

"No, you can. You're choosing not to because you're paranoid that something might happen to your daughter, which is a very reasonable reaction that I'm sure a lot of new parents go through. But you're not alone right now, Graham. I'm here."

I hesitated, and she nudged me slightly in the shoulder.

"Go. I can do this."

"You said you've nannied before, right?"

"Yes, a set of twins and their little brother. I was there from the first week up until they went off to school. Graham, I promise you, Talon's okay."

"Okay." I brushed my hand over my hairy chin and started in the direction of my bedroom. A shower sounded nice. I couldn't remember the last time I'd showered—or eaten. *When was my last meal? Do I even have food in my fridge? Is my fridge even still running?*

Bills.

Did I pay my bills? My phone hasn't been shut off yet, which is a good sign, because I have to call Talon's pediatrician in the morning.

Doctor.

Doctor's appointment—I have to set up doctor's appointments.

Nanny? I need to interview nannies.

"Shut up," Lucy barked at me.

"I didn't say anything."

"No, but your mind is spinning with everything you could be doing instead of sleeping. Before you can be productive, you gotta rest and, Graham?"

I turned to see her kind eyes staring my way. "Yes?"

"You're doing everything right, you know, with your daughter."

I cleared my throat and stuffed my hands into my jeans pockets. *Laundry—when was the last time I did laundry?* "She cries all the time. She's not happy with me."

Lucy laughed, the kind of laugh where she tossed her head backward and her smile stretched so far. She laughed too loud and at the wrong times. "Babies cry, Graham. It's normal. This is all new for both of you. It's a brand-new world, and you are both doing the best you can to adjust."

"She doesn't cry with you."

"Trust me." Lucy grinned, looking down at the somewhat calm Talon in her hold. "Give her a few minutes, and I'll be begging for you to switch spots with me, so go. Go rest for a bit before I hand her back over."

I nodded, and before I left, I cleared my throat once more. "I apologize."

"For?"

"The way I pushed you away this morning. It was rude, and for that, I'm sorry."

Her head tilted, and she stared at me with questioning eyes. "Why do I feel like there are a million words floating around in your mind, but you only allow a certain number to escape?"

I didn't reply.

As I stared at her rocking my daughter, who was growing more and more upset, Lucy smiled and winked my way. "See? Told you. She's just being a baby. I'll take care of her for a while. You go ahead and take care of yourself."

I thanked her in my mind, and she smiled as if she heard me.

The moment my head hit the pillow, I was fast asleep. I hadn't known I was so tired until I truly had a moment to rest. It was as if my body melted into my mattress and sleep swallowed me whole. No nightmares or dreams found me, and for that, I was thankful.

It wasn't until I heard Talon screaming that I tossed and turned in my bed. "Jane, can you get her?" I whispered, half asleep. Then my eyes opened, and I glanced at the other side of my bed—it was still completely made, no wrinkles in the sheets. My hand grazed over the empty spot that reminded me I was in this alone.

I climbed out of bed, and as I walked through the hallways, I heard a soft whisper.

"You're okay. You're okay."

The closer I grew to the nursery, the more the gentle voice calmed me. I stood in the doorway, watching Lucy as she held Talon and fed her.

Maybe in many ways, staring at my empty bed was a reminder that Jane was gone, but seeing Lucy before me was a small reminder that I wasn't alone.

"Is she okay?" I asked, making Lucy turn, surprised.

"Oh yeah. Just hungry, that's all." Her eyes traveled across my body. "I see you don't smell like a sewer anymore."

My hands ran through my still damp hair. "Yeah, I took a quick shower and a quicker nap."

She nodded and walked over to me. "Want to feed her?"

"I—no. She doesn't…"

Lucy nodded me over to the glider chair. "Sit." I started to protest, but she shook her head. "*Now*."

I did as she told me, and when I sat, she placed the baby in my arms. The moment the exchange happened, Talon started to cry, and I tried to quickly give her back to Lucy, but she refused to take her.

"You're not going to break her."

"She doesn't like it when I hold her. She's not comfortable."

"No, *you're* not comfortable, but you can do this, Graham. Just breathe and calm your energy."

I grimaced. "Your hippie weirdo side is showing."

"And your fear is showing," she countered. She bent down, placed Talon's bottle in my hand, and helped me feed her. After a few moments, Talon began to drink and calm down, her tired eyes closing. "You're not going to break her, Graham."

I hated how she could read my mind without my permission. I was terrified that each touch from me would be the one that would end Talon. My father once told me everything I touched, I ruined, and I was certain that would be the case with my baby.

I could hardly even get her to take a bottle, let alone raise her.

Lucy's hand was still wrapped around mine as she helped me feed Talon. Her touch was soft, gentle, and surprisingly welcoming to my unwelcoming soul.

"What's your greatest hope?"

Confusion hit me at her question. "What does that mean?"

"What's your greatest hope for life?" she asked again. "My mother used to always ask us girls that question when we were kids."

"I…I don't hope."

Her lips turned down, but I ignored her disappointment in my reply. I wasn't a man to hope; I was a man who simply existed.

When Talon was finished with her bottle, I handed her to Lucy, who burped her, then laid her back in her crib. We both stood over the crib, staring down at the resting child, but the knot that had been in my stomach since Talon was born remained.

She twisted a bit with a tiny grumpy look on her face before she relaxed into a deeper rest. I wondered if she dreamed while her eyes were shut and if someday, she'd have a greatest hope.

"Wow," Lucy said, a tiny smile on her lips. "She definitely has your frown."

I chuckled, making her turn my way.

"I'm sorry. Did you just…?" She pointed a finger at me and poked me in the arm. "Did Graham Russell just laugh?"

"A lapse in judgment. It won't happen again," I said dryly, standing up straight.

"Oh, how I wish that it would." Our eyes locked as we stood inches away from each other, no words finding either of us. Her blond hair was wild with tight curls, and it seemed to be her natural state; even at the funeral, her hair had been a mess.

A beautiful mess, somehow.

A loose curl fell over her left shoulder, and I reached out to move it when I saw something caught in it. The closer my hand got to her, the more I noticed her tensing up. "Graham," she whispered. "What are you doing?"

I combed my fingers through her hair, and she shut her eyes, her nervousness plain to see. "Turn around," I commanded her.

"What? Why?"

"Just do it," I told her. She cocked an eyebrow, and I rolled my eyes before tossing in a "Please." She did as I said, and I grimaced. "Lucille?" I whispered, leaning in closer to her, my mouth inches away from her ear.

"Yes, Graham Cracker?"

"There's vomit all over your back."

"What?!" she exclaimed, twisting around in circles, trying to view the back of her sundress, which was covered in Talon's spit-up. "Oh my God," she groaned.

"It's in your hair too."

"Oh, fuck me backward." She realized her words and covered her mouth. "Sorry, I mean, oh crap. I was just hoping to not go back into the real world covered in vomit."

I almost laughed again. "You can use my shower, and I can loan you some clothes while I toss this into the washer."

She smiled, something she did quite often. "Is that your sly way of asking me to stay to help with Talon for a few more hours?"

"No," I said harshly, offended by her comment. "That's ridiculous."

Her grin dropped, and she laughed. "I'm just kidding, Graham. Don't take everything so seriously. Loosen up a little. But yes, if it's okay, I'd love to take you up on your offer. This is my lucky dress."

"It can't be that lucky if it has vomit on it. Your definition of *luck* is off."

"Wow." Lucy whistled, shaking her head. "Your charm is almost sickening," she mocked.

"I didn't mean it in…" My words died off, and even though she kept smiling, I saw the small tremble in her bottom lip. I'd offended her. Of course I'd offended her—not on purpose, but still, it had happened. I shifted around before standing taller. I should've said more, but no words came to mind.

"I think I'll head home to wash it," she said, her voice lowering as she reached for her purse.

I nodded in understanding. I wouldn't want to stay near me either.

As she walked outside, I spoke. "I'm bad with words."

She turned around and shook her head. "No, I've read your books, and you're great with words—almost too good. What you lack are people skills."

"I live in my head a lot. I don't interact with people very often."

"What about my sister?"

"We didn't speak much."

Lucy laughed. "That makes for a hard relationship, I'm sure."

"We were close enough to being content."

Her head shook back and forth, and her eyes narrowed. "No one in love should ever be anything less than content."

"Who ever said anything about love?" I replied. The sadness that flooded her stare made me shift.

When she blinked, the sadness was gone. I appreciated the way she didn't live too long in the emotion. "You know what will help your people skills?" she asked. "Smiling."

"I do smile."

"No." She laughed. "You frown. You scowl. You grimace. That's about it. I haven't seen you smile once."

"When I encounter a valid reason to do so, I'll be sure to notify you. By the way, I am sorry, you know—for offending you. I-I know I can come off as somewhat cold."

"Understatement of the year." She laughed.

"I know I don't say much, and what I do say is normally the wrong thing, so I apologize for offending you. You've been nothing but giving to Talon and me, which is why I'm a bit thrown off. I'm not used to people giving just to…give."

"Graham—"

"Wait, let me finish before I say something else to ruin it all. I just wanted to say thank you for today and for the hospital visits. I know I'm not easy to deal with, but the fact that you still helped means more to me than you'll ever know."

"You're welcome." She bit her bottom lip and groaned as she muttered the word maktub repeatedly before she spoke to me again. "Listen, I might really, really end up regretting this, but if you want, I can stop by early mornings before work, and I can come help afterward. I know at some point you'll have to get back to writing your next bestseller, and I can watch her as you write."

"I…I can pay you for your services."

"It's not services, Graham, it's help, and I don't need your money."

"I'd feel better if I paid you."

"And I'd feel better if you didn't. Seriously. I wouldn't offer if I didn't mean it."

"Thank you, and, Lucille?"

She raised an eyebrow, waiting for my comment.

"That's a very nice dress."

She slightly twirled on her tiptoes. "Vomit and all?"

"Vomit and all."

Her head lowered for a moment before she looked back toward me. "You're both hot and cold all at once, and I cannot for the life of me figure you out. I don't know how to read you, Graham Russell. I pride myself on being able to read people, but you are different."

"Perhaps I'm one of those novels where you have to keep turning the page until the very end to understand the meaning."

Her smile stretched, and she started walking backward toward my bathroom to clean off the vomit. Her eyes stayed locked with mine. "A part of me wants to skip to the last page to see how it ends, but I hate spoilers, and I love a good suspense." After she finished cleaning up, she headed to the foyer. "I'll text to see if you need me tonight. Otherwise, I'll stop by early tomorrow morning, and, Graham?"

"Yes?"

"Don't forget to smile."

CHAPTER 10
Lucy

The next few weeks revolved around flower arrangements and Talon. If I wasn't at Monet's Gardens, I was helping Graham out. Whenever I went to his house, we hardly spoke. He'd pass Talon to me, then head into his office, where he'd close the door and write. He was a man of very few words, and if I'd learned anything, it was that his few words were harsh. Therefore, his silence didn't bring me any harm.

If anything, it brought me peace.

Sometimes I'd wander by his office, and I'd hear him leaving voice messages for Lyric. Each message was an update on Talon's life, detailing her highs and lows.

One Saturday evening when I pulled up to Graham's house, I was somewhat surprised to see a brown station wagon sitting in the driveway. I parked my car, walked up to the front door, and rang the doorbell.

As I waited, swaying back and forth, my ears perked up when I heard laughter coming from inside.

Laughter?

From Graham Russell's home?

"I want you to have less fat and more muscle next time I come back," a voice said seconds before the door opened. When I saw the man, I smiled wide. "Oh, hello there, young lady," he said cheerfully.

"Professor Oliver, right?"

"Yes, yes, but please, call me Ollie. You must be Lucille." He extended his hand for a shake, and I gave him mine.

"You can call me Lucy," I told him. "Graham just so happens to think Lucy is too informal, but I'm a pretty informal girl." I smiled at Graham, who stood a few feet back, not speaking a word.

"Ah, Graham, the formal gentleman. You know, I've been trying to get him to stop calling me Professor Oliver for years now, but he refuses to call me Ollie. He thinks it's childish."

"It *is* childish," Graham insisted, grabbing Ollie's brown fedora and handing it to him pointedly. "Thank you for stopping by, Professor Oliver."

"Of course, of course. Lucy, it's a pleasure to meet you. Graham speaks very highly of you."

I laughed. "I find that hard to believe."

Ollie wiggled his nose and snickered. "True, true. He hasn't said much about you. He's a bit of a silent asshole in that way, isn't he? But you see, Lucy, if I could let you in on a secret?"

"I'd love to hear any secrets and tips I can get."

"Professor Oliver," Graham said sternly. "Didn't you say you have another engagement to be off to?"

"Oh, he's getting testy, isn't he?" Ollie laughed and continued talking. "But here's a clue for dealing with Mr. Russell: he doesn't say much with his mouth, but he tells a full story with his eyes. If you watch closely, his eyes will tell you the complete story of how he's feeling. He's truly an open book if you learn how to read his language, and when I asked him about you, he said you were fine, but his eyes told me he was thankful for you. Lucy, girl with the brown doe eyes, Graham thinks the world of you, even if he doesn't say it."

I looked up at Graham, and there was a frown on his lips but also a small spark of softness in his eyes that melted my heart. Talon had that same beauty in her gaze.

"All right, old man, I think we've had enough of your mumbo jumbo. It's clear you've overstayed your welcome."

Ollie's grin stretched far, and he was completely unmoved by Graham's coldness. "Yet you keep asking me back. I'll see you next week, son, and please, less fat, more muscle. Stop selling yourself short with average writing when you are far above it." Ollie turned to me and bowed slightly. "Lucy, it was a pleasure."

"The pleasure was all mine."

As Ollie walked past me, he tipped his hat, and he whistled the whole way to his car with a bit of a hop in his step.

I smiled at Graham, who didn't smile back. We stood in the foyer for a few moments in silence, simply staring at each other. It was awkward, that was for sure.

"Talon's sleeping," he told me, breaking his stare from mine.

"Oh, okay."

I smiled.

He grimaced.

Our usual.

"Well, I can go do a bit of meditation in your sunroom if that's okay? I'll take the baby monitor with me, and I'll check in on Talon if she wakes up."

He nodded once, and I walked by him before he spoke again. "It's six in the evening."

I turned around and raised an eyebrow. "Yeah, it is."

"I eat dinner at six in my office."

"Yes, I know."

He cleared his throat and shifted around in his shoes. His stare fell to the floor for a few beats before he looked up at me. "Professor Oliver's wife, Mary, sent me two weeks of frozen dinners."

"Oh wow, that was sweet of her."

He nodded once. "Yes. One of the meals is in the oven now, and she made each pan enough for more than one person."

"Oh."

He kept staring at me but didn't say anything.

"Graham?"

"Yes, Lucille?"

"Are you asking me to eat dinner with you tonight?"

"If you would like to, there's enough."

A moment of uncertainty hit me as I wondered if I was dreaming or not, but I knew if I didn't reply quickly enough, the moment would be gone in a flash. "I'd love to."

"Do you have any food allergies? Vegetarian? Gluten free? Lactose intolerant?"

I laughed, because everything about Graham was so dry and serious. The look on his face when he listed each item was so stern and intense, I couldn't help but giggle to myself. "No, no, whatever it is will be fine."

"It's lasagna," he said, his voice heightening as if it might not be okay.

"That's fine."

"Are you sure?"

I snickered. "Graham Cracker, I'm sure."

He didn't display any emotion, only one nod. "I'll set the table."

His dining room table was ridiculously large, big enough to seat twelve people. He set the plating and silverware at each end of the table, and he motioned for me to take a seat. It was hauntingly quiet as he served the meal, and he took his seat at the other end.

There weren't many lights in Graham's home, and oftentimes the shades were drawn, not letting much sunlight through at all. His furniture was dark too and sparse. In his whole home, I was certain I was the brightest item to exist, with my colorful clothing and outrageous, wild blond hair.

"The weather's nice outside, ya know, for a spring day in Wisconsin," I said after several minutes of uncomfortable silence. Weather talk was the blandest of bland, but it was all I could think of. In the past, that flavor of small talk had always helped ease any situation.

"Is it?" he muttered, uninterested. "I haven't been out."

"Oh. Well, it is."

He didn't comment at all, just kept eating his dinner.

Hmph.

"Have you thought about putting a garden outside?" I asked. "It's the perfect time to start planting stuff, and you have such a beautiful backyard. All it would need is a bit of a trim, and you could really brighten the place up."

"I'm not interested in that. It's a waste of money."

"Oh. Well, okay."

Hmph.

"Ollie seems sweet," I mentioned, trying one last time. "He's quite the guy, isn't he?"

"He's fine for what he is," he muttered.

I tilted my head, watching his stare, applying the tip Ollie had shared with me. "You really care for him, don't you?"

"He was my college professor and now serves as my writing coach—nothing more, nothing less."

"I heard you laughing with him. You don't really laugh with a lot of people, but I heard you laughing with him. I didn't know you had a sense of humor."

"I don't."

"Right, of course," I agreed, knowing he was lying. "But it did seem as if you two were close."

He didn't reply, and that was the end of our discussion. We continued dinner in silence, and when the baby monitor alerted us of Talon crying, we both leaped up to go check on her.

"I'll get her," we said in unison.

"No, I—" he started, but I shook my head.

"That's why I'm here, remember? Finish your meal, and thank you for sharing it with me."

He nodded, and I went to check on Talon. Her eyes were wide, and she stopped crying, the tears replaced by a small smile on her face. It was what I imagined Graham's grin would look like. As I prepared a bottle for her and began feeding her, Graham entered the room and leaned against the doorframe.

"Is she all right?" he asked.

"Just hungry."

He nodded and cleared his throat. "Professor Oliver has a loud personality. He's forward, talkative, and full of nonsense ninety-nine percent of the time. I have no clue how his wife or his daughter put up with his ridiculousness and wild antics. For a man in his eighties, he acts like a child and oftentimes appears like a well-educated clown."

"Oh." Well, at least I knew Graham disliked everyone equally as much as he seemed to dislike me.

Graham's head lowered, and he stared at his fingers, which he latched together. "And he's the best man and friend I've ever known."

He turned and walked away without another word, and just like that, for a small fraction of a second, Graham Russell showed me a glimpse of his heart.

Around eleven that night, I finished cleaning up Talon's room and headed to Graham's office, where he was writing, his focus completely zoomed in on his words.

"Hey, I'm heading home."

He took a beat, finished typing his sentence, and turned to face me. "Thank you for your time, Lucille."

"Of course. Oh, and just a heads-up, on Friday, I don't think I can make it. My boyfriend is having an art show, so I'll have to be there."

"Oh," he said, a small twitch finding his bottom lip. "Okay."

I tossed my purse strap over my shoulder. "You know, if you want, you can bring Talon to the show. It might be nice to get her out and about to places other than the doctor's office."

"I can't. I have to finish these next few chapters by Saturday."

"Oh, okay. Well, have a great night."

"What time?" he said right as I stepped into the hallway.

"Hmm?"

"What time is the show?"

A lump of hope formed in my gut. "Eight o'clock, at the art museum."

He nodded once. "I might finish early. Fancy attire?"

I couldn't even hold the smile to myself. "Black tie."

"Noted." He must've noticed my excitement, because he narrowed his eyes. "It's not a promise that I'll make it. I just prefer to be informed in case I do attend."

"No, of course. I'll put you on the guest list, just in case."

"Good night, Lucille."

"Good night, Graham Cracker."

As I walked away, I couldn't help but think about the way the evening had progressed. To the average person, his interactions would've seemed normal at best, but I knew for Graham, it had been an extraordinary day.

Sure, he hadn't given me a guarantee that he'd make it to the show, but there was a small chance. If this was the man he became after a visit from Professor Oliver, I secretly prayed he'd stop by each day.

There were small moments that I sometimes witnessed with Graham as he cared for his daughter. Those moments were what I held on to when he was colder than cold. Oftentimes, I'd walk in on him shirtless, lying on the couch with Talon in his arms. Each day, he did the kangaroo care, out of fear of not bonding with Talon. But they were bonded more than he could've noticed. She adored him, just as he adored her. Once as I rested in the living room, I overheard him on the baby monitor speaking to his daughter as he tried to soothe her crying.

"You are loved, Talon. I promise to always take care of you. I promise to be better for you."

He would've never shown that side of his heart if he was standing near me. He would've never been seen in such a vulnerable state of mind. Yet the fact that he wasn't afraid to love his daughter so carefully in the quietness of his home lit me up inside. It turned out the beast wasn't such a monster after all. He was simply a man who'd been hurt in the past and was slowly opening back up due to the love of his daughter.

I arrived at the museum a little after eight due to a late floral delivery, and when I walked in wearing my sparkly purple dress, I was shocked by the number of people already there. Richard's display was in the west end of the museum, and the individuals who'd shown up were dressed as if they were at the Met Gala in New York City.

I'd found my dress on sale at Target.

My eyes darted around the room in search of Richard, and when I spotted him, I hurried over. "Hey." I smiled, stepping into the conversation he was having with two women about a piece of his artwork. The women were stunning in their red and gold gowns, which traveled to the floor. Their hair was pinned up perfectly, and their makeup was flawless.

Richard looked up at me and gave me a half smile. "Hey, hey, you made it. Stacy, Erin, this is Lucy."

The two ladies eyed me up and down as I eased my way closer to Richard and held my hand out to each of them. "His *girlfriend*."

"I didn't know you had a girlfriend, Richie," Erin said, shaking my hand with a look of distaste on her lips.

"Me neither," Stacy replied.

"Of five years," I gritted through my teeth, trying my best to give a fake smile.

"Oh," they said in unison, disbelief dripping from the word.

Richard cleared his throat, placed his hand on my lower back, and started to guide me away. "Ladies, go grab yourselves a drink. I'm going to show Lucy around a bit." They walked off, and Richard leaned slightly in to me. "What was that about?"

"What are you talking about?" I asked, trying to play off the fact that I had not been completely normal in that interaction.

"Your whole, this-is-my-man-back-off-bitches persona back there."

"Sorry," I muttered, standing up straighter. I wasn't a jealous girl, but the feeling those ladies had given me was so uncomfortable; it was as if they were displeased by my whole existence.

"It's fine, really," Richard said, taking off his glasses and cleaning them with a pocket cloth. "Your dress is short," he mentioned, looking around the room.

I spun a bit. "Do you like it?"

"It's short, that's all. Plus, your high heels are bright yellow and *really* tall. You're taller than me."

"And that's an issue?"

"It just makes me feel a bit undermined is all. When I introduce you, I'll look like the small guy next to his giant girlfriend."

"It's only a few inches."

"But still, it's belittling."

I wasn't sure how to take his words, and before I could reply, he commented on my hair.

"And there are rose petals in your hair."

I smiled and patted the flower crown I'd crafted at the floral shop before I came. It was made up of roses, tulips, and baby's breath, and it sat on top of my hair, which was placed in a big French braid that lay over my left shoulder. "Do you like it?" I asked.

"It just seems a bit childish," he replied, placing his glasses back on. "I just…I thought I told you how important this event is to me, Lucy. To my career."

I narrowed my eyes. "I know. Richard, this is all amazing. What you've done is amazing."

"Yeah, but it just looks a bit odd for you to arrive dressed in such a way."

My lips parted, uncertain what to say, but before I could reply, he excused himself, saying he needed to go say hello to some very important people.

Clearing my throat, I walked off by myself and wandered around the room before eventually making my way to the bar, where a nice gentleman smiled at me. "Hey there, what can I get you?"

"A different dress," I joked. "And maybe a shorter pair of heels."

"You look beautiful," he remarked. "And between you and me, I think you're the best dressed in the room, but what do I know? I'm just a bartender, not an artist."

I smiled. "Thank you. I'll just take a water with a lemon slice for now."

He cocked an eyebrow. "You sure you don't want vodka? This seems like a room that needs serious quantities of vodka."

I laughed, shaking my head. "While I agree, I think I'm already drawing enough attention to myself. No need to allow the drunken version of myself to escape." I thanked him for the ice water, and when I turned around, I saw the back of a man standing in front of one of Richard's paintings. Beside him sat a car seat that held the most beautiful child in the world.

A wave of comfort washed through me at seeing them before me. It was hard to explain how seeing those two familiar faces brought me a level of confidence.

"You made it," I exclaimed, going over to Talon and bending down to lightly kiss her forehead.

Graham turned my way just a bit before looking back at the painting. "We did." He stood tall in an all-black suit with a deep gray tie and gray cuffs. His shoes were shiny, as if freshly polished for the gala. His hair was slicked back with a bit of gel, and his beard was nicely groomed.

"Does that mean you finished your chapters?"

He shook his head once. "I'll finish once I get home."

My chest tightened. He hadn't even finished his work, but he'd still made time to make an appearance.

"Lucille?"

"Yes?"

"Why am I staring at a twelve-by-twelve-foot painting of your naked boyfriend?"

I giggled to myself, sipping my water. "It's a self-discovery collection where Richard dived deep to express his inner thoughts, fears, and beliefs through how he sees himself using different mediums, such as clay, charcoal, and pastels."

Graham glanced around the room at the rest of Richard's self-portraits and clay creations. "Is that a six-foot-tall statue of his penis?" he asked.

I nodded uncomfortably. "That is indeed a six-foot-tall statue of his penis."

"Hmph. He's quite confident in his"—he tilted his head slightly and cleared his throat—"manhood."

"I like to believe *confidence* is my middle name," Richard joked, walking up to our conversation. "I'm sorry, I don't believe we've met."

"Oh yes, right, sorry. Richard, this is Graham. Graham, this is Richard."

"Lucy's *boyfriend*," Richard said with a bit of bite to his words as he reached out to shake Graham's hand. "So you're the one who's been stealing my girlfriend's time day and night, huh?"

"More so Talon than me," Graham replied, dry as ever.

"And you're an author?" Richard asked, knowing very well that Graham was indeed G.M. Russell. "I'm sorry. I'm not exactly sure I've heard of your novels. I don't think I've ever read anything you've published." He was being oddly aggressive, making the whole situation uncomfortable.

"That's fine," Graham responded. "Enough other people have, so your lack of awareness doesn't inflict any damage on my success."

Richard laughed obnoxiously loud and slugged Graham in the shoulder. "That's funny." He chuckled awkwardly, then slid his hands into his pockets. Richard's eyes traveled to the glass in my hand, and he raised an eyebrow. "Vodka?"

I shook my head. "Water."

"Good, good. It's probably best for you not to drink tonight, right, sweetheart?"

I gave him a tight smile but didn't reply.

Graham grimaced. "Why's that?" he asked.

"Oh, well, when Lucy drinks, she becomes a bit…goofy. Very talkative, if you can believe it. It's like it heightens all her quirks, and it can be a lot to handle at times."

"She seems grown-up enough to make her own choices," Graham countered.

"And her choice was not to drink tonight," Richard replied, smiling.

"I'm sure she can speak for herself," Graham said, his voice cold. "After all, she was given her own vocal cords."

"Yes, but she would've just said exactly what I have stated."

Graham gave a forced, tight grin. It was the unhappiest smile I'd ever witnessed in my lifetime. "Please excuse me. I must go someplace other than right here," Graham stated coldly, lifting the car seat and walking off.

"Wow." Richard whistled low. "What an asshole."

I lightly pushed his shoulder. "What was that? You were a bit aggressive, don't you think?"

"Well, I'm sorry. I just don't know how comfortable I am with you being at his place all the time."

"I'm there helping taking care of Talon, who is my niece, my family. You know this."

"Yeah, but you seem to have left out the fact that he looks like a freaking Greek god, Lucy. I mean, Jesus Christ, what kind of author has arms the size of the *Titanic*?" Richard exclaimed, his jealousy loud and clear.

"He works out when he has writer's block."

"There must be a lot blocking that writer. Anyway, come over here. There are some people I need you to meet." He took my arm and started pulling me forward.

When I turned around to check on Graham, he was sitting on a bench, holding Talon and staring my way. His stare was intense, as if his mind was running with a million thoughts.

Richard took me around the room, introducing me to a bunch of people who were dressed much fancier than me. Every time, he'd speak about my outfit, mentioning how it was quirky, like my heart. He said it with a smile, but I could sense the frown underneath it.

"Can I take a break?" I asked after speaking to a woman who looked at me as if I were trash.

"Just two more people. This is important. They are *the* couple to talk to tonight."

Apparently my break would have to wait.

"Mr. and Mrs. Peterson," Richard said, reaching his hand out for handshakes. "I'm so happy you could make it."

"Please, don't be so formal, Richard. Just call us Warren and Catherine," the gentleman said as they both greeted us with warm smiles.

"Right, of course. Again, I'm so happy you're here."

Catherine wore a fur shawl around her shoulders, and she was decked out in expensive jewelry, making her smile shine even more. Her lips were painted fuchsia, and she carried herself as if she were royalty.

"We wouldn't have missed it for the world, Richard. And you must be Lucy." She grinned and took my hand in hers. "I've been asking a lot about the lady in this talented man's life."

"That's me." I laughed unenthusiastically, tugging on the bottom of my dress with my free hand, hoping Richard wouldn't comment on it. "I'm sorry, how do you both know—"

"Mr. Pet—*Warren* is one of the greatest artists in the world, and he's from Milwaukee, Lucy," Richard explained. "I've told you about him many times."

"No," I said softly. "I'm not sure you have."

"Yes, I have. I'm sure you've just forgotten."

Warren chuckled. "Don't worry about it, Lucy. My own wife forgets me about fifty times a day. Isn't that right, Catherine?"

"I'm sorry, do I know you?" Catherine joked, winking at her husband.

While they were nothing but pleasant, I could tell Richard was somewhat annoyed with me, though I was certain I'd never heard of them.

"So, Richard, what's the next step in your career?" Warren asked.

"Well, I was invited to a showcase in New York City by a friend of mine," he stated.

"Oh?" I asked, surprised to just be hearing about it right then. "I had no clue."

"It just happened this afternoon actually," he said, leaning in and giving me a kiss. "Remember Tyler? He's going to this big art gala in the city and said I could crash at his apartment."

"Oh, the Rosa Art Gala?" Warren asked, nodding. "I spent many years at the Rosa. It's a week of magic. I swear every artist must partake in it at least once. I've found some of my strongest artistic influences during those times."

"And lost plenty of brain cells too," Catherine joked. "From paint fumes, alcohol, and marijuana."

"It's going to be amazing, that's for sure," Richard agreed.

"Are you going too, Lucy?" Warren asked.

"Oh no. She's actually running a floral shop," Richard cut in, not even giving me a chance to answer. I hadn't been invited in the first place. "But I wish she could make it."

"You're a florist?" Warren asked eagerly. "You should consider pairing with an artist for the floral show that the museum hosts here. You make a floral arrangement, and then the artist paints a piece based on your creation. It's quite fun."

"That sounds amazing," I agreed.

"If you need an artist, let me know, and I'll see what I can do. I'm sure I can get your name on the program too." Warren grinned.

"Now's the time for the most important question of the night: What are you drinking, Lucy?" Catherine asked.

"Oh, just water."

She looped her arm with mine and started to walk off with me. "Well, that won't do. Are you a gin lady?" she asked.

Before I could reply, Richard spoke. "Oh, she loves gin. She'll have whatever you're having, I'm sure."

As the four of us started walking to the bar, Catherine paused.

"Oh my God, Warren! Warren, *look*!" She nodded in the direction of Graham, who was putting a sleeping Talon back into her car seat. "Is that G.M. Russell?"

Warren reached into his pocket and pulled out his glasses. "I think it is."

"You know his work?" Richard asked, unamused.

"Know it? We're in love with it. He's one of the best authors out there—besides his father, of course. May he rest in peace," Warren said.

"Oh no. He's much better than Kent was. He writes with so much pain, it's hauntingly beautiful."

"Yes." Richard nodded. "I completely agree. In fact, my Shadows series was inspired by his novel *Bitter*."

"That's one of my favorites." I smiled, remembering the novel that had a permanent spot on my bookcase. "And that twist!"

"Oh my gosh, honey, that twist!" Catherine agreed, her cheeks turning red. "Oh, I'd just love to meet him."

I wasn't certain if it was possible for my boyfriend to be full of any more crap in one night, but he for sure continued to amaze me with his out-of-this-world lies. "He's actually a good friend of Lucy's," he said effortlessly.

Graham was far from my friend, even though he was the only thing that felt right in the room that evening.

"Lucy, do you think you can introduce him?"

"Um, sure, of course." I smiled at the excited couple and led them over to speak with Graham. "Hey, Graham."

He stood up and smoothed out his suit, then placed his hands in front of him, fingers knotted. "Lucille."

"Are you having a good time?" I asked.

He remained silent, awkwardly so. After a moment, I cleared my throat and gestured toward the couple. "This is Warren and Catherine. They are—"

"Two of your biggest fans," Catherine exclaimed, reaching out and grabbing Graham's hand, shaking it rapidly.

Graham gave her a big smile, which was fake and forced, also known as his "author brand" smile, I assumed.

"Thank you, Catherine. It's always a pleasure to meet readers. I've been informed tonight that some have not heard of my work, but the fact that you both have is refreshing," Graham replied.

"Haven't heard of your work? Blasphemy! I can't think of a soul who wouldn't know of you," Warren said. "You're a living legend in a sense."

"Sadly, good ol' Richard seems to disagree," Graham mocked.

"Really, Richard? You don't know Graham's work?" Catherine said, a tinge of disappointment in her voice.

Richard laughed nervously, rubbing the back of his neck. "Oh no, of course I know his work. I was just teasing."

"Your definition of teasing is a bit inaccurate," Graham replied dryly.

Talon started to fuss a bit, and I bent down to pick her up, grinning at her sweet face as Graham and Richard waged their own odd war against each other.

The group could feel the tension building, and Warren broke out a large smile before glancing around the room. "So, Richard, your work is quite unique."

Richard stood up, proud. "Yes. I like to think of it as an awakening to all my deepest and darkest shadows. It's been a process for me to dig so deep, and for a long time, I had a lot of emotional breakdowns about being so vulnerable and open with myself, let alone the idea of allowing others into my soul. It was a very hard time for me, that's for sure, a lot of tears, but I made it."

Graham huffed, and Richard shot him a stern look.

"I'm sorry. Did I say something funny?"

"No, except for every single word that just came out of your mouth," Graham replied.

"You seem to know it all, don't you? Well, go ahead. Tell me what you see when you look around," Richard urged.

Don't do it, Richard. Don't awaken the beast.

"Trust me, you don't want to know my thoughts," Graham said, standing tall.

"No, come on. Enlighten us, because I'm kind of sick of the attitude," Richard replied. "Your pretentious tone is extremely unwarranted and frankly extremely disrespectful."

"Disrespectful? Pretentious?" Graham asked, arching an eyebrow.

Oh no. I took note of the vein popping out of the side of Graham's neck, and even though he kept his voice calm, he was growing more and more irritated as he spoke.

"We're standing in a room full of paintings and sculptures of your penis, which, if I'm honest, seems to be nothing more than a little man trying hard to overcompensate for something he's lacking in his life. Judging by his height and need to force people into a room to stare at his cartoonish oversize genitals, he's lacking quite a bit."

Everyone's mouths hung open, stunned by Graham's words.

My eyes stayed wide, my chest tight as I yanked on Graham's arm. "Can I please have a word in the other room?" I asked, but it was much more a demand than a polite request. "What was that about?!" I whisper-shouted, carrying Talon into the darkened exhibit where Graham headed.

"What are you talking about?"

"You. That whole act back there."

"I don't know what you're talking about," he replied.

"Come on, Graham! For once in your life, can you not be condescending?"

"Me? Condescending? Are you joking? He made portraits of himself, *naked*, and deemed it artwork when truly it's just some kind of hipster bullshit that doesn't belong in this museum."

"He's talented."

"Your idea of talent is jaded."

"I know," I replied harshly. "I do, after all, read your books."

"Oh, good one, Lucille. You really told me," he said, rolling his eyes. "Yet unlike your so-called boyfriend, I know my flaws when it comes to my craftsmanship. He believes he's the best of the best."

"What do you mean? What do you mean *so-called boyfriend*?"

"He doesn't know you," he said assertively, making me raise an eyebrow.

"We've been together for more than five years, Graham."

"Yet he still hasn't a clue who you are, which isn't shocking, because he seems to have his head so far up his own ass he has no time to focus on anyone else."

"Wow," I said, completely baffled by his words. "You don't know him."

"I know his type, the type of people who get the smallest taste of success and feel as if they can toss away the things and people from their past. I don't know how he used to look at you, but he stares at you as if you're nothing now. As if you're below him. I give your relationship two weeks. I bet it's over in a month, tops."

"You're being a jerk."

"I'm telling you the truth. He's a self-righteous piece of shit. Do you know what the nickname for Richard is? It's Dick, which is so fitting. I mean really, Lucille, you sure know how to pick 'em."

He was fuming, his face bright red as he fiddled with his cuffs nonstop. I'd never seen him so mad, so far from his normal unemotional self.

"Why are you so angry? What's wrong with you?"

"Never mind. Forget it. Hand Talon over."

"No, you don't get to do that. You don't get to explode and be disrespectful to my boyfriend and then tell me to forget it."

"I can, and I did."

"No. Graham, stop it. For once in your life, just say what you are actually feeling!"

He parted his lips, but no words escaped him.

"Really? Not a word?" I asked.

"Not a word," he softly replied.

"Then I think you're right. I think it's time for you to go."

"I agree." He stood inches away from me, his hot breaths melting against my skin. My heart pounded against my rib cage as I wondered what he was doing, and he took a few seconds before moving in closer. He straightened his tie, lowered his voice, and spoke so sternly. "Just because you smile and act free doesn't mean the cage doesn't exist. It merely means you lowered your standards for how far you'll allow yourself to fly."

Tears burned at the backs of my eyes as he took Talon from my grip and turned to leave. Right before he stepped out of the darkened area, he paused and took a few deep breaths. He turned back my way, locking eyes with mine, and his lips parted slightly as if he were going to speak again, but I held my hand up.

"Please, just go," I whispered, my voice shaky. "I don't think I can take any more tonight, Mr. Russell."

The coldness of me using his last name made him stand up straighter, and when he disappeared, my tears began to fall.

My fingers wrapped around my necklace, and I took in a few deep breaths. "Air above me, earth below me, fire within me, water surround me…" I repeated the words until my heartbeat returned to a normal pace. I repeated the words until my mind stopped spinning. I repeated the words until I erased the shock Graham had caused to my soul. Then I headed back to the gala with a fake smile on my lips, and in my head, I repeated my words some more.

CHAPTER 11
Lucy

He's still calling you?" Richard asked, cleaning up his paintbrushes in the bathroom sink.

I leaned against the wall in the hallway, staring down at Graham's name flashing against the screen. "Yup." I hadn't seen Graham since he exploded at Richard's gala five days ago, and he hadn't stopped calling me since then.

"And he doesn't leave a message?"

"Nope."

"Block him. He's the definition of a psychopath."

"I can't. What if something happens to Talon?"

Richard glanced my way with an arched brow. "You do know she's not actually your responsibility, right? As in she's not your kid."

"I know. It's just…" I bit my bottom lip and stared down at the phone. "It's hard to explain."

"No, I get it, LuLu. You're a giving person, but you gotta be careful, because a man like him is just a taker. He'll take all he can from you and treat you like crap."

My mind thought back on the dinner Graham and I had a week before, the night when he showed me a small, softer side of him I'd wondered about. The thing about Graham Russell was he lived almost completely inside his mind. He never really invited a person to see his inner thoughts or feelings. So the night he exploded at the art show, it was a complete 180 from who I'd come to know him to be.

Instead of engaging in more talk about Graham, I shifted the conversation. "Do you really have to be gone for a week?"

Richard walked past me, out to the living room, where his suitcases were lying open. "I know. I wish I didn't have to, but now that I hit the museum, I have to keep the momentum going, and when you're invited to a gala in New York City, you go."

I walked up behind him and wrapped my arms around him. "Are you sure girlfriends can't tag along?" I joked.

He turned around with a smile and kissed my nose. "I wish. I'm gonna miss you."

"I'm gonna miss you too." I grinned, giving him a light kiss. "And if you want, I can show you exactly how much I'm going to miss you."

Richard grimaced and glanced at his watch. "While that sounds ridiculously enticing, I gotta leave for the airport in, like, twenty minutes, and I'm hardly done packing." He unwrapped our bodies and went back to his suitcases to pack his brushes.

"Okay. Well, are you sure you don't want me to drive you to the airport?"

"No, it's fine, really. I'll just get a Lyft. You're training the new girl at work today, aren't you?" He glanced at his watch one more time before looking up at me. "I think you're already late."

"Yeah, you're right. Well, okay. Text me before your plane takes off, and call when you land." I bent down and kissed him on the lips.

"Okay, sounds good. And, babe?" he called after me as I scooped up my keys to leave.

"Yes?"

"Block that number."

"I'm sorry I'm late," I said, hurrying into Monet's Gardens through the back door.

Mari was going over the weekly orders with Chrissy, our new florist. Chrissy was a beautiful woman in her seventies who'd once owned her own floral shop. Teaching her the ins and outs of the shop was easy—she knew more than both Mari and me when it came to flowers.

When we mentioned that she was overqualified for the position, she disagreed, saying she'd been a busy florist and shop owner for many years, but it was a lot of work for her to keep up with. She said her friends told her to retire, but her heart knew she needed to be surrounded by flowers for a bit longer, and the position at our shop was perfect.

"No worries." Chrissy smiled. "I already started arranging the orders for today."

"Yeah, and she also taught me this new computer organization system. In other words, I think we hired a wizard," Mari joked. "Is Richard off to New York?"

"Yup, sadly enough, but he'll be back soon."

Mari narrowed her eyes. "This is the first time you two have spent a week apart. Are you sure you can handle the separation?"

"I'm planning to binge on comfort foods—kale chips and guacamole."

"Sweetheart, no offense, but kale chips are not comfort food," Chrissy sassed.

"That's what I've been telling her for the past million years!" Mari said with a sigh as she walked over to unlock the front door and open the shop. "But okay, I'm going to take Chrissy with me to set up a wedding in Wauwatosa. Do you need anything from us?"

I shook my head. "No. Have fun! I'll be here when you get back."

As they walked out of the back door, an older gentleman with a fedora walked in the front and was quick to take off his hat. My chest tightened seeing him, and when his stare found mine, he smiled wide. "Lucy," he said warmly, tipping his hat my way.

"Hi, Ollie. What are you doing here?"

He walked around a bit, studying the flowers in the shop. "I was hoping to buy a few roses for a special lady." He gave me his charming smile and started whistling as he wandered around the shop. "Though I'm not certain which ones she'd like. Will you help?"

"Of course. Tell me a little about her."

"Well, she's beautiful. She has these eyes that just pull you in, and when she looks at you, she makes you feel like the most important person in the room."

My heart warmed hearing him talk so endearingly about the woman. As he continued, we walked around the shop, pulling a flower for each facet of her seemingly vibrant personality.

"She's gentle and caring. Has a smile that lights up a room. She's smart too, so smart. She's not afraid to give a helping hand, even when it's tough. And the last word to describe her," he said, reaching out and picking out a deep red rose, "is pure. She's pure, untainted by the world's cruelty. Just simply, easily, and beautifully pure."

I took the rose from him, a grin resting on my lips. "She sounds like a wonderful woman."

He nodded. "She is indeed."

I walked to the counter and started to trim the flowers for Ollie as he picked out a red vase. The flowers were an arrangement of different colors and styles—a stunning collection. That was my favorite part of my job: when people came into the store and had no idea what they wanted. Roses were gorgeous, yes, and tulips were pretty too, but there was something so creatively rewarding about being able to have free range and create a piece that expressed the artistic personality of the customer's loved one.

As I tied a bow around the vase, Ollie narrowed his eyes at me. "You're ignoring his calls."

I grimaced for a second, fumbling with the ribbon. "It's complicated."

"Of course it is," he agreed. "We are, after all, talking about Graham." He lowered his voice and held his fedora to his chest. "Sweetheart, whatever he did, he's sorry."

"He was cruel," I whispered, the bow not quite perfect enough, leading me to untie the ribbon to begin again.

"Of course he was," he agreed. "We are, after all, talking about Graham." He softly snickered. "But then again, he's Graham, which means he didn't mean it."

I didn't say anything else on the subject. "So the flowers are $44.32, but I'll give you the first-time visit discount, bringing it to $34.32."

"That's very kind of you, Lucy. Thank you." He reached into his wallet and handed me the money. Then he placed his fedora back on his head and turned to leave.

"Ollie, you're forgetting your flowers," I called after him.

He turned back to me and shook his head. "No, ma'am. A friend of mine asked me to stop in to pick those out for you. I asked him some characteristics about you, and that is the creation that came to be."

"Graham said those things about me?" I asked, my chest tightening a bit as I stared down at the arrangement.

"Well, he gave me one of the words, and I just kind of gathered the others on my own, based on the few moments we spent together." He cleared his throat and tilted his head. "Listen, I'm not saying you have to go back, but if you do, you'll prove him wrong."

"Prove him wrong?"

"Graham lives a life where he believes everyone leaves. If his past has taught him anything, it's that. So a part of him feels relief that you left. After all, he was certain you'd disappear eventually anyway. That's why he can't for the life of him stand me. No matter what, I keep showing up, and it drives him bonkers. So if you in any way, shape, or form want to get back at Graham for hurting you, the best revenge is proving to him that he's wrong, that not everyone is going to walk out. I promise you, he'll act like he hates you for it, but remember: the truth lies within his eyes. His eyes will thank you a million times over."

"Ollie?"

"Yes?"

"Which word did he give you? To describe me?"

"Pure, my dear." He tipped his hat one last time and opened the door. "He called you pure."

His brow was knitted and his arms crossed when I approached him. "You came back," Graham stated, sounding surprised as I stood on his front porch. "Honestly, I thought you would've come back days ago."

"Why would you have thought that?" I asked.

"Professor Oliver told me you received the flowers."

"Yes."

He raised an eyebrow. "That was four days ago."

"Uh-huh."

"Well, it took you long enough to come say thank you." His stern, dry words were not shocking, but still, for some reason, they shook me.

"Why would I thank you for the flowers? You didn't even pick them out."

"What does that matter?" he asked, brushing the back of his neck. "You still received them. You seem ungrateful."

"You're right, Graham. *I'm* the rude one here. Anyway, I'm only here because you left a message saying Talon was sick." I walked into the house without being invited and took off my jacket, then laid it on his living room chair.

"A small fever, but I wasn't certain that…" He paused. "You came back because she was sick?"

"Of course I came back," I huffed. "I'm not a monster. If Talon needs me, I'm here for her. You just didn't leave a message before today."

"Yes, of course." He nodded. "Listen…"

"Don't apologize. It seems too weak."

"I wasn't going to apologize. I was going to say I forgive you."

"Forgive me?! For what?"

He shifted around, picking up my jacket from the couch and hanging it in the front closet. "For being childish and disappearing for days."

"You're joking, right?"

"I'm not one to joke."

"Graham…" I started to speak, then closed my eyes and took a few deep breaths to stop myself from saying something I'd regret. "Can you at least for a second accept some kind of blame for how you acted at the museum?"

"Blame? I meant every word I said to you that night."

"Every word?" I huffed, shocked. "So you're not sorry?"

He stood taller and placed his hands in his jeans pockets. "Of course not. I only spoke the truth, and it's a pity you're just too emotional to fully accept it."

"Your definition of truth and my definition of truth are wildly different. Nothing you said held any truth to it. You were just stating your opinionated thoughts, which weren't asked for."

"He treated you like—"

"Just stop, Graham. No one asked you how he treated me. No one came to you for your thoughts. I just invited you to the event because I thought it would be nice to get you and Talon away from staring at the same four walls. My mistake."

"I didn't ask for your pity."

"You're right, Graham. Silly me for reaching out a hand to someone, for trying to build a relationship of some sort with the father of my niece."

"Well, that's your fault. Your need to find life in everything and everyone is ridiculous and reveals your childish ways. You let your emotions drive everything you are, which in turn makes you weak."

My lips parted in disbelief, and I slightly shook my head. "Just because I'm not like you doesn't mean I'm weak."

"Don't do that," he said softly.

"Do what?"

"Make me regret my comments."

"I didn't make you do that."

"Then what did?"

"I don't know. Maybe your conscience."

His dark eyes narrowed, and as Talon started crying, I started in her direction. "Don't," he said. "You can go, Lucille. Your services are no longer needed."

"You're being ridiculous," I told him. "I can get her."

"No. Just go. It's obvious that you want to leave, so leave."

Graham was a monster born from the ugliest of circumstances. He was painfully beautiful in such a dark, tragic way. His words urged me to go while his eyes begged me to stay.

I walked past him, our shoulders brushing against each other, and I stood tall, staring into his dark eyes. "I'm not going anywhere, Graham, so you can stop wasting your breath telling me to go."

Walking into Talon's room, I partly expected Graham to try to stop me, but he never followed.

"Hey, honey," I said, reaching down to Talon and taking her in my arms. I knew it had only been about a week since I last saw her, but I swore she was bigger. Her blond hair was growing in, and her chocolate eyes smiled all on their own.

She smiled more too, even with her tiny cough and somewhat warm forehead. I laid her on the floor to change her diaper and quietly hummed to myself as she smiled brightly at me.

I wondered if her father's smile would look like hers if he ever took part in the expression. I wondered what his full lips would look like if they curved up.

For about thirty minutes, Talon sat in her swing, and I read her books that sat on her small bookcase. She smiled and giggled, and she made the cutest sounds in the world as her tiny nose ran. Eventually, she fell asleep, and I didn't have the nerve to try to move her back into her crib. She looked beyond comfortable as the chair swayed back and forth.

"I'll need to give her medicine in about an hour," Graham said, breaking my stare away from the sleeping baby. I looked up at the doorway, where he stood with a plate in his hand. "I…um…" He shifted his feet around and avoided eye contact. "Mary prepared meat loaf and mashed potatoes. I figured you might be hungry and that you wouldn't want to eat with me, so…" He placed it on the dresser and nodded once. "There you go."

He hurt my mind with the way he twisted my opinions about the person he truly was compared to the person he presented himself to be. It was hard to keep up.

"Thank you."

"Of course." He still avoided eye contact, and I watched as his hands clenched and released repeatedly. "You asked me what I was feeling that night. Do you remember?" he asked.

"Yes."

"Can I share now?"

"Of course."

When his head rose and our eyes locked, I swore he somehow squeezed my heart with his stare. When his lips moved, I drank in every word that spilled from his tongue.

"I felt anger. I felt so much anger at him. He looked at you as if you were unworthy of his attention. He insulted your clothing all night long as he introduced you to people. He discussed you as if you weren't good enough, and for the love of God, he gawked at other women whenever you turned your back to him. He was insensitive, rude, and a complete idiot." He dropped his head for a split second before bringing his eyes back to mine, his once-cold stare now soft, gentle, caring as his lips continued to move. "He was a complete idiot for thinking you weren't the most beautiful woman in that room. Yeah, I get it, Lucille—you're a hippie weirdo and everything about you is loud and outlandish, but who is he to demand that you change? You're a prize of a woman, rose petals in your hair and all, and he treated you as if you were nothing more than an unworthy slave."

"Graham—" I started, but he held a hand up.

"I do apologize for hurting you and for offending your boyfriend. That night just reminded me of a past I once lived, and I am ashamed that I let it get to me in such a way."

"I accept and appreciate your apology."

He gave me a half smile and turned to walk away, leaving me wondering what had happened in his past that upset him so much.

CHAPTER 12
New Year's Eve

It hit the New York Times *bestseller list, on today of all days. You know what that means, Graham?"* Rebecca asked, spreading a new tablecloth on the dining room table.

"It means another reason for Dad to get drunk and show off his house to people," he muttered, just loud enough for her to hear.

She snickered and grabbed the fancy table runner, handed him one end, and took the other in her hands. "It won't be that bad this year. He hasn't been drinking as much lately."

Poor, sweet, naïve Rebecca, Graham thought to himself. She must've been blind to the whisky bottles that sat in his father's desk drawer.

As he helped her set the dinner table for the sixteen guests coming over in two hours, his eyes traveled across the room to her. She'd been living with him and his father for two years now, and he'd never known he could be so happy. When his father was angry, Graham had Rebecca's smile to fall back on. She was the flash of light during the dark thunderstorms.

Plus, every year, he had a birthday cake.

She looked beautiful that night in her fancy New Year's Eve dress.

When she moved, the gold dress traveled with her, slightly dragging on the floor behind her. She wore high-heeled shoes that stretched out her small body, and still she seemed so tiny.

"You look pretty," Graham told her, making her look up and smile.

"Thank you, Graham. You look quite handsome yourself."

He smiled back, because she always made him smile.

"Do you think any kids are gonna come tonight?" he asked. He hated how the parties always had grown-ups and never any kids.

"I don't think so," she told him. "But maybe tomorrow I can take you to the YMCA to hang out with some of your friends."

That made Graham happy. His father was always too busy to take him places, but Rebecca always made time.

Rebecca glanced at the fancy watch on her hand, one his father had given her after one of their many fights. "Do you think he's still working?" she asked, raising an eyebrow.

He nodded. "Uh-huh."

She bit her bottom lip. "Should I interrupt?"

He shook his head. "Nuh-huh."

Rebecca crossed the room, still glancing at her watch. "He'll be mad if he's late. I'll go check." She walked toward his office, and it was only seconds before Graham heard the shouting.

"I'm working! This next book isn't going to write itself, Rebecca!" Kent hollered right before Rebecca came hurrying back into the dining room, visibly shaken, her lips now twisted in a frown.

She smiled at Graham and shrugged. "You know how he is on deadlines," she said, making up excuses.

Graham nodded. He knew better than most.

His father was nothing more than a monster, especially when he was behind on his word count.

Later that night, right before the guests began arriving, Kent changed into his brand-name suit just in time. "Why didn't you get me earlier?" he shouted to Rebecca as she set up appetizers in the living room. "I would've been late if I hadn't seen the time because when I went to use the bathroom."

Graham turned his back to his father and rolled his eyes. He always had to turn his back to mock his father. Otherwise, his father's backhand would mock him right back.

"I'm sorry," Rebecca replied, not wanting to dig any deeper and upset Kent. It was New Year's Eve, one of her favorite holidays, and she refused to get into an argument.

Kent huffed and puffed, straightening his tie. "You should change," he told Rebecca. "Your outfit is too revealing, and the last thing I need is for my friends to think my wife is a floozy." His voice was short, and he didn't even look at Rebecca as he spat out the words.

How did he miss it? Graham thought to himself. How did his father not notice how beautiful Rebecca looked?

"I think you look beautiful," Graham voiced.

Kent cocked an eyebrow and looked over at his son. "No one asked you for your thoughts."

That night, Rebecca changed into something else, and she still looked beautiful to Graham.

She still looked beautiful, but she smiled less, which simply broke his heart.

During dinner, Graham's role was to sit and be quiet. His father preferred when he blended in, almost as if he weren't in the room. The grown-ups talked about how great Kent was, and Graham internally rolled his eyes repeatedly.

"Rebecca, what a delicious meal," a guest commented.

Rebecca parted her lips to speak, but Kent spoke before her. "The chicken is a bit dry and the salad a little underdressed, but otherwise it's edible," he said with a laugh. "My wife isn't known for her cooking skills, but boy, does she try."

"She's better than me," a woman chimed in, winking at Rebecca to ease the sting of Kent's passive-aggressive comment. "I can hardly make macaroni and cheese from a box."

The meal went on with a few more cuts from Kent, but he stated his grievances about Rebecca with such humor that most people didn't think he was serious.

Graham knew better, even though he wished he didn't.

When she reached for more wine, Kent placed his hand on top of hers, halting her. "You know how wine affects you, my love."

"Yes, you're right," Rebecca replied, retracting her hand and placing it in her lap. When a woman inquired about it, she grinned. "Oh, it just makes me a bit dizzy, that's all. Kent's just watching out for me." Her smile became more fake as the night went on.

After dinner was served, Graham was sent to his room for the remainder of the evening, where he spent time playing video games and watching the New Year's Eve countdown on ABC. He watched the ball drop first in New York City and then again when they replayed the clip to celebrate midnight in Milwaukee. He listened to the grown-ups cheering in the other room and could faintly hear the sounds of the fireworks exploding over Lake Michigan.

If Graham stood on his tiptoes, glanced out his window to the left, and looked way up high, he could see some of the fireworks painting the sky.

He used to watch them all the time with his mother, but that was so long ago that he sometimes wondered if it was a real memory or one he made up.

As the people began to leave the house, Graham crawled into bed and pushed the palms of his hands over his ears. He was trying his best to drown out the sound of his father drunkenly yelling at Rebecca about all her mistakes that night.

It was amazing how Kent could hold in his anger until his company left.

Then, it just spilled out of all his pores.

A toxic amount of anger.

"I'm sorry," Rebecca always ended up saying, even though she never had anything to apologize for.

How could his father not see how lucky he was to have a woman like her? It hurt his heart knowing that Rebecca was hurting.

When Graham's door opened a few minutes later, he pretended to be sleeping, unsure if it was his father or not.

"Graham? Are you awake?" Rebecca whispered, standing in his doorway.

"Yes," he whispered back.

Rebecca walked into the room and wiped at her eyes, removing any evidence that Kent had caused her pain. She wandered over to his bed and combed his curly hair out of his face. "I just wanted to say Happy New Year. I wanted to stop by earlier, but I had to clean up a bit."

Graham's eyes filled with tears as he stared at Rebecca's eyes, which were heavy with exhaustion. She used to smile more.

"What is it, Graham? What's wrong?"

"Please don't…" he whispered. As the tears began to roll down his cheeks and his body began to shake in the bed, he tried his hardest to be a man, but it wasn't working. His heart was still the heart of a young boy, a child who was terrified of what would happen if his father didn't ease up on Rebecca.

"Please don't what, sweetie?"

"Please don't leave," he said, his voice strained with fear. He sat up in his bed and placed his hands in Rebecca's. "Please don't leave, Rebecca. I know he's mean and he makes you cry, but I promise you're good. You're good, and he's mean. He pushes people away, he does, and I can tell he makes you so sad. I know he tells you you're not good enough, but you are. You are good enough, and you're pretty, and your dress was beautiful, and your dinner was perfect, and please, please don't leave us. Please don't leave me." He was now crying full-blown tears, his body shaking from the idea that Rebecca was two suitcases away from leaving him forever. He couldn't imagine what his life would be like if she was gone. He couldn't even begin to envision how dark his life would become if she walked away.

When he was only with his father, he was so very much alone.

But when Rebecca came, he remembered how it felt to be loved again.

And he couldn't lose that feeling.

He couldn't lose his light.

"Graham." Rebecca smiled, tears falling from her own eyes as she tried to wipe his away. "You're okay. Please, it's okay. Calm down."

"You're going to leave me. I know you are." He sobbed, covering his face with his hands. That was what people did—they left. "He's so mean to you. He's too mean to you, and you're going to leave."

"Graham Michael Russell, you stop it right now, okay?" she ordered, holding his hands tightly in hers. She placed his hands against her cheeks and nodded once. "I'm here, all right? I'm here, and I'm not going anywhere."

"You're not leaving?" he asked, hiccupping as he tried to catch his next breath.

She shook her head. "No. I'm not leaving. You're just overthinking everything. It's late, and you need rest, okay?"

"Okay."

She laid him back down and tucked him in, kissing his forehead.

As she stood up to leave, he called after her one last time. "And you'll be here tomorrow?"

"Of course, honey."

"Promise?" he whispered, his voice still a bit shaky, but Rebecca's remained strong and sure.

"Promise."

CHAPTER 13
Graham

Lucy and I fell back into our normal routine. In the mornings, she'd show up with her yoga mat and do her morning meditation in the sunroom, and whenever she wasn't working a special event, she'd come over to my house at night to help take care of Talon while I worked on my novel. We ate dinner together at the dining room table almost every night but didn't have much to talk about other than the cold that had found its way into both Talon's body and mine.

"Drink it," Lucy told me, bringing me a mug of tea.

"I don't drink tea." I coughed into my hands. My desk was still scattered with tissues and cough syrup bottles.

"You will drink this twice a day for three days, and it will make you one hundred percent better. I have no clue how you're even functioning with that nasty cough. So drink," she ordered.

I smelled the tea and made a face.

She laughed. "Cinnamon, ginger, fresh lemons, hot red peppers, sugar, black pepper, and peppermint extract—plus a secret ingredient I can't tell you about."

"It smells like hell."

She nodded with a small smirk. "A perfect drink for the devil himself."

For the following three days, I drank her tea. She pretty much had to force-feed it to me, but by day four, the coughing had disappeared.

I was almost positive Lucy was a witch, but at least with her tea, I was able to clear my head for the first time in weeks.

The following Saturday evening, dinner sat on the table, and when I went to get Lucy to eat, I noticed her in the sunroom on her cell phone.

Instead of interrupting, I waited patiently, until the roasted chicken was cold.

Time passed quickly. She'd been standing in the sunroom on her cell phone for hours now. Her eyes were glued to the rain cascading down from the sky as she moved her lips, speaking to whoever was on the other end of the line.

I wandered past the room every now and then, watching her move her hands to express herself, watching the tears fall from her eyes. They fell heavily, like the rain. After a while, she hung up and lowered herself to the floor, sat with her legs crossed, and stared out the window.

When Talon was down, I stepped into the sunroom to check on her.

"Are you all right?" I asked, concerned about how someone as bright as Lucy could appear so dark that evening. It was almost as if she blended into the gray clouds herself.

"How much do I owe you?" she asked, not turning my way.

"Owe me?"

She turned around, sniffling, and allowed the tears to keep falling down her cheeks. "You bet me that my relationship would be over in a month tops, and you win. So how much do I owe you? You win."

"Lucille…" I started, but she shook her head.

"He…um…he said New York is the place for artists. He said it's the place for him to grow his craft, and there are opportunities there that he wouldn't have in the Midwest." She sniffled some more and wiped her nose on her sleeve. "He said his friend offered him a couch in his apartment, so he's going to stay there for a while. Then he said a long-distance relationship wasn't something he was really interested in having, so my stupid heart tightened, thinking he was inviting me out there to be with him. I know what you're thinking too." She giggled nervously, then shrugged and shook her head. "Silly, immature, naïve Lucille, believing love would be enough, thinking she was worthy of being someone's forever."

"That's…not what I was thinking."

"So how much?" she asked, standing up. "How much do I owe you? I have some money in my purse. Let me go grab it."

"Lucille, stop."

She walked in my direction and put on a fake smile. "No, it's fine. A bet is a bet, and you won, so let me go get the money."

"You don't owe me anything."

"You're good at reading people, you know. That's probably what makes you a fantastic author. You can look at someone for five minutes and know their entire story. It's a gift really. You saw Richard for a moment and knew he'd end up breaking me. So what's my story, huh? I hate spoilers, but I'd love to know. What's going to happen to me?" she asked, her body shaking as the tears kept rolling down her cheeks. "Am I always going to be the girl who feels too much and ends up alone? Because I…I…" Her words became a blurred mess as her emotions began to overpower her. She covered her face with her hands and broke down right in the middle of the sunroom.

I didn't know what to do.

I wasn't made for these kinds of moments.

I wasn't one to give comfort.

That was true, but when her knees started to tremble and her legs began to look as if they were going to collapse, I did the only thing I could think to do.

I wrapped her in my arms, giving her something to hold on to, giving her something to hold her up before gravity forced her down to the solid ground. She wrapped her fingers in my shirt and cried into me, soaking my shoulder as my hands rested against her back.

She didn't let go, and I figured I shouldn't ask her to pull her emotions together.

It was all right that she and I handled things in a different fashion. She wore her heart on her sleeve, and I kept my heart wrapped in steel chains deep within my soul.

Without thought, I held her closer as her body continued to shake. The woman who felt everything leaned in closer to the man who felt nothing at all.

For a split second in time, I felt a little of her pain while she encountered my coldness, and neither one of us seemed to mind.

"You can't go home," I told her, glancing at my watch, seeing that it was almost midnight. "It's pouring rain, and you rode your bike to my house."

"It's fine. I'll be okay," she told me, trying to grab her jacket from the front closet.

"It's not safe. I'll drive you."

"No way," she argued. "Talon has a cold. She shouldn't be leaving the house, especially in the pouring rain. Plus, you're a bit sick your-self," she told me.

"I can handle a cold," I stated.

"Yes, but your daughter cannot. I'll be okay. Plus, there's whisky back home," she joked, her eyes still swollen from her emotional break-down over Dick.

I shook my head slightly, disagreeing. "Stay here for a moment." I hurried into my office, picked up three of the five whisky bottles that sat on my desk, and took them back to the foyer where Lucy stood. "Yours for the choosing. You can have all the whisky you want and one of the spare rooms for the night."

She narrowed her eyes. "You're not going to let me ride my bike home tonight, are you?"

"No, definitely not."

She bit her bottom lip and narrowed her eyes. "Fine, but you cannot judge me for the intense romance Johnnie and I are about to have," she said, taking the bottle of Johnnie Walker whisky from my hand.

"Deal. If you need anything, you can knock on my office door. I'll be up and can assist you."

"Thank you, Graham."

"For what?"

"Catching me before I hit the ground."

Knock, knock, knock.

I glanced over at my closed office door and raised an eyebrow as I typed the final few sentences in chapter twenty of my manuscript. My desk was covered in tissues, and a half bottle of cough syrup sat beside me. My eyes burned a bit from exhaustion, but I knew I still needed another five thousand words before I could call it a night. Plus, Talon would be awake in a few hours for a bottle, so it seemed pointless to even consider going to bed.

Knock, knock, knock.

Standing up, I stretched a bit before opening the door. Lucy stood there with a glass of whisky in her hand and a remarkably wide smile on her lips.

"Hi, Graham Cracker," she said, stumbling a bit as she swayed back and forth.

"Do you need something?" I asked, completely aware and alert. "Are you all right?"

"Are you a psychic?" she asked, placing her glass to her lips and taking a sip. "Or a wizard?"

I cocked an eyebrow. "I beg your pardon?"

"I mean, it has to be one of those," she said, dancing down the hallway, back and forth, swirling, twirling, humming. "Because how did you know that Richard—er, *Dick*—would break up with me? I've been thinking about that repeatedly with Johnnie tonight, and I've concluded that the only way you could've known is if you are a psychic." She came closer to me and tapped my nose once with her pointer finger. "Or a wizard."

"You're drunk."

"I'm happy."

"No, you're drunk. You're simply covering your sadness with a blanket of whisky."

"Que será, será." She giggled before trying to peer into my office. "So is that where the magic happens?" She giggled again, then covered her mouth for a second before leaning in closer and whispering, "I mean *magic* as in your stories, not your sex life."

"Yes, I figured, Lucille." I closed my office door, leaving us standing in the hallway. "Would you like some water?"

"Yes, please. The kind that tastes like wine."

We walked past the living room, and I told her to wait on the couch for me to grab the drink.

"Hey, Graham Cracker," she called. "What's your greatest hope?"

"I already told you," I yelled back. "I don't hope."

When I walked back, she was sitting straight up on the couch with a smile on her face.

"Here you go," I said, handing her the glass.

She took a sip of the water, and her eyes widened, stunned. "Oh my gosh, I know who you are now. You aren't a psychic; you aren't a wizard—you're Reverse Jesus!" she exclaimed, her doe eyes wide with wonderment.

"Reverse Jesus?"

She nodded quickly. "You turned wine into water."

Even I couldn't hold in my smile at that one, and she was quick to notice.

"You did it, Graham Cracker. You smiled."

"A mistake."

She tilted her head, studying me. "My favorite mistake thus far. Can I tell you a secret?"

"Sure."

"You may not be a psychic, but sometimes I think I am, and I have this psychic feeling that one day, I'm going to grow on you."

"Oh, I doubt that. You're pretty annoying," I joked, making her laugh.

"Yes, but still. I'm like an ingrown toenail. Once someone lets me in, I dig my claws in."

"What a disgusting thing to compare yourself to." I grimaced. "I mean, that's literally the worst comparison I've ever heard before."

She poked me in the chest. "If you end up using that in one of your novels, I want royalties."

"I'll have my lawyer talk to your lawyer." I smirked.

"Oh, you did it again," she said, leaning in toward me in awe. "Smiling looks good on you. I have no clue why you avoid doing it."

"You just think it looks good on me because you're intoxicated."

"I'm not intoxicated," she insisted, slurring her words a bit in the process. "I'm perfectly sober."

"You couldn't walk a straight line if your life depended on it," I told her.

She took it as a challenge and leaped up from the sofa. As she began walking, she stretched out her arms as if she were walking an invisible tight rope. "See!" she said a second before stumbling over, forcing me to lunge to catch her. She lay in my arms, looked up into my eyes, and smiled. "I totally had it."

"I know," I told her.

"This is the second time you've caught me in one day."

"Third time's a charm."

Her hand rested on my cheek, and she stared into my eyes, making my heart stop for a few moments. "Sometimes you scare me," she said candidly. "But most of the time, your eyes just make me sad."

"I'm sorry for anything I've done to scare you. It's the last thing I'd want to do."

"It's okay. Every time I walk in on you playing peekaboo with Talon, I see your true aura."

"My aura?"

She nodded once. "To the rest of the world, you seem so dark and grim, but when you look at your daughter, everything shifts. Everything in your energy changes. You become lighter."

"You're drunk," I told her.

"I can walk a straight line!" she argued again, trying to stand but failing. "Oh wait, I can't, can I?"

I shook my head. "You definitely can't."

She kept touching my face, feeling my beard in her hands. "Talon is very lucky to have you as her father. You're a really shitty human but a pretty awesome dad." Her voice was soaked in kindness and misplaced trust, which made my heart beat in a way I was certain would kill me.

"Thank you for that," I said, fully accepting both of her comments.

"Of course." She giggled before clearing her throat once. "Graham Cracker?"

"Yes, Lucille?"

"I'm going to vomit."

I scooped her up into my arms and rushed her to the bathroom. The moment I placed her on the floor, she wrapped her arms around the toilet, and I wrapped her wild hair in my hands, holding it out of the way as Lucy appeared to lose everything she'd ever put into her stomach.

"Better?" I asked after she finished.

She sat back a bit and shook her head. "No. Johnnie Walker was supposed to make me feel better, but he lied. He made me feel worse. I hate boys who lie like that and break hearts."

"We should get you to bed."

She nodded and went to stand up but almost tumbled over.

"I got you," I told her, and she nodded once before allowing me to lift her into my arms.

"Third time's a charm," she whispered. She closed her eyes as she laid her head against my chest, and she kept them shut the whole time I pulled the covers back, laid her down, and pulled the blanket over her small body. "Thank you," she whispered as I shut off the light.

I doubted she'd remember any of the night's events come morning, which was probably for the best.

"Of course."

"I'm sorry my sister left you," she said, yawning with her eyes still closed. "Because even though you're cold, you're still very warm."

"I'm sorry Dick left you," I replied. "Because even when you're upset, you're still very kind."

"It hurts," she whispered, wrapping her arms around a pillow and pulling it closer to her chest. Her eyes stayed closed, and I watched a few tears slip out. "Being left behind hurts."

Yes.

It did.

I stood still for a few moments, unable to leave her side. As someone who'd been left behind before, I didn't want her to fall asleep alone. Perhaps she wouldn't remember me standing there in the morning, and maybe she wouldn't even care. But I knew what it felt like going to bed alone. I knew the cold chill that loneliness left drifting through a darkened room, and I didn't want her to suffer from that same feeling. Therefore, I stayed.

It didn't take long for her to fall asleep. Her breaths were gentle, her tears stopped, and I shut the door. I couldn't for the life of me understand why a person would leave someone as gentle as her behind—with or without her weird sage stick and crystals.

CHAPTER 14

Lucy

O *uch, ouch, ouch.*

I slowly sat up in bed, realizing quickly it wasn't my bed at all. My eyes examined the room, and I shifted around in the sheets a bit. My hands fell against my forehead.

Ouch!

My mind was spinning as I tried to recall what happened the night before, but everything seemed to be a blur. The most important piece of information came flooding back to me though—Richard had chosen New York City over me.

I turned to my left and found a small tray sitting on the nightstand with a glass of orange juice, two pieces of toast, a bowl of berries, a bottle of ibuprofen, and a small note.

> *Sorry for misleading you last night.*
> *I'm a jerk. Here's some medicine and breakfast to*
> *make up for me making you feel like shit this morning.*
>
> —*Johnnie Walker*

I smiled and popped a few berries into my mouth before washing down the ibuprofen. Pulling myself up, I walked to the bathroom and washed my face. My mascara was smeared all over, making me look like a raccoon. Then I used the toothpaste in the top drawer and my finger as the brush to clean my nasty morning-after-whisky breath.

As I finished washing up, I heard Talon crying and hurriedly went to check on her. I walked into her nursery and paused when I saw an older lady standing over her, changing her diaper.

"Hello?" I asked.

The woman turned for a moment, then went back to her task.

"Oh, hello, you must be Lucy," the woman exclaimed, lifting Talon into her arms and bouncing the smiling girl. She turned my way with a big grin. "I'm Mary, Ollie's wife."

"Oh, hi! It's nice to meet you."

"You too, darling. I've heard so much about you from Ollie. Not as much from Graham, but, well, you know Graham." She winked. "How's your head?"

"It's somehow still there," I joked. "Last night was rough."

"You kids and your coping mechanisms. I hope you're feeling better soon."

"Thank you." I smiled. "Um, where's Graham exactly?"

"He's in the backyard. He called me early this morning to ask me to come watch Talon while he went to run some errands. As you know, that's a big deal for Graham—asking people for help—so I swooped in to watch her while he left and you rested."

"Did you leave me the breakfast?" I asked. "With the note?"

Her lips stretched farther, but she shook her head. "No, ma'am. That was all Graham. I know. I'm as surprised as you are. I didn't know he had it in him."

"What is he doing in the backyard?" I asked, walking in that direction.

Mary followed me, bouncing Talon the whole way. We walked into the sunroom and stared out the floor-to-ceiling windows at Graham as he cut the grass. Against the small shed lay bags of soil and shovels.

"Well, it seems he's making a garden."

My chest tightened at the idea, and no words came to me.

Mary nodded once. "I told him to wait to cut the grass seeing as how it rained last night, but he seemed eager to get started."

"That's amazing."

She nodded. "I thought so too."

"I can take Talon for you if you need to get going," I offered.

"Only if you're feeling up to it. I do need to get going if I'm going to make the afternoon church service. Here you go." She handed Talon over and kissed her forehead. "It's amazing, isn't it?" she asked. "How a few months ago, we weren't sure she was going to make it, but now she's more here than ever before."

"So, so amazing."

She placed her hand on my forearm, a gentle touch, and gave me a warm smile, just like her husband. "I'm glad we were finally able to meet."

"Me too, Mary. Me too."

She left the house a few minutes later. Talon and I stayed in the sunroom, watching Graham working hard outside, turning his head every now and then to cough. It had to be freezing out there after the cold rain the night before, and it couldn't have been doing anything great for his cold.

I walked to the back door that led out to the yard and pushed it open, a cold breeze brushing against me. "Graham, what are you doing?"

"Just fixing up the backyard."

"It's freezing out here, and you're making your cold worse. Get inside."

"I'm almost finished, Lucille. Just give me a few more minutes."

I arched an eyebrow, confused as to why he was so determined. "But why? What are you doing?"

"You asked me to make a garden," he said, wiping his brow with the back of his hand. "So I'm making you a garden."

My heart.

It exploded.

"You're making a garden? For me?"

"You've done plenty for me," he replied. "You've done even more for Talon. The least I can do is build you a garden so you can have another place to meditate. I bought a ton of organic fertilizer. They told me it was the best kind, and I figured a hippie weirdo like yourself would enjoy the organic part." He wasn't wrong. "Now please close that door before you make my daughter freeze."

I did as he said, but not for a second did I take my eyes off him. When he finished, he was covered in dirt and sweat. The backyard was beautifully trimmed, and all that was missing was the plants.

"I figure you can pick out the flowers or seeds or whatever garden-ers garden," he told me as he wiped his brow. "I know nothing about these kinds of things."

"Yeah, of course. Wow, this is just…" I smiled, staring at the yard. "Wow."

"I can hire someone to plant whatever you choose," he told me.

"Oh no, please let me. That's my favorite part of spring—digging my hands into the earth's soil and feeling myself reconnect with the world. It's very grounding."

"And once again, your weird is showing," he said with a small twinkle in his eye, as if he were...teasing me? "If it's all right with you, I'd like to shower. Then I can take Talon so you can start your day."

"Yes, for sure. No rush."

"Thank you."

He started to walk away, and I called after him. "Why did you do this?" I asked. "The garden?"

He lowered his head and shrugged his shoulders before looking into my eyes. "A smart woman once told me I was a shitty human, and I'm trying my best to be a little less shitty."

"Oh no." I pulled the collar of my shirt over my face and scrunched up my nose. "I said that last night, didn't I?"

"You did, but don't worry. Sometimes the truth needs to be voiced. It was much easier to hear it from someone as giggly, drunk, and kind as you."

"I'm sorry, come again?" Mari asked me that afternoon as we walked our bikes to the hiking trail. Spring was always exciting because we could bike a lot more and explore nature. Sure, I loved it more than my sister, but somewhere deep, deep, *deep* inside her soul, I was sure she was thankful to have me to keep her healthy.

"I know." I nodded. "It's weird."

"It's beyond weird. I cannot believe Richard would break up with you via a phone call," she gasped. Then she grimaced. "Well, on second thought, I'm surprised it took this long for you to break up."

"What?!"

"I mean, I'm just saying. You two were so much alike in the beginning, Lucy. It was kind of annoying how much of a match made in heaven you two were, but over time, you both seemed to… shift."

"What are you talking about?"

She shrugged. "You used to laugh all the time with Richard, but lately…I can't even think of the last time he made you giggle. Plus, tell me the last time he asked how you were doing. Every time I saw him, he was talking about himself."

Hearing that from Mari didn't make it any easier to deal with the fact that Richard had broken up with me. I knew she was right too. The truth of the matter was Richard wasn't the same man who fell in love with me all those years ago, and I was far from the girl he knew me to be.

"Maktub," I whispered, looking down at my wrist.

Mari smiled my way and hopped on her bike. "Maktub indeed. You can move in with me so you're not stuck in his apartment. It will be perfect. I needed more sister time. Look at it this way—at least now you don't have a mustache going down on you."

I laughed. "Richard hasn't gone down on me in what feels like years."

Her mouth dropped open in disbelief. "Then you should've broken up with him years ago, sister. A boy who doesn't go down doesn't have the right to your services once he goes up."

My sister was filled with irrefutable knowledge.

"You don't seem that sad about it at all," Mari mentioned. "I'm a bit surprised."

"Yeah, well, after drinking my weight in whisky last night and spending the rest of the morning meditating today, I'm feeling okay. Plus, Graham made me a garden this morning."

"A garden?" she asked, surprised. "Is that his form of an apology?"

"I think so. He bought a ton of organic fertilizer too."

"Well, he gets an A for that one. Everyone knows the way to Lucy's forgiveness is through dirt and organic fertilizer."

Amen, sister.

"So are we still on for going to visit Mama's tree up north for Easter?" I asked as we started biking the trail. Every holiday, Mari and I tried our best to make it up to visit Mama. One of Mama's old friends had a cabin up north that she didn't use often, and that was where we'd planted Mama's tree all those years ago, surrounded by people from all around the country who made up her family.

If I'd learned anything from all my traveling with Mama, it was that family wasn't built by blood—it was built by love.

"So you're going to hate me, but I'm going to be visiting a friend that weekend," Mari said.

"Oh? Who?"

"I was going to catch the train to Chicago to see Sarah. She's back in the States visiting her parents, and I thought I'd swing by, seeing as how I haven't seen her since I got better. It's been years."

Sarah was one of Mari's closest friends and a world traveler. It was almost impossible to pinpoint where Sarah would be one month to the next, so I completely understood Mari's choice. It just sucked because with Richard gone, it would be the first holiday I'd be spending alone.

Alas, maktub.

CHAPTER 15

Graham

Professor Oliver sat across from me at my desk, his eyes roaming over the first draft of chapters seventeen through twenty of my novel. I sat impatiently waiting as he flipped each page slowly, his eyes narrowed, deep in thought.

Every now and then, he'd glance my way, make a low hum, and then go back to reading. When he finally finished, he set the papers back on my desk and remained silent.

I waited, arched an eyebrow, but still, no sound.

"Well?" I asked.

Professor Oliver removed his glasses and crossed his leg over his knee. With a very calm voice, he finally spoke. "It's kind of like a monkey took a big shit and tried to spell their name in it with their tail. Only, the monkey's name is John, and he wrote *Maria*."

"It's not that bad," I argued.

"Oh no." He shook his head. "It's worse."

"What's wrong with it?" I asked.

He shrugged his shoulders. "It's just fluff. All fat, no meat."

"It's the first draft. It's supposed to be shit."

"Yes, but it's supposed to be human shit, not monkey shit. Graham, you're a *New York Times* bestseller. You're a *Wall Street Journal* best-seller. You have millions of dollars in your bank account from your craftsmanship in creating stories, and there are numerous fans around the world with your words tattooed on their bodies. So it's a shame that you had the nerve to hand this complete and utter bullshit to me." He stood up, smoothed out his velvet suit, and shook his head. "Talon can write better than this."

"You're joking. Did you read the part about the lion?" I asked.

He rolled his eyes so hard, I was certain his eyeballs were going to get lost in the back of his head. "Why the hell is there a lion loose in Tampa Bay?! No. Just—no. Find a way to relax, okay? You need to loosen up, break free a bit. Your words read as if you have a stick up your ass, and the stick isn't even teasing you right."

I cleared my throat. "That's a really weird thing to say."

"Yes, well, at least I don't write monkey shit."

"No." I smiled. "You only speak it."

"Listen closely, okay? As the godfather to Talon, I am proud of you, Graham."

"Since when are you her godfather?"

"It's a self-proclaimed title, and don't kill my spirit, son. As I was saying, I am proud of how great of a father you are to your daughter. Every minute of your day is spent caring for her, which is amazing, but as your writing mentor, I am demanding that you take some time for yourself. Go smoke some crack, hump a stranger, eat some weird mushrooms. Just loosen up a bit. It will help your stories."

"I've never had to loosen up before," I told him.

"Were you getting laid before?" he countered with an eyebrow arched.

Well, fuck.

"Goodbye, Graham, and please, don't call me until you are high or having sex."

"I'm probably not going to call you while I'm having sex."

"That's fine," he said, grabbing his fedora off the desk and placing it on his head. "It probably wouldn't last long enough for you to dial my number anyway," he mocked.

God, I hated that man.

Too bad he was my best friend.

"Hey, Talon's down for a nap. I just wanted to see if you wanted me to order a piz—" Lucy's words faded away as she stepped into my office. "What are you doing?" she asked warily.

I set my phone down on my desk and cleared my throat. "Nothing."

She smirked and shook her head. "You were taking a selfie."

"I was not," I argued. "A pizza is fine. Just cheese on my half."

"No, no, no, you cannot change the subject. Why are you taking selfies while dressed in a suit and tie?"

I straightened my tie and went back to my desk. "Well, if you have to know, I need a picture of myself to upload on this site."

"What site? Are you joining Facebook?"

"No."

"Then which site?" She giggled to herself. "Anything but Tinder, and you'll be okay."

My jaw tightened, and she stopped laughing.

"*Oh my God*, you're joining Tinder?!" she hollered.

"Say it a bit louder, Lucille. I'm not certain the neighbors heard you."

"I'm sorry. I just…" She walked into my office and sat on the edge of my desk. "G.M. Russell is joining the world of Tinder. I knew it felt a little cold in the house."

"Huh?"

"I mean, when I first met you, I figured you were the devil, which meant your home was hell, which means with it now being cold that—"

"Hell has finally frozen over. Clever, Lucille."

She reached for my cell phone and started trying to unlock it. "Can I see your photos?"

"What? No."

"Why not? You do know Tinder is, like, a hookup site, right?"

"I'm fully aware of what Tinder is."

Her cheeks reddened, and she bit her bottom lip. "You're trying to get laid, eh?"

"Professor Oliver is convinced my writing is suffering from the fact that I haven't had sex in a while to loosen myself up. He thinks I'm uptight."

"What?!" she gasped. "You?! Uptight?! No way!"

"Anyway, he's one hundred percent wrong about the manuscript. It's good."

She rubbed her hands together, giddy. "Is it? Can I read it?"

I hesitated, and she rolled her eyes.

"I'm your biggest fan, remember? If I don't love it, you'll know Ollie was right. If I do love it, you'll know you're right."

Well, I did love to be right.

I handed her the chapters, and she sat reading, her eyes darting back and forth over the pages. Every now and then, she'd glance at me with a concerned look. Finally, she finished and cleared her throat. "A lion?"

Shit.

I rolled my eyes. "I need to get laid."

"Take off your tie, Graham."

"Excuse me?"

"I need you to unlock your phone and take off your tie and the suit jacket. No girl who is trying to have sex is in search of a man with a freaking suit and tie on. Plus, you buttoned the top button on your shirt."

"It's classy."

"It looks like your neck has a muffin top."

"You're being ridiculous. This is a custom-made designer suit."

"You rich people and your labels. All I hear is that it's not a penis, and therefore it eliminates your opportunities to get laid. Now, unlock your phone, and take off the tie."

Annoyed, I followed her orders. "Better?" I asked, crossing my arms.

She grimaced. "A little. Here, unbutton the top three buttons on your shirt."

I did as she said, and she nodded, taking photographs.

"Yes! Chest hair—women who are trying to get it on love some chest hair. It's like the three little pigs; it has to be the right amount. Not too much, not too little, your hair is juuuuust right." She grinned.

"Have you been drinking again?" I asked.

She laughed. "No. This is just me."

"That's what I was afraid of."

After taking some shots, she studied them with the biggest frown I'd ever seen. "Yeah, no. You have to take off your shirt completely."

"What? Don't be ridiculous. I'm not taking off my shirt in front of you."

"Graham," Lucy whined, rolling her eyes. "You have your shirt off every other day doing that kangaroo thing with Talon. Now shut up and take off your shirt."

After some more arguing, I finally gave in. She even had me switch into dark black jeans—to "look more manly." She started snapping photographs, telling me to turn left and right, to smile with my eyes—whatever that meant—and to be moody but sexy.

"Okay, one more. Turn to the side, drop your head a little, and slide your hands into your back pockets. Look as if you hate everything about me taking pictures of you."

Easy enough.

"There," she said, grinning from ear to ear. "Your pictures are now uploaded. Now all that's left to do is perfect your bio."

"No need," I told her, reaching for my cell phone. "I already did that part."

She raised an eyebrow, seeming unsure, and then went to read it. "*New York Times* bestselling author who has a six-month-old child. Married, but the wife ran away. Looking to hook up. Also, I'm five foot eleven."

"Everyone seems to put their height. I guess it's a thing."

"This is awful. Here. I'll fix it."

I hurried over to her, standing behind to watch what she typed.

> Looking for sex. I am a big dick.

"I think you meant I *have* a big dick," I remarked.

She wickedly replied, "No, I meant what I wrote."

I groaned and went to grab my phone.

"Okay, okay, I'll try again!"

> Looking for casual sex, no strings attached.
> Unless you're into being tied up.
> Looking at you, Anastasia.

"Who's Anastasia?" I asked.

Lucy tossed me my phone and laughed to herself. "All that matters is that the women will understand. Now all you have to do is swipe right if you find them attractive, left if you think they're not. Then, just wait for the magic to happen."

"Thank you for your help."

"Well, you gave me a garden, so the least I can do is get you laid. I'm going to order the pizza now. I'm exhausted after all that."

"Only cheese on my half! Oh, Lucille?"

"Yes?"

"What's Snapchat?"

She narrowed her eyes and shook her head twice. "Nope, not even touching that one. Only one social media adventure a night. We'll save the snapping for another day."

CHAPTER 16
Lucy

Graham's first Tinder date was on Saturday, and before he left, I forced him to change out of his suit and tie and into a plain white T-shirt and dark jeans.

"It feels too casual," he complained.

"Um, it's not like your clothes are going to stay on anyway. Now go. Go on and spread some legs, do some pelvic thrusts, and then come back home and write about horror stories and monsters."

He left at eight thirty that night.

By nine, he'd returned.

I arched an eyebrow. "Um, not to sound totally disrespectful to your manhood and all, but that was legit the fastest round of sex in the history of sex."

"I didn't sleep with her," Graham replied, dropping his keys on the table in the foyer.

"What? Why?"

"She turned out to be a liar."

"Oh no!" I frowned, feeling my chest tighten for him. "Married?

Kids? Three hundred pounds bigger than her picture? Did she have a penis? Was her name George?"

"No," he said harshly, plopping down on the living room couch.

"Then what was it?"

"Her hair."

"Huh?"

"Her hair. On the app, she was a brunette, but when I got there, she was a blond."

I blinked repeatedly. Full-on blank stare. "Come again?"

"I'm just saying, it's obvious that if she'd lie about something like that, she'd lie about gonorrhea and chlamydia."

The way he said it with such a straight face made me burst out into a giggling fit.

"Yes, Graham, that's exactly how it works." I laughed, my stomach hurting from laughing so hard.

"This isn't funny, Lucille. It turns out I'm not a person who can just randomly sleep with someone. I'm on a deadline, and I cannot for the life of me figure out how I'm going to loosen up in time to send the book to my editor. It was supposed to be done by the time Talon was born. That was over six months ago."

I smiled widely and bit my bottom lip. "You know what? I think I have an idea, and I'm one hundred and ten percent sure you're going to hate it."

"What is it?" he asked.

"Have you ever heard of hot yoga?"

"I'm the only man in here," Graham whispered as he walked into the yoga studio with me that Sunday morning. He was in a white tank top with gray sweatpants, and he looked terrified.

"Don't be silly, Graham Cracker. The instructor is a guy. Toby. You'll fit right in."

I lied.

He didn't fit right in, but at least watching a grown man with muscles on top of muscles trying to do a sun salutation was the highlight of my life—and of the lives of all the women in class that morning.

"Now travel from cobra to downward dog to pigeon with controlled movement," Toby instructed.

Graham groaned, doing the movements but complaining the whole time. "Cobra, pigeon, camel—why is every move named after a sex position?" he asked.

I giggled. "You know, most people would say those are named after animals, Graham Cracker, not sex positions."

He turned my way, and after a second, realization broke through. A tiny smile formed. "Touché."

"You're super tight," the instructor noted to Graham as he walked around to help him.

"Oh no, you don't have to—" Graham started, but it was too late. Toby was helping adjust his hips.

"Relax," Toby said in his soothing voice. "Relax."

"It's hard to relax when a stranger is touching my—" Graham's eyes widened. "Yup, that's my penis. You are actually touching my penis," Graham muttered as the instructor helped him with one of the positions.

I couldn't stop giggling at how ridiculous and uncomfortable Graham looked. His face was so stern, and when Toby made Graham pop his butt out, I had tears rolling down my cheeks from laughter.

"Okay, class, one final breath. In with the good energies, out with the bad. Namaste." Toby bowed to us all, and Graham just stayed there, lying on the floor in a pile of sweat, tears, and his manhood.

I kept giggling to myself. "Come on. Get up." I reached down to him, and he took my hand as I pulled him up. As he stood up, he shook his nasty, sweaty hair all over me. "Ew! That's disgusting."

With a sly smile, he said, "You made me get touched in public, so you get to enjoy the sweat."

"Trust me, you're lucky it's Toby who touched you instead of the women who are currently gawking at you over in the corner right now."

He turned to see the women staring his way, waving. "You women and your sex-driven minds," he joked.

"Says the man who does camel as a sex position. What do you do exactly? Do you just sit on your knees and like"—I thrust my hips—"do this repeatedly?" I kept making the humping motion, which turned Graham's face even redder than it had been during the class.

"Lucille."

"Yes?"

"Stop humping the air."

"I would, but your embarrassment is too rewarding right now." I laughed. He was so easily humiliated, and I knew being around me in public would be awful for him. I'd take every opportunity to make myself look like a fool. "Okay, so needless to say, hot yoga isn't your thing."

"Not at all. If anything, I feel more stressed out and a pinch violated," he joked.

"Well, let me try a few more things to see if they help you."

He cocked an eyebrow as if he could read my mind. "You're going to sage my house, aren't you? Or put crystals on my windowsills?"

"Oh yeah." I nodded. "I'm going to hippie-weirdo the crap out of your house, and then you're going to help me in the garden."

I spent the next few weeks out in the backyard, teaching Graham the ins and outs of gardening. We planted fruits, vegetables, and beautiful flowers. I made lines of sunflowers that would look so beautiful as they grew tall over time. In one corner of the yard was a stone bench, which would be perfect for morning energy meditations and great as an afternoon reading corner. I surrounded it with beautiful flowers that would light up the area—Peruvian lilies, nepeta, coreopsis, forget-me-nots, and gloriosa daisies. The colors would be beautiful mixed together. The pinks, blues, yellows, and purples would add a pop of color to Graham's life, that was for sure.

As the baby monitor started going off, Graham stood up from the dirt. "I'll get her."

Only a few minutes passed before I heard him shouting my name. "Lucille!"

I sat up in the dirt, alarmed by the urgency in Graham's shout.

"Lucille, hurry!"

I shot up to my feet, my heart pounding in my chest, dirt across my face, and I sprinted into the house. "What is it?!" I hollered back.

"In the living room! Hurry!" he shouted once more.

I ran, terrified about what I was about to witness, and when I made it into the space, my heart landed in my throat as I wrapped my hands over my mouth. "Oh my gosh," I said, my eyes watering over as I looked at Talon.

"I know, right?" Graham said, smiling at his daughter. For a long time, he'd tried his best to hold in his grins, but he hadn't been able to lately. The more Talon laughed and smiled, the more she opened Graham's heart.

He was holding Talon in his arms, feeding her.

Well, he wasn't feeding her. She was feeding herself, holding the bottle in her own hands for the first time.

My heart exploded with excitement.

"I was feeding her, and she wrapped her hands around the bottle and started to hold it herself," he told me, his eyes wide with pride.

As we cheered her on, Talon started giggling and spat milk into Graham's face, making us both laugh. I grabbed a cloth and wiped the milk from his cheek.

"She amazes me every day," he said, staring at his daughter. "It's too bad that Jane..." He paused. "That *Lyric* is missing out on it. She has no clue what she left behind."

I nodded in agreement. "She's missing everything. It's just sad."

"What was it like, growing up together?" he asked.

I was a bit surprised. We'd spent months together, and he hadn't once asked me any questions about my sister.

I sat on the couch beside him and shrugged. "We moved around a lot. Our mom was a bit of a floater, and when my dad couldn't take any more, he left us. Lyric was older and noticed more issues than Mari and I did. Every day with my mother felt like a new adventure. The lack of a real home never bothered me because we had each other, and whenever we needed something, some kind of miracle would happen. But Lyric didn't see it that way. She was very much like our father—grounded. She hated not knowing where our next meal would come from. She hated that sometimes Mama would give what little money we did have to help out a friend in need. She hated the instability of our lives, so when she'd finally had enough, when she could no longer take the person Mama was, she did exactly as our father had—she left."

"She's always been a runner," he stated.

"Yes, and a part of me wants to hate her for how distant and cold she became, but another part understands. She had to grow up fast, and in a way, Lyric wasn't wrong. Our mother was kind of a child herself, which meant we didn't have much parenting growing up. Lyric felt as if she had to take on that role and parent her parent."

"Which is probably why she never wanted kids," he said. "She'd already done the parent role."

"Yeah. I mean, it doesn't forgive her actions at all, but it makes them more understandable."

"I think I could tell when I met her that she was a runner. Also, I'm certain she could tell I was cold, that I'd never once ask her to stay."

"Do you miss her?" I asked, my voice low.

"No," he answered quickly, no hesitation whatsoever. "She and I were never in love. We had an unspoken agreement that if one was ever ready to go, they were free to do so. The marriage arrangement was just something she thought would help her advance in her career. We were simply roommates who happened to have sex sometimes. Before Talon, it would've been fine if she left. It would've been completely acceptable. Hell, I was somewhat surprised she stayed as long as she did. I wouldn't have cared, but now…" He smiled down at Talon as she burped for him, and then he laid her on the blanket on the floor. "Now I call her each night, asking her to come back, not for me but for our daughter. I know what it's like to grow up without a mother, and I'd never want that for Talon."

"I'm so sorry."

He shrugged. "Not your fault. Anyway, how's the garden?"

"Perfect. It's perfect. Thank you again for the gift. It means more to me than you could imagine."

He nodded. "Of course. I'm guessing you're gone this weekend, for the holiday?" He climbed from the couch onto the floor and started playing peekaboo with Talon, which made my heart do cartwheels.

"I was supposed to be, but it turns out I'm spending the holiday alone."

"What? Why?"

I explained that Mari would be out of town and that I normally made the trip up north but didn't want to do the drive alone.

"You should come to Professor Oliver's house with Talon and me," Graham offered.

"What? No. No, it's really okay."

He pulled out his cell phone and dialed a number. "Hello? Professor Oliver, how are you?"

"Graham, no!" I whisper-shouted, reaching out my arm to stop him, but he stood up and wouldn't allow me to grab the phone.

"Good, I'm good." *Pause.* "No, I'm not trying to back out. I'm calling to see if you could add another chair to your table. It appears Lucille was going to sit in her apartment for Easter and cry into a pint of Ben & Jerry's, and while I think that's a completely normal thing to do, I thought I'd see if you could host her at your place."

Another long pause.

Graham smiled.

"Very well. Thank you, Professor Oliver. We'll see you this weekend." He hung up and turned my way. "They are having a brunch at one. It will be us, Professor Oliver and Mary, and their daughter, Karla, and her fiancée, Susie. You should bring a dish."

"I cannot believe you did that!" I hollered, grabbing a throw pillow from the couch and tossing it at him. He smiled even more.

God, that smile.

If he had smiled more often before, I was certain Lyric would've never been able to leave his side.

He picked up the pillow and threw it back at me, making me fall backward onto the couch. "We can drive over there together. I can pick you up from your house."

"Perfect." I grabbed the pillow and threw it back at him. "Dress code?"

He tossed it at me one last time and bit his bottom lip, allowing the small dimple in his right cheek to appear. "Anything you wear will be good enough for me."

CHAPTER 17
Graham

I arrived at Lucy's house to pick her up for Easter brunch, and when she walked down the apartment staircase, I sat in the driver seat of my car. Talon babbled, and I nodded once. "Exactly."

Lucy looked beautiful. She was wearing a yellow dress with tulle underneath the skirt that made it flare out. Her makeup was sparse except for the apple-red lipstick that matched her high heels. Her hair was braided up with daisies threaded throughout, like a crown.

I stepped out of the car and hurried to the passenger side to open the door for her. She smiled my way with a bouquet of flowers in one hand and a dish to pass in her other.

"Well, aren't you just dapper looking." She smirked.

"Just a suit and tie," I said, taking the dish from her. I walked around to the other side of the car and opened the door, placing the dish on the seat.

As I climbed back into the driver's seat, I closed the door and glanced once at Lucy. "You look beautiful."

She laughed and patted her hair before smoothing out her dress. "You're not wrong, sir."

We drove to Professor Oliver's home, and when we arrived, I introduced Lucy to Ollie's daughter, Karla, and her fiancée, Susie.

"It's lovely to meet you, Lucy," Karla said as we walked into the house. "I would say I've heard a lot about you, but you know Graham. The guy doesn't talk," she joked.

"Really?" Lucy asked sarcastically. "I can't get the guy to ever shut up."

Karla laughed, took Talon from my arms, and kissed her forehead. "Yeah, he's a real loudmouth, that one."

Karla was the closest thing I'd ever had to a sister, and we argued like it too. As a kid, she had been in and out of the foster program and had found herself in a lot of trouble with drugs and alcohol. I never knew her back then though. When I came across her, she had already kind of figured out life. She was this beautiful African American woman who was a strong activist for kids who have no place to call home.

Professor Oliver and Mary wouldn't give up on her when she was a teenager, and Karla always said because of that, something changed in her heart. Not many kids would be asked to be adopted at the age of seventeen, yet Oliver and Mary wouldn't let her go.

They had that skill about them—seeing people's scars and calling them beautiful.

"Here, I'll take that dish," Susie offered, taking Lucy's tray from her. Susie was also a stunning person. She was a beautiful Asian American woman who fought hard for women's rights. If ever there was a couple destined for a true love story, it was Karla and Susie.

I was never a people person, but these people were good.

Like Lucy.

Just wholeheartedly good people who didn't ask for anything but love.

When we walked into the kitchen, Mary was there, cooking, and she hurried over, giving me a kiss on the cheek and doing the same to Talon and Lucy. "You've been requested to join Ollie in his office, Graham. You were supposed to bring him new chapters of your book to read, and he's waiting," Mary said. I glanced over at Lucy, and Mary laughed. "Don't worry about her. She'll fit right in. We'll take good care of her."

Lucy smiled, my heart expanded, and then I headed to Professor Oliver's office.

He sat at his desk reading the newest chapters I'd presented to him, and I waited impatiently as his eyes darted back and forth. "I took out the lion," I told him.

"Shh!" he ordered, going back to reading. Every now and then, he made facial expressions as he flipped the pages, but mostly, nothing. "Well," he said, finishing and placing the papers down. "You didn't have sex?"

"No."

"And no cocaine?"

"Nope."

"Well." He sat back in his chair in disbelief. "That's shocking, because whatever it is that made you step up your game, it's mind-blowing. This…" He shook his head in disbelief. "This is the best work you've ever written."

"Are you shitting me?" I asked with a knot in my stomach.

"I shit you not. Best thing I've read in years. What changed?"

I shrugged my shoulders and stood up from the chair. "I started gardening."

"Ah." He smiled knowingly. "Lucy Palmer happened."

"So, Karla, I owe you fifty dollars," Oliver stated, coming to the dining room table for brunch after we finished talking shop in his office. He straightened his tie and sat down at the head of the table. "You were right about Graham—he still knows how to write. Turns out he's not a twenty-seven-book wonder."

Lucy chuckled, and it sounded beautiful. "You bet against Graham's words?"

He cocked an eyebrow. "Did you read his last draft?!"

She grimaced. "What was the deal with the lion?"

"I know, right?" he hollered, nodding in agreement. "That freaking lion!"

"Okay, okay, we get it. I suck. Can we move on with the conversation?" I asked.

Lucy nudged me in the arm. "But the lion."

"It was hideous," Professor Oliver agreed.

"Poorly written."

"Weird."

"Odd."

"Complete trash," the two said in unison.

I rolled my eyes. "My God, Lucille, you're like the female version of Oliver—my worst nightmare."

"Or your favorite dream come true," Professor Oliver mocked, wiggling his eyebrows in a knowing way. What he knew—hell if I could tell. He reached across the table for bacon, and Karla slapped his hand.

"Dad, no."

He groaned, and I welcomed the change in subject. "A few pieces of bacon won't kill me, darling. Plus, it's a holiday."

"Yeah, well, your heart doesn't know it's a holiday, so keep to the turkey bacon Mom made for you."

He grimaced. "That's *not* bacon." He smiled over at Lucy and shrugged his shoulders. "You have a mini heart attack once and three minor heart surgeries, and people take that stuff so seriously for the rest of your life," he joked.

Mary smiled over at her husband and patted his hand with hers. "Call us overprotective, but we just want you around forever. If that includes you hating us for forcing you to eat turkey bacon"—she put three strips onto his plate—"so be it."

"Touché, touché." Professor Oliver nodded, biting into the *nonbacon* bacon. "I can't really blame you all. I'd want to be forever surrounded by me too."

We spent the rest of brunch laughing with one another, exchanging embarrassing stories, and sharing memories. Lucy listened to everyone's words with such grace, asking questions, wanting more details, fully engaging in the conversation. I adored that about her, how she was such a people person. She made every room fill with light whenever she entered the space.

"Lucy, we're so happy you joined us today. Your smile is contagious," Mary said as we finished up the afternoon. We all sat at the dining room table, stuffed and enjoying the good company.

Lucy smiled wide and smoothed out her dress. "This has truly been amazing. I would've just been sitting at home lonely." She laughed.

"You don't normally spend holidays alone, do you?" Karla questioned with a frown.

"Oh no. I'm always with my sister, but this year, an old friend of hers is back in the States for such a short period of time, so she went to visit her. Normally Mari and I go up to a friend's cabin to visit my mother's tree every holiday."

"Her tree?" Susie asked.

"Yeah. After my mom passed away years ago, we planted a tree to honor her memory, taking a life and making it grow, even after death. So each holiday, we go, eat licorice—Mama's favorite candy—and sit around the tree, listening to music and breathing in the earth."

"That's so beautiful." Karla sighed. She turned to Susie and slapped her in the arm. "When I die, will you plant a tree in my memory?"

"I'll plant a beer. Seems more fitting," Susie replied.

Karla's eyes widened, and she leaned in to kiss Susie. "I'm going to marry you so hard in three months, woman."

Lucy's eyes widened with joy. "When are you two getting married?"

"Fourth of July weekend, the weekend we met," Karla said, giddy. "We were going to wait until next year, but I can't wait any longer." She turned to Professor Oliver, smiling wide. "I just need my papa to walk me down the aisle and give me away to my love."

"It's going to be the best day," Oliver replied, taking his daughter's hand and kissing it. "Only second best to the day you officially became my daughter."

My heart expanded even more.

"Well, if you need a florist, it'll be my treat," Lucy offered.

Susie's eyes widened. "Seriously? That would be amazing. Like, beyond amazing."

If it weren't for the love I saw between Professor Oliver and Mary and the love between Karla and Susie, I would've been certain love was an urban legend, something made only for fairy-tale books.

But the way those people stared at each other, the way they loved so freely and loudly…

True romantic love was real.

Even if I'd never been able to feel it for myself.

"You know, Graham still needs a plus-one for the ceremony. Hint, hint." Susie smirked widely.

I rolled my eyes, feeling a knot in my stomach. A quick change of subject was needed. "Susie and Karla are amazing singers," I told Lucy, leaning in and nudging her in the side. "That's how they met—at a Fourth of July music showcase. You should ask them to sing something."

"Graham is full of crap," Karla replied, throwing a piece of bread at him.

"No, he's not." Mary smiled. "I might be a bit biased, but they are amazing. Come on, girls. Sing something."

Right at that moment, Talon's baby monitor started going off, telling us she was up from her nap.

"I'll grab her, and you ladies pick out a song," Mary ordered.

"Mom, geez, no pressure, huh?" Karla rolled her eyes, but there was a bit of light in her gaze that revealed how much she loved to perform. "Fine. What do you think, Susie? Andra Day?"

"Perfect," she agreed, standing up. "But I'm not singing at the table. This diva needs a stage."

We all headed to the living room, and I sat on the sofa next to Lucy. Mary walked in with my daughter in her arms, and for a moment, I considered that was what a grandmother should've looked like. Happy. Healthy. Whole. Filled with love.

Talon had no clue how lucky she was to have a Mary.

I hadn't had a clue how lucky I was to have a Mary either.

Karla sat down at the piano in the corner, stretched out her fingers, and began to play "Rise Up" by Andra Day. The music floating from the piano was stunning all on its own, but when Susie started to sing, I thought the whole room felt the chills. Lucy's eyes were glued to the performance, while mine stayed glued to her. Her body started to tremble, and her legs shook as she watched the girls perform. It was as if the words were swallowing her whole as tears began to stream down her cheeks.

Her tears fell faster and faster as the lyrics of the song found her heart and planted their seeds. She blushed nervously and tried to wipe her tears away, but when she wiped some away, more came.

The next time she went to wipe them, I took her hand in mine, stopping her. She turned my way, confused, and I squeezed her hand lightly. "It's okay," I whispered.

Her lips parted as if she were going to speak, but then she just nodded once before turning back to the girls and closing her eyes. The tears kept falling as she listened to the beautiful vocals, her body rocking slightly as I held her hand.

For the first time, I began to understand her fully.

The beautiful girl who felt everything.

Her emotions weren't what made her weak.

They were her strength.

When the girls finished performing, Lucy started clapping, the tears still falling. "That was so amazing."

"Are you sure you're not crying because we suck?" Karla laughed.

"No, it was so amazing. My mom would have…" Lucy paused for a moment and took a deep breath. "She would've just loved it."

My eyes fell to our hands, which were still clasped together, and I released my hold, along with the tugging feeling in my chest.

When night came, we packed up our things, thanking everyone for including us.

"It was amazing," Lucy told Mary and Oliver as she hugged them both tightly. "Thank you for keeping me from sitting on my couch eating Ben & Jerry's tonight."

"You're always welcome here, Lucy," Mary said, kissing her cheek.

"I'll go put Talon in her car seat," Lucy said to me, taking Talon from my arms before thanking everyone once more.

Mary gave me a tight smile and pulled me into a hug. "I like her," she whispered as she patted me on the back. "She has a good heart."

She wasn't wrong.

Once she went back inside, Professor Oliver stood on the front porch, grinning wide.

"What?" I asked, my eyebrows knotted.

"Oh, Mr. Russell," he sang, placing his hands in his pockets, rocking back and forth.

"*What*?!"

He whistled low, shaking his head back and forth. "It's just funny that it's happening to you of all people, and you seem one hundred percent ignorant to it."

"What are you talking about?"

"I guess it's harder to see the plotline when you're the one living the story."

"Is someone living in a fictional world again?" I asked.

"In every story, there's the moment when the characters go from act one, the old world, into act two, the new world. You know this."

"Yes…but what does that have to do with anything?"

Professor Oliver nodded toward Lucy. "It has everything to do with everything."

Realization set in, and I cleared my throat, standing up straighter. "No, that's ridiculous. She's just helping with Talon."

"Mm-hmm," he said, almost mockingly.

"No, really, and regardless of your batty mind games, she's Jane's sister."

"Mm-hmm," he replied, driving me wild. "The thing is, the heart never listens to the brain's logic, Mr. Russell." He nudged me in the side with an all-knowing hitch in his voice. "It just feels."

"You're really starting to annoy me."

He laughed and nodded. "It's just funny, isn't it? How the main characters never know about the adventures they're about to go on?"

What bothered me the most about his words was how much truth was contained in them. I knew my feelings for Lucy were growing, and I knew how dangerous it was to allow myself to develop any kind of emotions toward her.

I couldn't remember the last time I felt the way I did when I held her hand, when I saw her caring for Talon, or even when I saw her merely existing.

"What do you think of her, Graham?" Professor Oliver asked.

"What do I think of Lucille?"

"Yes. Maybe if you can't be with her, perhaps you still have room for a friendship."

"She's my complete opposite," I told him. "Lucille is such an odd character, a freak of nature. She's clumsy and always speaks out of turn. Her hair's always wild, and her laughter is at times annoying and too loud. Everything about her is disastrous. She's nothing more than a mess."

"And yet?" he urged me on.

And yet I wanted to be just like her. I wanted to be an odd character, a freak of nature. I wanted to stumble and laugh out loud. I wanted to find her beautiful disaster and mix it together with my own mess. I wanted the freedom she swam in and her fearlessness of living in the moment.

I wanted to know what it meant to be a part of her world.

To be a man who felt everything.

I wanted to hold her but still have her move freely in my arms. I wanted to taste her lips and breathe in a part of her soul as I gave her a glimpse of mine.

I didn't want to be her friend—no.

I wanted to be so much more.

Yet I knew the possibility of that was impossible. She was the one thing off-limits and the only thing I'd ever craved. It wasn't fair, the way this story was unfolding for me, yet it wasn't at all shocking. I never wrote happily ever afters, and Lucy would never be featured in my final chapter.

"You're overthinking something right now, Graham, and I urge you to believe in the opposite," he told me. "Jane has been gone for almost a year now, and let's face it—you never looked at her the way you stare at Lucy. Your eyes never lit up the way they do whenever she walks into a room. You spent most of your life struggling to avoid embracing a form of happiness, my son. When in the world will you allow yourself to be free of the chains you placed upon yourself? This life is short, and you never know how many chapters you have left in your novel, Graham. Live each day as if it's the final page. Breathe each moment as if it's the final word. Be brave, my son. Be brave."

I rolled my eyes and started walking down the steps. "Professor Oliver?"

"Yes?"

"Shut up."

CHAPTER 18
Lucy

I have to stop by the store to grab some diapers. I hope that's okay," Graham told me as he pulled the car into the parking lot of a twenty-four-hour grocery store.

"That's fine."

He hurried inside, and when he came out, he tossed a few bags into the trunk and hopped back into the car. "Okay," he said, putting the car in drive. "Which way do we go to get to the cabin?"

"What?"

"I said which way do we go? To visit your mother's tree?"

My chest tightened, and I shook my head. His words replayed in my head as I stared blankly his way. "What? No way, Graham. You're already behind on your book, and I can't imagine having you drive that far just to—"

"Lucille Hope Palmer."

"Yes, Graham Michael Russell?"

"You've never missed a holiday visiting your mother, right?"

I bit my bottom lip and nodded. "Right."

"Okay then. Which way do we go?"

My eyes closed, and my heart beat faster and faster as I realized Graham wasn't going to let this one go. I hadn't even mentioned how much my heart ached not seeing Mama that day. I hadn't even mentioned how hard it was to watch Susie and Karla love on Karla's mother that evening. A tear rolled down my cheek, and a smile found its way to my lips. "You can take Highway 43 north for two hours."

"Perfect," he said as he pulled out of the parking spot. When I opened my eyes, I glanced back at a sleeping Talon, and my hands wrapped around my heart-shaped necklace.

When we arrived, it was pitch-dark out until I plugged the extension cord into the outlet outside the cabin. The plug lit up the area with the white lights Mari and I had hung in December for our Christmas visit. Mama's tree lit up bright, and I walked over to it, standing still as I watched the lights sparkle. I sat down on the ground and clasped my fingers, looking up at the tree. It was bittersweet, staring at the beautiful branches. Each day it grew was a day Mama was gone, but visiting her in the spring was my favorite time to come, because that was when the leaves began to bloom.

"She's beautiful," Graham said, walking over to me with Talon bundled up in his arms.

"Isn't she?"

He nodded. "She takes after her daughter."

I smiled. "And her granddaughter."

He reached into his coat pocket and pulled out a pack of licorice, making my heart skip a beat.

"You picked it up at the grocery store?" I asked.

"I just wanted today to be good for you."

"It is," I replied, overwhelmed by his kindness. "It's a very good day."

As we sat there staring, breathing, existing, Graham pulled out his cell phone and started playing "Rise Up" by Andra Day.

"You said she might like it," he told me.

Once again, I began to cry.

And it was beautiful.

"Are we friends, Lucille?" Graham asked.

I turned to him, my heart feeling tight in my chest. "Yes."

"Then can I tell you a secret?"

"Yes, of course. Anything."

"After I tell you, I need you to pretend I never spoke of it, all right? If I don't say it now, I fear the feeling will only grow, and it will mess with my head even more than it is now. So after this, I need you to pretend I never said this. After this, I need you to go back to being my friend, because being friends with you makes me a better person. You make me a better human."

"Graham—"

He turned and placed sleeping Talon into her car seat. "Wait, just tell me first—do you feel anything? Anything more than friendship when we do this?" He reached out and took my hand in his.

Nerves.

He moved in closer to me, our bodies closer than they'd ever been. "Do you feel anything when I do this?" he whispered, slowly grazing the back of his hand against my cheek. My eyes shut.

Chills.

He moved in even closer, his small exhales hovering over my lips, his exhales becoming my inhales. I couldn't open my eyes, because I would see his lips. I couldn't open my eyes, because I would crave being closer. I couldn't open my eyes, because I could hardly breathe.

"Do you feel anything when we're this close?" he asked softly.

Excitement.

I opened my eyes and blinked once.

"Yes."

A wave of relief traveled through him, and he reached into his back pocket, pulling out two pieces of paper. "I made two lists yesterday," he told me. "I sat at my desk all day listing all the reasons why I shouldn't feel the way I feel about you, and that list is long. It's detailed with bullet points expressing every single reason why this—whatever this is between us—is a bad idea."

"I get it, Graham. You don't have to explain yourself. I know we can't—"

"No, just wait. There's the other list. It's shorter, much shorter, but in that list, I tried to not be so logical. I'm trying to be more like you."

"Like me? How so?"

"I'm trying to *feel*. I imagined what it would be like to be happy, and I think you are the definition of happiness." His dark eyes locked with mine, and he cleared his throat twice. "I tried to list the things I find pleasant, outside of Talon of course. It's a short list, really, only two things so far, and oddly enough, it begins and ends with you."

My heart pounded against my chest, my mind spinning faster and faster each second that passed. "Me and me?" I asked, feeling his body's warmth. I felt his words grazing across my skin and seeping so deep into my soul.

His fingers slowly trailed along my neck. "You and you."

"But…" *Lyric.* "We can't."

He nodded. "I know. That's why after I tell you this last thing, I need you to pretend we are only friends. I need you to forget everything I've said tonight, but first, I need to tell you this."

"What is it, Graham?"

His body slowly turned away from me, and he stared at the blinking lights on the tree. My eyes watched as his lips moved so slowly. "Being around you does something strange to me, something that hasn't happened in such a long time."

"What happens?"

He took my hand in his, then led it to his chest, and his next words came out as a whisper. "My heart begins to beat again."

CHAPTER 19
Lucy

A re we okay?" Graham asked a few days after Easter as I drove him to the airport to catch his flight. His publisher needed him to fly out to New York City to do interviews and a few book signings around the city. He'd been putting off taking trips ever since Talon was born, but he was being forced to attend the meetings. It was the first time he'd be away from Talon for a weekend, and I could tell he was filled with nerves about the separation. "I mean, after our talk the other night?"

I gave him a smile and nodded. "It's fine, really."

It was a lie.

Ever since he mentioned that feelings for me lived inside his chest, I hadn't been able to stop thinking about it. But since he had been brave enough to be more like me by feeling everything that night, I was forcing myself to be more like him by trying to feel a little less.

I wondered if this was what his whole life was like, feeling everything only in the shadows.

"Okay."

As we pulled up to the airport, I climbed out to help him with his suitcases. I grabbed Talon from the back seat, and Graham held her so close to his chest. His eyes glassed over as he looked at his daughter.

"It's only three days," I told him.

He nodded once. "Yes, I know. It's just…" His voice dropped, and he kissed Talon's forehead. "She's my world."

Oh, Graham Cracker.

He made it so hard not to fall for him.

"If you need anything, day or night, call me. I mean, I'll be calling you every break I get." He paused and bit his bottom lip. "Do you think I should cancel and stay home? She had a bit of a fever this morning."

I laughed. "Graham, you can't cancel. Go to work, and then come back to us." I paused at my word choice and gave him a tight smile. "Back to your daughter."

He nodded, then kissed her forehead once more. "Thank you, Lucille, for everything. I don't trust many people, but I trust you with my world." He touched my arm lightly before handing Talon over to me and leaving.

The moment I placed Talon in her car seat, she started screaming, and I tried my best to calm her down. "I know, little lady." I buckled her in and kissed her forehead. "I'm gonna miss him too."

The next day, Mari asked me to take a bike ride with her, but since I had Talon, it became a stroller hike. "She's just beautiful," Mari said, smiling down at Talon. "She has Mama's eyes, just like Lyric, doesn't she?"

"Oh yeah, and Mama's sassiness too." I laughed as we started walking toward the beginning of the trail. "I'm glad we're finally getting to spend some time together, Mari. I feel like even though we live in the same apartment, I hardly ever see you. I didn't even get to ask how seeing Sarah went."

"I didn't see her," she blurted out, making me pause my steps.

"What?"

"She wasn't even in town," she confessed, her eyes darting around nervously.

"What are you talking about, Mari? You were gone all weekend. Where were you?"

"With Parker," Mari said nonchalantly, as if her words weren't drenched in toxicity.

My eyes stayed narrowed. "I'm sorry. Come again?"

"A while back, he stopped by Monet's again when you were out, and I agreed to see him. We've been talking for a few months now."

Months?!

"You're mad." She grimaced.

"You lied to me. Since when do we lie to each other?"

"I knew you wouldn't approve of me seeing him, but he wanted to talk to me about things."

"Talk about things?" I echoed as anger rocketed through me. "What in the world could there be to talk about?"

Her head lowered, and she started tracing her shoe in the dirt.

"Oh my gosh, he wants to talk about getting back together, doesn't he?"

"It's complicated," she told me.

"How so? He walked out on you during the worst time of your life, and now he wants to walk back in during the best."

"He's my husband."

"*Ex*-husband."

Her head lowered. "I never signed the papers."

My heart shattered.

"You told me—"

"I know!" she cried, running her hands through her hair, pacing back and forth. "I know I told you it ended, and it did. Mentally, I was done with my marriage, but physically...I never signed the papers."

"You have got to be kidding me, Mari. He *abandoned* you when you had *cancer*."

"But still..."

"No. No 'but still.' He doesn't get a pass, and you lied about being *divorced*! To *me*! You're supposed to be my person, Pea. We're supposed to be able to tell each other everything, and this whole time, you've been living a lie with me. You know what Mama always said about lying? If you have to lie about it, you probably shouldn't be doing it anyway."

"Please don't quote Mama to me right now, Lucy."

"You have to leave him, Mari. Physically, emotionally, mentally. He's toxic for you. No good is going to come from this."

"You have no clue what it's like to be married!" Her voice heightened. Mari never raised her voice.

"But I do have a clue what it's like to be respected! Jesus, I cannot believe you've been lying this whole time."

"I'm sorry I lied, but if we're honest, you haven't been the most honest person lately."

"What?"

"This," she said, gesturing toward Talon. "This whole Graham thing is weird. Why are you taking care of his kid? She's obviously old enough for him to take care of himself, or hell, he could hire a nanny. Tell me the truth. Why are you still there?"

My gut tightened. "Mari, that's not the same thing..."

"It's exactly the same thing! You say I'm staying in a loveless marriage because I'm weak, and you're pissed that I lied to you, but you've been lying to me and to yourself. You're staying with him because you're falling for him."

"Stop it."

"You are."

My jaw dropped open. "Mari…this, right now, this isn't about me or Graham or anything other than you. You're making a huge mistake talking to him. It's not healthy and—"

"I'm moving back home."

"What?!" I exclaimed, shock reverberating through me. I stood up straighter. "That's not your home. I'm your home. We are each other's home."

"Parker thinks it will be best for us, to work on our marriage."

What marriage?! "Mari, he called you after you were in remission for two years. He waited it out to see if the cancer would come back. He's a snake."

"Stop it!" she screamed, shaking her hands back and forth in annoyance. "Just stop. He's my husband, Lucy, and I'm going home to him." Her head lowered, and her voice cracked. "I don't want to end up like her."

"Like who?"

"Mama. She died alone, because she never let any man get close enough to love her. I don't want to die without being loved."

"He doesn't love you, Pea."

"But he can. I think if I just change a little, if I just become a better wife…"

"You were the best wife out there, Mari. You were everything to him."

Tears fell from her eyes. "Then why wasn't I enough back then? He's giving me another chance, and I can do better this time."

It was unbelievable how fast it happened, how quickly my anger transformed into pure sadness for my sister. "Mari," I said softly.

"Maktub," she said, looking down at the tattoo on her wrist.

"Don't do that." I shook my head, hurting more than she'd ever know. "Don't take our word and give it some kind of dirty meaning."

"It means *it is written*, Lucy. It means everything that happens was meant to be, not only what you believe to be destined. You can't only accept the positive in life. You must accept it all."

"No. That's not true. If a bullet is coming toward you and you have enough time to move, you don't just stand there and wait for it to hit. You step sideways, Mari. You dodge the bullet."

"My marriage is not a bullet. It's not my death. It's my life."

"You're making a huge mistake," I whispered, tears falling down my cheeks.

She nodded. "Maybe, but it's my mistake to make, just like it's yours to make with Graham." She crossed her arms and shivered as if a chill had found her. "Listen, I didn't want to tell you like this but…I'm glad you know. My lease is up soon, so you'll have to find a place. Look…we can still go on the hike if you want, to clear our heads."

"You know what, Mari?" I grimaced and shook my head. "I'd rather not."

The hardest part of life was watching a loved one walk straight into fire when all you could do was sit and watch them as they burned.

"You'll stay with us," Graham said over FaceTime from his hotel room in New York.

"No, don't be ridiculous. I'll find something. I'll start searching the minute you get back in two days."

"Until then, you'll stay with us, no ifs, ands, or buts. It's fine. My house is big enough. I'm sorry, though, about Mari."

I shivered at the thought of it all, at the idea of her going back to Parker. "I just don't get it. How can she just forgive him?"

"Loneliness is a liar," Graham told me, sitting down on the edge of his bed as he spoke. "It's toxic and deadly most of the time. It forces people to believe they are better off with the devil himself than being alone, because somehow being alone means a person failed. Somehow being alone means a person isn't good enough. So more often than not, the poison of loneliness seeps in and makes a person believe that any kind of attention must stand for love. Fake love that is built on a bed of loneliness will fail. I should know. I've been alone all my life."

"I hate that you just did that." I sighed. "I hate that you just took my annoyance with my sister and made me want to go hug her."

He chuckled. "Sorry. I can call her names if you'd—" His eyes narrowed as he stared at his phone. I noticed the panic in his stare instantly. "Lucille, I have to call you back."

"Is everything okay?"

He hung up before I received a response.

CHAPTER 20
Graham

I was a master of stories.

I knew how a great novel came to exist.

A great novel didn't involve tossing together words that didn't interconnect. In a great novel, each sentence mattered, each word had a meaning to the overall story arc. There was always forewarning to the plot twists and the different paths the novel would travel down too. If a reader looked closely enough, they could always witness the warning signs. They could taste the heart of every word that bled on the page, and by the end, their palate would be satisfied.

A great story always had structure.

But life wasn't a great story.

Real life was a mess of words that sometimes worked and other times didn't. Real life was an array of emotions that hardly made sense. Real life was a first draft novel with scribbles and crossed-out sentences, all written in crayon.

It wasn't beautiful. It came without warning. It came without ease.

And when the novel of real life came to fuck you up, it made sure to knock the air from your lungs and leave your bleeding heart for the wolves.

The message was from Karla.

She tried to call me, but I sent her to voicemail.

I was looking at Talon.

She left a voice message, but I ignored it.

I was staring into Lucille's eyes.

She then sent me a text message that made a part of me die.

Dad's in the hospital.

He had another heart attack.

Please come home.

I took the next flight home, my hands clenched the whole time, too nervous to take a full breath. When the plane landed, I grabbed the first taxi I could find and rushed to the hospital. Hurrying inside, I felt like my chest was on fire. The burning sensation shook me as I tried to blink away the emotion racing through my veins.

He must be okay.

He has to be okay...

If Professor Oliver didn't make it through this, I wasn't certain I'd survive. I wasn't certain I'd survive if he wasn't going to always be there for me.

When I made it to the waiting room, my eyes fell to Mary and Karla first. Then I noticed Lucy sitting with Talon sleeping in her lap.

How long had she been there? How had she even known? I hadn't mentioned I was coming back. Every time I'd tried to type out the words, I'd deleted them instantly. If I'd sent out the words that Professor Oliver had had a heart attack, it would be real. If I'd thought it was real, I would've died on the flight home for sure.

It couldn't be real.

He couldn't die.

Talon wouldn't even remember him.

She needed to remember the greatest man in the world.

She needed to know my father.

"How did you know?" I asked Lucy, walking over and gently kissing Talon's forehead.

Lucy nodded over to Karla. "She called me. I came right away."

"Are you all right?" I asked.

"I'm okay." Lucy grimaced, took my hand in hers, and lightly squeezed it. "Are you?"

I narrowed my eyes and swallowed hard, speaking so low that I wasn't certain the word actually left my lips. "No."

My eyes darted over to Mary, and I told Lucy I'd be back. She told me to take all the time I needed. I was thankful for that, for her watching over Talon, for her being there for my daughter and for me while I needed to be there for others.

"Mary," I said, calling after her. She looked up, and my heart cracked seeing the pain in her stare. Karla's broken stare cracked my heart once more.

"Graham," Mary cried, hurrying over to me.

I wrapped my arms around her, holding her so close to me. She parted her mouth to say more, but no words came out. She began sobbing uncontrollably, as did her daughter, who I pulled into the tight hug. I held them both against me, trying to convince their shaky bodies that everything would be okay.

I stood tall like a tree, not shaking, because they needed me as their foundation. They needed strength, and I played the role.

Because that was what he would've wanted me to be.

Brave.

"What happened?" I asked Mary once she could calm down. I led her to the waiting room chairs, and we sat down.

Her back was curved as she clasped her fingers together, a little tremble still in her soul. "He was in his office reading, and when I went to check on him…" Her bottom lip started to tremble. "I have no clue how long he was down. If I could've gotten there faster…if…"

"No ifs just now," I told her. "You did everything you could. This isn't your fault, Mary."

She nodded. "I know, I know. We've been preparing for this day, but I just didn't think it would come so soon. I thought we had more time."

"Preparing?" I asked, confused.

She grimaced and tried to wipe away her tears, but more continued to fall. "He didn't want me to tell you…"

"Tell me what?"

"He's been sick for a while, Graham. A few months ago, he was told if he didn't have surgery, he'd only have a few months before his heart gave out. The surgery was very risky too, and he didn't want to do it. Not after all the surgeries he had beforehand. I fought long and hard to get him to do it, but he was too afraid he'd go in that day and not come back instead of spending each and every day he had left surrounded by love."

He knew?

"Why didn't he tell me?" I asked, a bit of anger rising in my chest.

She took my hands in hers and lowered her voice. "He didn't want you to push him away. He thought if you learned about his sickness, you'd become cold, to protect yourself from feeling too much. He knew you'd go deeper into your mind, and that idea broke his heart, Graham. He was so terrified of losing you, because you were his son. You are our son, and if you left during his final days…he would've left this world brokenhearted."

My chest was tight, and it took everything inside me to not cry. I lowered my head a bit and shook it back and forth. "He's my best friend," I told her.

"And you are his," she replied.

We waited and waited for the doctors to come tell us what was happening. When one finally returned, he cleared his throat. "Mrs. Evans?" he asked. We all shot up from our chairs, our nerves shot.

"Yes, I'm right here," Mary replied as I took her trembling hand in mine.

Be brave.

"Your husband suffered from heart failure. He's in the ICU on breathing machines, and the truth of the matter is that if those came off, there's a significant chance he wouldn't make it. I'm so sorry. I know this is a lot to take in. I can arrange for you to meet with a specialist to help you decide what the best choice is for moving forward."

"You mean we have to decide to either unplug the machines or keep him in his current state?" Mary asked.

"Yes, but please understand, he's not in a good state. There's not much we can do for him except keep him comfortable. I'm so sorry."

"Oh my God," Karla cried as she fell into Susie's arms.

"Can we see him?" Mary asked, her voice trembling.

"Yes, but only family for now," the doctor said. "And maybe only one person at a time."

"You go first," Mary said, turning to me, as if the idea that I wasn't family was ridiculous.

I shook my head. "No. You should, really. I'm good."

"I can't," she cried. "I can't be the first to see him. Please, Graham? Please go first so you can tell me how he is. Please."

"Okay," I told her, still a little worried about not being there to hold her up. Before I could say anything else, Lucy was standing on the other side of Mary, holding her hand tight and promising me with her gentle eyes that she wouldn't let go.

"I'll take you to the room," the doctor told me.

As we walked down the hallway, I tried my best to keep it together. I tried my best to not show how much my heart was hurting, but the moment I was left alone with Professor Oliver in that room, I lost it.

He looked so broken.

So many machines beeping, so many tubes and IVs.

I took a deep breath, pulled a chair up to his bed, and then cleared my throat. "You're a selfish asshole," I stated, stern, angry. "You're a selfish asshole for doing this to Mary. You're a selfish asshole for doing this to Karla weeks before her wedding. You're a selfish asshole for doing this to me. I hate you for thinking if I knew, I'd run. I hate you for being right about it too, but please, Professor Oliver…" My voice cracked, and my eyes watered over. They burned, the way my heart was burning from the pain. "Don't go. You can't go, you selfish fucking asshole, okay? You can't leave Mary, you can't leave Karla, and you absolutely, one hundred percent, cannot leave *me*."

I fell apart, taking his hand in mine, and I prayed to a god I didn't believe in as my cold heart, which had only recently thawed, began to shatter.

"Please, Ollie. Please don't go. Please, I'll do anything…just… just…"

Please don't go.

CHAPTER 21
Christmas Day

*H*e hadn't liked her gift, so he allowed himself a drink. Kent never only had one drink though. One led to two, two led to three, and three led to a number that brought out his shadows. When Kent lived in his shadows, there was nothing able to bring him back.

Even though Rebecca was beautiful.

Even though Rebecca was kind.

Even though Rebecca tried hard each day to be enough.

She was more than enough, Graham thought.

For the past five birthdays, she'd watched him blow out his candles.

She was his best friend, the proof that good existed, but that wouldn't last, because Kent had had a drink—or ten.

"You are shit!" he screamed at her, throwing his glass of whisky at the wall, where it shattered into a million pieces. He was more than a monster; he was darkness, the worst kind of man that ever existed. Kent didn't even know why he was so angry, but he took it all out on Rebecca.

"Please," she whispered, shaken as she sat on the couch. "Just rest, Kent. You haven't taken a break since you started writing."

"*Don't tell me what to do. You ruined Christmas,*" *he slurred, stumbling over to her.* "*You ruined it all, because you are shit.*" *He raised his hand to take his anger out on her, but before he could slap her, his palm slammed against Graham's forehead as he stepped in the way to protect Rebecca.* "*Move!*" *Kent ordered, wrapping his hands around his son and tossing him to the side of the room.*

Graham's eyes filled with tears as he watched his father hit her.

How?

How could he hit someone so good?

"*Stop!*" *Graham cried, rushing over and hitting his father repeatedly. Each time, Kent would push him away, but Graham didn't stop. He kept rising from the floor and going back for more, unafraid of how his father would hurt him. All he knew was that Rebecca was being hurt, and he knew he had to protect her.*

What lasted for minutes felt like hours. The room spun as Graham got hit and Rebecca got hurt, and it wasn't until both lay there still, not trying to fight back, that it finally stopped. They took the hits and punches and stayed quiet until Kent grew tired of it all. He wandered off to his office, where he slammed his door and probably found some more whisky.

Rebecca wrapped her arms around Graham the second Kent was gone, and she let him fall apart in her arms. "*It's okay,*" *she told him.*

He knew better than to believe such a thing.

Late into that night, Rebecca stopped by Graham's room. He was still awake, sitting in the darkness of his room, staring at the ceiling.

When he turned her way, he saw her in her winter coat and boots. Behind her was a suitcase.

"*No,*" *he said, sitting up. He shook his head.* "*No.*"

Tears rolled down her cheeks, which were bruised from the hands of darkness. "*I'm so sorry, Graham.*"

"Please," he cried, running over to her and wrapping his arms around her waist. "Please don't go."

"I can't stay here," she told him, her voice shaking. "My sister is waiting outside, and I just wanted to tell you face-to-face."

"Take me with you!" he begged, tears falling faster and faster as the panic of her leaving him with the darkness set in. "I'll be good, I swear. I'll be good enough for you."

"Graham." She took a deep breath. "I can't take you. You're not mine."

Those words.

Those few and hurtful words cracked his heart in half.

"Please, Rebecca, please…" He sobbed into her shirt.

She pulled him back a few inches and bent herself down so they were eye level. "He told me if I take you, he'll send his lawyers. He told me he'd fight. I have nothing, Graham. He had me quit my job years ago. I signed a prenup. I have nothing."

"You have me," he told her.

The way she blinked and stood up told him he wasn't enough.

In that moment, the young boy's heart began to freeze.

She walked away that evening and never looked back.

That night, Graham sat at his window, staring out at where Rebecca had driven off, and he felt sick to his stomach as he tried to understand. How could someone be there for so long and then just let go?

He stared at the road covered in snow. The tire tracks were still on the ground, and Graham didn't take his eyes off them once.

Over and over again in his head, three words repeated.

Please don't go.

CHAPTER 22
Lucy

His eyes were swollen when he walked back into the waiting room. Karla and Susie wandered off to find coffee, and Graham gave Mary a fake smile and a quick hug before she went to visit Ollie.

"Hey." I stood up and walked over to him. "Are you okay?"

He grimaced, his stance strong but his eyes so heartbroken. "If anything happens to him…" He swallowed hard and lowered his head. "If I lose him…"

I didn't give him a chance to say another word. I wrapped my arms around him as his body started to shake. For the first time, he let himself feel, let himself hurt, and I was there to hold him close.

"What can I do?" I asked, holding him closer. "Tell me what I can do."

He placed his forehead against mine and closed his eyes. "Just don't let go. If you let go, I'll run. I'll let it overtake me. Please, Lucille, just don't let go."

I held him for minutes, but it felt like hours. Against his ear, I softly spoke. "Air above me, earth below me, fire within me, water surround me, spirit becomes me." I kept repeating the words, and I felt his emotions overtake him. Each time he felt himself slipping, he held my body closer, and I refused to let him go.

It wasn't long until Talon woke up in her car seat and started fussing. Graham slowly let go of me and walked over to his daughter. When her eyes met his, she stopped her fussing, and she lit up as if she'd just met the greatest man alive. There was complete love in her eyes, and I saw it happen—the moment of relief she had delivered to her father. He lifted her up into his arms and held her close. She placed her hands on his cheeks and started babbling, making noises with that same beautiful smile that matched her father's.

For that one moment in time, for that small second, Graham stopped hurting.

Talon filled his heart with love, the same love he had once believed didn't even exist.

For that one moment in time, he seemed okay.

Mary decided to wait to see if things changed. She lived those weeks with a knot in her stomach, and Graham stayed by her side throughout it all. He showed up at her house with food, forcing her to eat and forcing her to sleep when all she wanted to do was stay in the waiting room at the hospital.

Waiting for a change.

Waiting for a miracle.

Waiting for her husband to come back to her.

Karla called me when it came time to make the toughest decision of her family's life. When we arrived at the hospital, the light in the hallway flickered repeatedly, as if it were going to die any moment.

The chaplain walked into the room, and we all stood around Ollie, our hands joined together as we prepared for our final goodbyes. I wasn't certain how anyone would come back from a loss like this. I'd only known Ollie for such a short period of time, but I knew he'd already changed my life for the better.

His heart was one that was always filled with love, and he'd be missed forever.

After the chaplain's prayer, he asked if anyone had any final words to say. Mary couldn't speak as the tears flowed down her cheeks. Karla's face was wrapped in Susie's shoulder, and my lips refused to move.

Graham held us all up. He became our strength. As words flowed from his soul, I felt the squeezing of my heart. "Air above me, earth below me, fire within me, water surround me, spirit becomes me."

In that moment, we all began to crumble into the realm of nothingness.

In that moment, a part of each of us left with Ollie's soul.

CHAPTER 23
Graham

Everyone was gone. Mary, Karla, and Susie had left to deal with the next steps, and I knew I should've gone with them, but I couldn't force myself to move. I stood still in the hospital hallway with the flickering light. His room had been emptied, and there wasn't anything else that could be done. He was gone. My professor. My hero. My best friend. My father.

Gone.

I hadn't cried. I hadn't processed it at all.

How was it possible for this to be the outcome? How could he fade so fast? How could he be gone?

Footsteps were walking in my direction, nurses moving on to their next patients, doctors checking in on those who still had a pulse, as if the world hadn't just stopped spinning.

"Graham."

Her voice was deep, drenched in pain and sorrow. I didn't look up to see her; my head wouldn't turn away from the room where I had just said my final goodbye.

"He was right," I whispered, my voice shaky. "He thought if I knew about his heart, if I knew he was about to die at any moment, I would've run. I would've been selfish, and I would've left him, because I would've closed myself off. I wouldn't have been able to mentally deal with him dying. I would've been a coward."

"You were here," she said. "You were always here. There was nothing cowardly about you, Graham."

"I could've talked him into the surgery though," I argued. "I could've convinced him to fight."

I stopped speaking. For a moment, it felt as if I were floating, as if I were in the world but no longer a part of it, floating high in disbelief, denial, guilt.

Lucy parted her lips as if she were going to offer some kind of comfort, but then no words came out. I was certain there weren't any words that could make this better.

We stayed still, staring at the room as the world kept moving on around us.

My body started to tremble. My hands shook uncontrollably at my sides as my heart caved into my chest. *He's gone. He's really gone.*

Lucy lowered her voice and whispered, "If you need to fall, fall into me."

Within seconds, gravity found me. Every sense of floating was gone, every sense of strength no longer mine. I began to descend, faster and faster, crashing down, waiting for the impact to hit, but she was there.

She was right beside me.

She caught me before I hit the ground.

She became my strength when I could no longer be brave.

"She's finally sleeping, though she put up quite the fight." Lucy's eyes were heavy, as if she were exhausted but forcing her eyes to stay open. "How are you feeling?" she asked, leaning against my office doorframe.

I'd been sitting at my desk, staring at my blinking cursor for the past hour. I wanted to write, wanted to escape, but for the first time in my life, there were truly no words to be found. She came closer to me and placed her hands on my shoulders. Her fingers started kneading into my tense shoulder blades, and I welcomed her touch.

"It's been a long day," I whispered.

"It's been a very long day."

My eyes moved over to the windows, watching the rain falling outside. Sheets of water pounded against the exterior of my home. Professor Oliver would've rolled his eyes at the coincidence of rain on the day he passed away. *What a cliché.*

I shut off my computer.

No words were going to come that night.

"You need to sleep," Lucy told me.

I didn't even disagree. She reached out for my hands, and I allowed her to take them. She pulled me up and walked me to my room so I could try to shut my eyes for some rest.

"Do you need water? Food? Anything?" she asked, her eyes filled with concern.

"There is one thing."

"Yeah? What can I do for you?" she asked.

"Stay with me. Tonight, I just…" My voice cracked, and I bit the inside of my cheek to hold back the emotion. "I don't think I can be alone tonight. I know it's a weird thing to ask, and you are free to go of course. It's just…" I took a deep breath and slid my hands into the pockets of my slacks. "I don't think I can be alone tonight."

She didn't say another word. She simply walked over to the bed, turned down the blanket, and lay down. Lucy's hand patted the spot beside her, and I walked over, lying down beside her. It started slow, our fingers moving closer to one another. I shut my eyes, and tears started falling down my cheeks. Then somehow, our fingers locked, Lucy's warmth slowly filling up my cold heart. Her body inched closer and closer. My arms somehow found their way around her, and as I lay there holding her close, I allowed sleep to find its way to me.

Oh, how badly I needed someone to stay that night.

I was so thankful it was her.

CHAPTER 24
Lucy

When the day came for Ollie's funeral, there were not nearly as many people as there'd been at the last funeral I'd attended; it was nothing like Kent's service. We stood in an open field, surrounded by nature, in the place where he'd proposed to Mary many moons ago. She said it was the day her life began, and it only seemed right to go back there to absorb that same love she'd felt years ago.

And oh, there was love. So, so much love showed up for Ollie, including former students, colleagues, and friends. Although the space wasn't packed with reporters, fans, or cameras, it was filled with the only important thing in the world: love.

Everyone made sure to comfort Karla and Mary to the best of their ability, and the two were never alone. As the service went on, there were tears, laughter, and stories filled with light and love.

The perfect tribute to a perfect man.

When the pastor asked if anyone would like to share words, it only took Graham a second to rise from his seat. My eyes locked with his as he handed Talon over to me.

"A eulogy?" I whispered, my heart racing fast. I knew how hard something like this would be for Graham.

"Yes." He nodded. "It might not be any good."

I shook my head slowly and took his hand, squeezing it lightly. "It will be perfect."

Each step he took to the podium was slow, controlled. Everything about Graham had always been controlled. He almost always stood tall, never wavering back and forth. As my eyes stayed glued to him, my stomach tightened when I saw him stumble a bit. He grabbed the podium and refocused his stance.

The space was silent, and all eyes were on him. I could smell the lilacs and jasmine surrounding us as the wind blew through them. The earth was still wet from all the rain we'd received over the past few days, and whenever the air brushed past, I could almost taste the moisture. My eyes didn't move from Graham. I studied the man I had learned to quietly love as he prepared to say goodbye to the first man who ever taught me what love was meant to look like.

Graham cleared his throat and loosened his slim black tie. He parted his lips, looking down at his sheets of paper, which were filled with words front and back. Once more, his throat was cleared. Then he tried to speak. "Professor Oliver was a…" His voice cracked, and he lowered his head. "Professor Oliver…" His hands formed fists on the podium. "This isn't right. You see, I wrote this long speech about Oliver. I spent hours upon hours crafting it, but let's be honest. If I turned this paper in to him, he would call it complete shit." The field filled with laughter. "I'm certain many of the people here have been his students, and one thing we all know is that Professor Oliver was a hard-ass when it came to grading papers. I received my first F on a paper from him, and when I challenged him about it in his office, he looked at me, lowered his voice, and said, 'Heart.' I didn't have a clue what he was talking about, but he gave me a tiny smile and repeated, 'Heart.' I later realized he meant that was what was missing from my paper.

"Before his classes, I had no clue how to put heart into a story, but he took the time to teach me what it looked like—heart, passion, love. He was the greatest teacher of those three subjects." Graham picked up his pieces of paper and ripped them in half. "And if he were to grade this speech of mine, he'd fail me. My words speak on his achievements in his career. He was an amazing scholar and received numerous awards that recognized his talents, but that's just fluff." Graham chuckled, along with other students who'd had Ollie as a professor. "We all know how Oliver hated when people added extra fluff to their papers to reach the required word count. 'Add muscle, not fat, students.' So now, I'll just add the strongest muscle—I'll add the heart. I'll tell you the core of who Professor Oliver was.

"Oliver was a man who loved unapologetically. He loved his wife and his daughter. He loved his work, his students, and their minds. Oliver loved the world. He loved the world's flaws, he loved the world's mistakes, he loved the world's scars. He believed in the beauty of pain and the glory of better tomorrows. He was the definition of love, and he spent his life trying to spread that love to as many people as he could.

"I remember my sophomore year, I was so mad at him. He gave me my second F, and I was so pissed off. I marched straight to his office, barged in uninvited, and right as I was about to shout at him for this outrageous issue, I paused. There he was, sitting at his desk crying with his face in the palms of his hands."

My stomach tightened as I listened to Graham's story. His

shoulders drooped, and he tried his best to hold himself together as he continued speaking.

"I'm the worst person in those situations. I don't know how to comfort people. I don't know how to say the right things. That was normally his job. So I just sat. I sat across from him as he sobbed uncontrollably. I sat and allowed him to feel his world falling apart until he could voice what was hurting him so deeply. It was the day one of his former students committed suicide. He hadn't seen the student in years, but he remembered him—his smile, his sadness, his strength—and when he learned that the student passed away, Ollie's heart broke. He looked at me and said, 'The world's a little darker tonight, Graham.' Then he wiped away his tears and said, 'But still, I must believe that the sun will rise tomorrow.'"

Tears flooded Graham's eyes, and he took a beat to catch his breath before continuing, speaking directly to Ollie's family. "Mary, Karla, Susie, I tell stories for a living, but I'm not very good with words," he said softly. "I don't know what I can say to make any sense of this. I don't know what the meaning of life is or why death interrupts it. I don't know why he was taken away, and I don't know how to lie to you and tell you everything happens for a reason. What I do know for a fact is that you loved him, and he loved you with every ounce of heart that he possessed.

"Maybe someday that fact will be enough to help you through each day. Maybe someday that fact will bring you peace, but it's okay if that day's not today, because it's not that day for me. I don't feel peace. I feel cheated, sad, hurt, and alone. All my life, I never had a man to look up to. I never knew what it meant to be a true man until I met Professor Oliver. He was the best man I've ever known, the best friend I've ever had, and the world's a lot darker tonight because he's gone. Ollie was my father," Graham said, tears freely falling down his cheeks as he took one final deep breath. "And I will forever be his son."

For the past few nights, I'd been sharing a bed with Graham. He seemed to be more at peace when he wasn't alone, and all I wanted was for him to find a little bit of peace. The May rain showers had been coming down heavily, and it was our background music as we fell asleep.

One Sunday morning, I woke up in the middle of the night due to the sound of thunder, and I rolled over in the bed to see that Graham was missing. Climbing out of bed, I went to see if he was with Talon, but once I reached her nursery, I saw she was sleeping calmly.

I walked throughout the house searching for him, and it wasn't until I stepped into the sunroom that I saw a shadow in the garden. I quickly tossed on my rain boots and grabbed an umbrella, walking outside to see him. He was soaked from head to toe with a shovel in his hands.

"Graham," I called after him, wondering what it was he was doing until I glanced over at the shed where a large tree was leaning, waiting to be planted.

Ollie's tree.

He didn't turn back to look toward me. I wasn't even certain he heard my voice. He just kept shoveling into the ground, digging a hole that would hold the tree. It was heartbreaking watching him get more soaking wet, dig deeper and deeper. I walked over to him, still holding my umbrella, and lightly tapped him on his shoulders.

He turned to me, surprised to see me standing there, and that was when I saw his eyes.

The truth lies in his eyes, Ollie had told me.

That night, I saw it, and I saw that Graham was breaking. His heart was breaking minute by minute, second by second, so I did the only thing I could think to do.

I placed the umbrella on the ground, picked up another shovel, and started to dig right there beside him.

No words were exchanged—none were needed. Each time we tossed the earth's soil to the side, we took a breath in honor of Ollie's life. Once the hole was large enough, I helped him carry the tree over, and we placed it down, covering the base back up with mud.

Graham lowered himself to the ground, sitting in the mess of nature while the rain continued to hammer down on us. I sat down beside him. He bent his knees and rested his hands on top of them with his fingers laced. I sat with my legs crossed and my hands in my lap.

"Lucille?" he whispered.

"Yes?"

"Thank you."

"Always."

CHAPTER 25
Graham

L ucille?" I called from my office late one afternoon. Over the past few weeks, I'd forced myself to sit at my desk and write. I knew that was what Professor Oliver would've wanted me to do. He would've wanted me to not give up.

"Yes?" she questioned, stepping into the room.

My heart skipped. She looked exhausted—no makeup, messy hair, and absolutely everything I'd ever wanted.

"I…um…I have to send a few chapters to my editor, and normally, Professor Oliver would read them, but…" I grimaced. "Do you think you could read them for me?"

Her eyes widened, and her smile stretched wide. "Are you kidding? Of course. Let me see."

I handed her the papers, and she sat down across from me. She crossed her legs and began to read, taking in all my words. As her eyes stayed glued to the paper, my stare was stuck on her. Some nights, I wondered what would've happened without her. I wondered how I would've survived without the hippie weirdo in my life.

I wondered how I'd gone so long without telling her she was one of my favorite people in the whole wide world.

Lucy Palmer had saved me from the darkness, and I'd never be able to thank her enough.

After some time, her eyes watered over, and she bit her bottom lip. "Wow," she whispered to herself as she kept flipping the pages. She was deeply focused as she read my words, taking her time. "Wow," she muttered again. When she finished, she placed all the pages in her lap and shook her head slightly before looking at me, and then she said, "Wow."

"You hate it?" I asked, crossing my arms.

"It's perfect. It's absolutely perfect."

"Would you change anything?"

"Not a single word. Ollie would be proud."

A small sigh left my lips. "Okay. Thank you." She stood up and started walking toward the door, and I called after her once. "Do you think you'd want to be my plus-one for Karla and Susie's wedding?"

A gentle smile landed on her lips, and she shrugged her left shoulder. "I've been waiting for you to ask me."

"I wasn't certain you'd want to come. I mean…it seems weird to take a friend to a wedding."

Her voice lowered, and her chocolate eyes showed a touch of sadness as she stared my way. "Oh, Graham Cracker," she said softly. Her voice was so low that for a moment, I wondered if I imagined the words. "What I wouldn't give to be more than your friend."

The day of the wedding, I waited in the living room as Lucy finished getting ready in her bedroom. My chest was tight waiting to see her, and when she appeared, it was better than I could've ever imagined.

She came out like a spark of perfection. She wore a floor-length baby-blue gown and had baby's breath twisted into her hair.

Her lips were painted pink, and her beauty was louder than ever. Each second I saw her, I fell a little more.

Plus, she held Talon in her arms, and the way my daughter, my heart, snuggled into this woman made me fall even more.

We weren't supposed to feel this way.

We weren't supposed to fall for each other, she and I.

Yet it seemed gravity had a way of pulling us closer.

"You look beautiful," I told her, standing up from the couch and smoothing out my suit.

"You don't look half-bad yourself." She smiled as she walked over to me.

"Dada," Talon said, babbling and reaching out to me. Every time she spoke, my heart grew in size. "Dadadada."

I'd never known love could be so real.

I took her into my arms and kissed her forehead as she kissed mine back. Lucy stepped forward, straightening out my bow tie, which she had picked out. She'd picked out my whole outfit. She was convinced my closet contained too much black, so she had forced me out of my comfort zone with a light gray suit and a baby-blue polka-dot bow tie.

We drove to Lucy's employee Chrissy's house before heading to the ceremony. Chrissy had said she'd take care of Talon for the evening, and a part of me worried. Talon had never spent time with anyone other than Lucy or me, but Lucy told me she trusted Chrissy, and in turn, I trusted Lucy.

"If you need anything, you have our numbers," I told Chrissy as I handed her Talon, who seemed timid at first.

"Ah, don't you worry. We're going to have a great time. All you two have to worry about is having a great time tonight. Embrace each moment."

I gave her a tight smile before leaning in to kiss Talon's forehead one last time.

"Oh, and, Graham? I'm sorry about your father. Professor Oliver seemed like a great man," Chrissy told me.

I thanked her as Lucy took my hand and squeezed it lightly.

As we walked to the car, I turned her way. "You told her he was my father?" I asked.

"Of course. He was your father, and you were his son."

I swallowed hard and opened her car door to help her in. As she climbed inside, I waited a second before shutting the door. "Lucille?"

"Yes?"

"You make the world a lot less dark."

We arrived at the ceremony about ten minutes before it was going to begin and sat in a middle row on the edge of the aisle. The space was surrounded by beautiful flowers, which Lucy herself had arranged for the event and set up earlier that morning. She was the best at making every moment beautiful.

When it was time, everyone in attendance stood up as Susie walked down the aisle first, with her arm looped through her father's. She was smiling wide and looked breathtaking in her white gown. Once she made it to the front, her father kissed her cheek and took his seat. Then the music shifted, and it was Karla's turn. She looked like an angel, holding her beautiful bouquet of pink and white roses. Her dress flowed effortlessly, but her steps seemed to be a struggle. With each one she took, I could tell what was weighing on her heart—she was missing her father, the man who was supposed to be walking her down the aisle on the happiest day of her life.

Halfway down the aisle, her steps stopped, she covered her mouth with her hand, and she began sobbing, the overwhelming pain of the situation swallowing her whole.

Within seconds, I was there. My arm wrapped around hers, I leaned in closer to her, and I whispered, "I have you, Karla. You're not alone."

She turned to me, her eyes filled with broken pieces of her soul, and she wrapped her arms around me. She took a few seconds to fall apart, and I held her each second that passed. When she was strong enough, I kept her arm linked with mine and walked her down the aisle.

The officiant smiled wide when we reached the end of the aisle. Susie's eyes locked with mine for a moment, and she silently thanked me. I simply nodded once.

"Who gives this beautiful bride away?" the officiant asked.

I stood tall, staring straight at Karla. "I do." I wiped a few of her tears away and smiled. "With every ounce of my being, I do."

Karla turned and hugged me so tight, and I held her close to me as she softly spoke. "Thank you, brother."

"Forever, sister."

I walked back to my seat and sat beside Lucy, who had tears streaming down her face. She turned to me and gave me the greatest smile I'd ever seen. Her lips parted, and she whispered, "I am in love with you," and then she turned to face the ceremony.

Within seconds, my heart filled with more love than I had thought possible.

Because that was the thing about hearts—when you thought

they were completely full, you somehow found room to add a little more love.

Loving Lucy Hope Palmer wasn't a choice; it was my destiny.

The rest of the ceremony ran smoothly. The evening was filled with love, laughter, and light—and dancing. So much dancing.

When a slow song came on, Mary walked over to me and held her hand out, asking me for a dance. I stood up and walked her to the dance floor. As she placed her hand on my shoulder, we started to sway.

"What you did for Karla…I'll never be able to thank you enough for that," Mary said, a tear rolling down her cheek.

I leaned in and kissed her tear away before it could hit the floor. "Anything you ladies need, I am here for you. Always, Mary. Always."

She smiled and nodded. "I always wanted a son."

"I always wanted a mom."

We danced, and she laid her head against my shoulder, allowing me to guide our moves. "The way you look at her," she said, speaking of Lucy. "The way she looks at you…"

"I know."

"Let her in, my dear. She makes you feel the way Ollie made me feel—whole—and a love like that isn't something one should ever pass up. There might be a million reasons why you think it couldn't work, but all you need is one reason why it could. That reason is love."

I knew she was right about Lucy and love.

If love were a person, it would be her.

When our dance finished, Mary kissed my cheek and said, "Tell her. Tell her everything that scares you, everything that excites you, everything that moves you. Tell her all of it, and let her in. I promise every moment will be worth it."

I thanked her and took a breath as I turned around to see Lucy finishing up a dance with one of the older gentlemen in his seventies. I could hear Professor Oliver in my head, and I could feel him in my heart as it beat.

Be brave, Graham.

I met her at our table, and she sat down, beaming with happiness. It was as if happiness was the only mode she knew.

"Thank you for bringing me, Graham. This has been—"

I cut her off. There wasn't a chance that I could wait one more minute. I couldn't waste another second of time where my lips weren't against hers. My mouth crashed into hers, making my mind swirl as I felt her lips on mine. I felt her entire being wrapping around my soul, soaking me in, changing me into a better man than I'd ever thought I could be. I'd died a million deaths before I gave living a chance, and my first breath of life was taken from her lips.

As I pulled away a bit, my hands stayed resting around her neck as my fingers slightly massaged her neck. "It's you," I whispered, our lips still slightly touching. "My greatest hope is and always will be you."

And then she kissed me back.

CHAPTER 26
Lucy

We didn't know how to act with each other after our first kiss. Our situation wasn't the norm when it came to building a relationship. We did everything backward. I fell in love with a boy before our first kiss, and he fell for a girl who he wasn't allowed to have. Our connection, our heartbeats, matched each other in our fairy-tale world, but in reality, society deemed us as an awful accident.

Maybe we were an accident—a mistake.

Maybe we were never supposed to cross each other's paths.

Maybe he was only meant to be a lesson in life and not a permanent mark.

But still, the way he kissed me…

Our kiss was as if heaven and hell collided together, and each choice was right and wrong at the same exact time. We kissed as if we were making a mistake and the best decision all at once. His lips made me float higher yet somehow descend. His breaths somehow made my heart beat faster as it came to a complete halt.

Our love was everything good and bad wrapped in one kiss.

A part of me knew I should've regretted it, but the way his lips warmed up the cold shadows of my soul…the way he left his mark on me…

I'd never regret finding him, holding him, even if we only had those few seconds as one.

He'd always be worth those tiny seconds we shared.

He'd always be worth that soul-connecting feeling we created when our lips touched.

He'd always be the one I spent my nights dreaming of being near.

He'd always be worth it to me.

Sometimes when your heart wanted a full-length novel, the world only gave you a novella, and sometimes when you wanted forever, you only had those few seconds of now.

And all I could do, all anyone could ever do, was make each moment count.

After we went home that night, we didn't talk about it at all. Not the following week either. I focused on Talon. Graham worked on his novel. I believed both of us were waiting for the right time to come up for us to speak about it, but that was the tricky thing about timing: it was never right.

Sometimes you just had to leap and hope you didn't fall.

Luckily, on a warm Saturday afternoon, Graham jumped.

"It was good, right?" he asked, surprising me as I was changing Talon's diaper in the nursery.

I turned slightly to see him standing in the doorway, looking my way. "What was good?" I asked, finishing up fastening the diaper.

"The kiss. Did you think it was good?"

My chest tightened as I lifted Talon into my arms. I cleared my throat. "Yeah, it was good. It was amazing."

He nodded, walking in closer. Each step he took made my heart ache with anticipation. "What else? What else did you think?"

"Truth?" I whispered.

"Truth."

"I thought I'd been in love before. I thought I knew what love was. I thought I understood its curves, its angles, its shape. But then I kissed you."

"And?"

I swallowed hard. "And I realized you were the first and only thing that ever made my heartbeat come to life."

He studied me, uncertain. "But?" he asked, moving in closer. He slid his hands into his pockets and bit his bottom lip before speaking again. "I know there's a *but*. I see it in your eyes."

"But…she's my sister."

He grimaced knowingly. "Jane."

I nodded. "Lyric."

"So you think never? You and I?"

The hurt in his eyes from his question broke my heart.

"I think society would have a lot to say about it. That's my biggest worry."

He was even closer than before, close enough to kiss me again. "And since when do we care what society thinks, my hippie weirdo?"

I blushed, and he moved my hair behind my ear.

"It's not going to be easy. It might be very hard and weird and out of the norm, but I promise you, if you give me a chance, if you give us a few moments, I'll make it worth all your time. Say okay?"

I lived in the moment, and my lips parted. "Okay."

"I want to take you out on a date. Tomorrow. I want you to wear your favorite outfit and allow me to take you out."

I laughed. "Are you sure? My favorite outfit involves stripes, polka dots, and a million colors."

"I wouldn't expect anything else." He smiled.

God. That smile. That smile did things to me. I placed Talon on the floor so she could crawl around as Graham kept speaking.

"And, Lucille?"

"Yes?"

"There's poop on your cheek."

My eyes widened in horror as I moved to a mirror and grabbed a baby wipe to clean my face. I looked at Graham, who was snickering to himself, and my cheeks didn't stop turning red. I crossed my arms and narrowed my stare. "Did you just ask me on a date even though there was poop on my face?"

He nodded without hesitation. "Of course. It's just a little poop. That wouldn't change the fact that I'm in love with you and want to take you out on a date."

"What? Wait. *What*? Say that again." My heart was racing, my mind spinning.

"I want to take you out a date?"

"No. Before that."

"That it's just a little poop?"

I waved my hands. "No, no. The part after that. The part about—"

"Me loving you?"

There it was again. The racing heart and the spinning mind. "You're in love with me?"

"With every piece of my soul."

Before I could reply, before any words left my mouth, a little girl walked past me. My eyes widened at the same exact moment as Graham's did as he stared at his daughter.

"Did she…?" he asked.

"I think…" I replied.

Graham scooped Talon into his arms, and I swore his excitement lit up the whole house. "She just took her first steps!" he exclaimed, swirling Talon in his arms as she giggled at the kisses he was giving to her cheeks. "You just took your first steps!"

We both began jumping up and down, cheering Talon on, who just kept giggling and clapping her hands together. We spent the rest of the evening on the floor, trying to get Talon to take more steps. Every time she did, we cheered as if she were an Olympic gold medalist. In our eyes, she was exactly that.

It was the best night of my life, watching the man who loved me love his baby girl so freely. When Talon finally fell asleep that night, Graham and I headed to his bedroom and held each other before sleep overtook us.

"Lucille?" he whispered against my neck as I snuggled myself closer to his warmth.

"Yes?"

"I don't want it to be true, but I want to prepare you. There's going to come a time when I let you down. I don't want to, but I think when people love each other, they sometimes let each other down."

"Yes." I nodded knowingly. "But I am strong enough to lift myself back up. There will be a day that I let you down too."

"Yes," he yawned before pulling my body closer to his. "But I'm certain on those days, I'll somehow love you more."

The next morning, I was still on my high from Graham and Talon. That was until I went in to work.

Mari sat in the office at Monet's Gardens with her fingers laced together as she examined the bookkeeping binders. Normally, she handled the paperwork side of the business while I handled the front of the house. She was good at what she did too, but when I walked into the office that afternoon, I could almost see the heavy cloud sitting over her.

I knew exactly what Mama would've said if she saw her baby girl in that moment.

Overthinking again, my Mari Joy?

"What is it?" I asked, leaning against the doorframe.

She looked up at me, her brow knitted, and leaned back in her chair.

"Those are pretty much the most words you've said to me since I—"

"Moved back in with your ex?"

"My husband," she corrected.

We hadn't really spoken since the Parker situation exploded and she moved back in with him. I avoided all conversation about it, because I knew she'd made a choice. That was one thing about Mari— she overthought everything, but when she made her final decision, she followed through. There was nothing I could say to make her leave the monster she was currently sharing a bed with.

All I could do was patiently wait to piece her heart back together when he destroyed her again.

"What is it?" I asked, nodding toward the paperwork.

She shook her head. "Nothing. I'm just trying to figure out numbers."

"It's not nothing," I disagreed, walking over to the desk and sitting across from her. "You have that look about you."

"That look?" she asked.

"You know, your worried look."

"What are you talking about? I don't have a worried look."

I gave her an *are-you-seriously-trying-to-say-you-don't-have-a-worried-look* look.

She sighed. "I don't think we can keep Chrissy on staff."

"What? She's great. She's actually way *too* good—better than both of us. We need her. I was actually going to talk to you about giving her a raise."

"That's the thing, Lucy. We don't have the money to give her a raise. We hardly have enough to keep her here. I think it's best if we let her go."

I narrowed my eyes, confused by her words and certain they had been tainted. "Is this you or Parker talking?"

"I'm my own person, Lucy, with a college degree. This is me."

"She loves her job," I told her.

Mari slightly shrugged. "I like her too, but this is business, nothing personal."

"Now you sound like Lyric," I huffed. "All business, no heart."

"She has heart, Lucy. The two of you together just never really worked."

I cocked an eyebrow, flabbergasted by Mari backing up Lyric. "She left her child, Mari."

"We all make mistakes."

"Yes." I nodded slowly, still confused. "But a mistake is spilling milk, burning a pizza, missing an anniversary. Walking out on your newborn child who was in the NICU for weeks? Staying gone when the child is fully okay? That's not a mistake—that's a choice."

She grimaced. "I just think it's odd how involved you are with it all. I mean, you didn't even know Graham, and it's clear that you and Lyric have your issues. Why make things worse? It just doesn't make sense. It's not normal."

"You could get to know her more too, you know. She's your niece, our niece. We are throwing her a first birthday party next weekend. Maybe if you come, you'll understand."

"*We* are throwing her a party? We? Don't you see how that's weird? Lucy, she's not your daughter."

"I know that. I'm just helping Graham—"

"You're living with him."

"You kicked me out!"

She shook her head. "I didn't kick you out exactly, and I definitely didn't push you into his home. Your heart did that."

"Stop," I said, my voice growing low as a knot formed in my stomach.

Mari gave me her knowing stare. "Lucy, I know you're falling for him."

I blinked away some tears that were trying to fall. "You don't know what you're talking about. You have no clue what you're talking about."

"You're making a mistake. He was with Lyric. She's your sister," Mari exclaimed. "I know you live by your emotions, but this isn't right."

I bit my bottom lip, feeling my anger building. "Oh, right, because you are the world's most knowledgeable on what a relationship should look like."

"A *relationship*?" she hissed. "Lucy, you're not in a relationship with Graham Russell. I know this will hurt to hear, but I get Lyric when it comes to you. You're too much like Mama. You're too free, and freedom can be suffocating. If you settle down, don't settle for him. He's not yours to love."

I didn't know what to do. The burning in my chest was so painful. I parted my lips to speak, but no sound came out. I couldn't think of the words I needed to say, so I turned around and left.

It didn't take long for me to find myself in nature. I headed to my favorite running trail, took a deep breath in, and let a heavy breath out before I started to run. I ran through the trees, allowing the air to slap against my skin as I ran faster and faster, trying to rid myself of the hurt and confusion.

Part of me hated Mari for the words she spoke, but another part wondered how right she was.

In my mind, I played out the fairy tale of what Graham and I would be. Selfishly, I thought how it could be if maybe someday our love led to forever. Selfishly, I allowed myself to feel completely.

I was a dreamer, like my mother, and while I'd always adored that fact, I was slowly beginning to see her flaws. She floated more than she walked, skipped more than she stood, and no matter what, she never faced reality.

So whenever reality came for her, she was always alone.

That terrified me—being alone.

But not being with Graham and Talon terrified me more than anything.

When I arrived at Graham's house, I didn't have the nerve to walk inside. Even the run hadn't cleared my mind, so instead, I went and sat in the backyard near Ollie's tree. I sat with my legs crossed, staring at the tiny tree that had so many years of growth to go. I stayed there for seconds, minutes, hours. It wasn't until the sun started setting that Graham joined me outside. He was dressed in a perfectly fitted suit and looked out-of-this-world amazing. I felt awful missing our date, but I knew due to my emotions I wouldn't have been ready to go out with him. Mari put more guilt in my heart than I knew I could hold. Maybe I was being naïve about the way Graham made me feel. Maybe I was being foolish.

"Hi," he said.

"Hi," I replied.

He sat.

He stared.

He spoke.

"You're sad."

I nodded. "Yes."

"You've been here for four hours."

"I know."

"I wanted to give you space."

"Thank you."

He nodded. "I think you've had enough space though. You can only be alone for so long before you start convincing yourself you deserve to be that way—trust me, I know—and you, Lucille Hope Palmer, do not deserve to be alone."

No more words were exchanged, but the feeling of wholeness was loud and clear. If only the world could feel the way our hearts beat as one, then maybe they wouldn't be so harsh to judge our connection.

"This is a terrible first date." I laughed, nerves shaking my vocals.

He reached into his suit pocket, pulled out a pack of licorice, and handed it to me. "Better?" he asked.

I sighed and nodded once before opening the package. "Better." Being beside him always felt right to me. Like home.

In that way, I was different from Mama. While she always wanted to float away, my heart craved staying beside Graham Russell.

For the first time in my life, I desperately wanted to stand on solid ground.

CHAPTER 27
Graham

You should call her," I told Lucy as she went around the house, making up reasons to keep distracted. For months, she and her sister Mari hadn't talked about anything but work-related issues, but apparently they'd had a big falling-out over something a few days before. I could tell the issues were eating her alive, but she tried her best not to talk about it.

"It's fine. We're fine," she replied.

"Liar."

She turned to me and cocked an eyebrow. "Don't you have a book to finish or something?"

I smiled at her sassiness.

I loved that side of her.

I loved all sides of her.

"I'm just saying, you miss her."

"I don't," she said, her poker face communicating the complete opposite of her words. She bit her bottom lip. "Do you think she's happy? I don't think she's happy. Never mind. I don't want to talk about it."

"Lucil—"

"I mean, he literally left her during the worst days of her life. Who does that?! Whatever. It's her life. I'm done talking about it."

"Okay," I agreed.

"I mean, he's a monster! And he's not even a cute monster! I just hate him, and I'm so angry with her for choosing him over me, over us. And now this afternoon is Talon's first birthday party, and Mari won't even be here for it! I can't believe—oh crap!" she screamed, running into the kitchen. I followed right behind her to witness her pulling out Talon's chocolate cake, which was badly burned. "No, no, no," she said, placing it on the countertop.

"Breathe," I told her, walking behind her and placing my hands on her shoulders. Her eyes watered over, and I laughed. "It's just a cake, Lucille. It's okay."

"No! No, it's not okay," she said, turning her body around to face me. "We were going to backpack across Europe. We started saving up when she got sick. We started a negative thoughts jar, and every time we thought something negative about her diagnosis or fear took over our minds, we had to put a coin in the jar. After the first week, the jar was filled to the brim, and we had to get another jar. She wanted to go right after she was in remission, but I was too scared. I was afraid she might not be strong enough, that it might be too soon, so I kept her home. I kept her locked away, because I wasn't strong enough to get on a plane with her." I swallowed hard. "And now she's not talking to me, and I'm not talking to her. She's my best friend."

"She'll come around."

"I invited her today, for Talon's party. That's what started the argument."

"Why was that an issue?"

"She…" Lucy's voice cracked, and she took a deep breath as we stood just inches apart. "She thinks this is all wrong, you and me, Talon. She thinks it's weird."

"It is weird," I told her. "But that doesn't mean it's not right."

"She told me you're not mine. She said you're not mine to love."

Before I could reply, the doorbell rang, and she tore herself away from me, finding a fake smile to plaster on her face.

"It's fine, really. I'm just upset that I burned the cake. I'll get the door."

I stood there, staring at the cake, and then I pulled out a knife to see if perhaps I could somehow save it by scraping off some of the inedible parts. Lucy needed a win that day. She needed something to make her smile.

"Oh my God," I heard from the other room. Lucy's voice sounded terrified, and when I walked into the living room, I knew exactly why.

"Jane," I muttered, staring at her standing in my doorway with a teddy bear and a gift in her other hand. "What the hell are you doing here?"

She parted her lips to speak, but then her eyes traveled back to Lucy. "What are you doing here?" she asked her, a bit of a sting lacing her words. "Why on earth would you be here?"

"I…" Lucy started, but I could tell her nerves were too shaken for words to come out.

"Jane, what are you doing here?" I asked her once more.

"I…" Her voice shook the same way Lucy's had a moment before. "I wanted to see my daughter."

"Your daughter?" I huffed, stunned by the nerve she had to walk into my home and use those words.

"I… Can we talk, Graham?" Jane asked. Her eyes darted to Lucy, and she narrowed them. "Alone?"

"Anything you say can be said in front of Lucille," I told her.

Lucy's already bruised heart was taking another beating. "No, it's okay. I'll go. I should probably get some work done at the floral shop anyway. I'll just grab my coat."

As she walked past me, I lightly grabbed her arm and whispered, "You do not have to go."

She nodded her head slowly. "I just think it's best if you two talk. I don't want to cause any more issues."

She gave my hand a light squeeze, then let go. When she grabbed her coat, she walked straight out of the house without another word, and the room somehow filled with darkness.

"What is it you want, Jane?"

"It's been a year, Graham. I just want to see her."

"What makes you think you have any right to see her? You abandoned her."

"I was scared."

"You were selfish."

She grimaced and shifted around in her shoes. "Still, you need to let me see her. As her mother, I deserve that much. It's my right."

"Mother?" I hissed, my gut filled with disgust. Being a mother didn't simply mean giving birth. Being a mother meant late-night feedings. Being a mother meant sleeping next to a crib because your child was sick and you needed to watch their breaths. Being a mother meant knowing Talon hated teddy bears. Being a mother meant you stayed.

Jane was not a mother, not for a minute.

She was a stranger to my child. A stranger in my house.

A stranger to me.

"You need to leave," I told her, uneasy about the fact that she apparently believed she could walk back into our lives after all this time.

"Are you sleeping with Lucy?" she questioned, throwing me for a complete loop.

"Excuse me?" I felt it form in my gut and start rising to my throat—my anger. "You abandoned your daughter months ago. You left without more than a bullshit note. You didn't take a second to look back once. Yet now, you think you have the right to ask me something like that? No, Jane. You don't get to ask me questions."

She pushed her shoulders back. Although she stood tall in her high heels, there was a tremble in her voice. "I don't want her near my child."

I walked over to the front door and opened it. "Goodbye, Jane."

"I'm your wife, Graham. Talon shouldn't be around someone like Lucy. She's a toxic person. I deserve—"

"*Nothing!*" I hollered, my voice hitting a new height of anger, panic, and disgust. "You deserve nothing." She'd crossed a line by using the word *wife*. She'd crossed a bigger line by speaking ill of Lucy, the one who had stayed. She'd crossed the biggest line by saying how Talon should be raised. "*Leave!*" I shouted once more. The second I hollered, Talon started crying, and I swallowed hard.

I had grown up in a home with screaming, and it was the last thing I ever wanted my daughter to witness.

My voice dropped low. "Please, Jane. Just go."

She stepped outside, her head still held high. "Think about what you're about to do, Graham. If you slam this door, it means we must fight. If you slam this door, it means there's going to be a war."

With no thought needed, I replied, "I'll have my lawyers call yours."

With that, I slammed the door.

CHAPTER 28
Lucy

Lyric's back in town," I said, hurrying into Monet's Gardens where Mari was putting together a new window display.

She glanced over at me and gave me a small nod. "Yeah, I know."

"What?" I asked, surprised. "When did you find out?"

"I saw her two days ago. She stopped by Parker's place to talk."

The way the words rolled off her tongue so effortlessly and carelessly confused me. Who had taken my sister, my favorite person in the world, and changed her?

What had happened to my Mari?

"Why didn't you tell me?" I asked, my chest hurting as my heart began to crack. "You saw me yesterday."

"I was going to mention it, but our last conversation didn't lead to the best place. You stormed off," she told me, picking up the vase and moving it over to the windows. "And what does it matter if she's back? Her family is here, Lucy."

"She abandoned them for months. She left her newborn in the NICU because she was selfish. Don't you think it's terrible for her to just walk back into Graham's life? Into Talon's life?"

"We don't really get a say in that, Lucy. It's none of our business."

More pieces of my heart shattered, and Mari acted as if she didn't even care.

"But..." Mari took a deep breath and crossed her arms, looking my way. "We do have to talk about the business. I thought I could hold out for a while longer, but since we're here now, we might as well talk."

"About what?" I asked, confusion filling me up.

"Lyric is a bit worried about how some of the things in the book-keeping are adding up, and I mean, I think she's right. I think we jumped the gun hiring Chrissy. We aren't bringing in enough profit."

"Why in the world are you talking to Lyric about the store?"

Mari grimaced, and I cocked an eyebrow.

"What aren't you telling me?"

"Don't freak out," she said, which of course made me freak out even more. "Remember when we were starting out and we couldn't get a loan to cover the rest of our needs?".

"Mari...you said you got another loan from the bank. You said after months of trying, it finally went through."

She continued, breaking her stare from mine. "I didn't know what to do. You were so happy and excited to move forward after me getting sick, and I didn't have the guts to tell you the truth. You gave up so much of your life for me, and all I wanted was to give you our shop."

"You lied to me about the loan?" I asked Mari, my chest tight. "You asked Lyric for a loan?"

"I'm sorry, Lucy. I really am. With the medical bills and everything piling up, I knew I'd never be able to get a bank to help me—"

"So you went behind my back and asked Lyric for the money."

"You would've never let me take it if I told you."

"Of course I wouldn't have! Do you think she gave it to you out of the goodness of her heart? Mari, everything is leverage with Lyric. She only does things that will benefit her."

"No," Mari swore. "She did this for us, to help us get back on our feet. There were no strings attached."

"Until now," I huffed, my hands falling to my waist. "If it weren't for you taking money from her, letting her hold something so big over us, this wouldn't even be a problem, Mari. Now she's trying to tell you how to run our shop. We could've worked harder to get the loan ourselves. We could've done it, but now she wants to ruin everything we've built, all because you trusted the snake. We need to destroy the deal."

"I won't," she said sternly. "I was talking to Parker about everything, and he thinks—"

I huffed again. "Why would I care what he thinks? It's none of his business."

"He's my husband. His opinion matters to me."

"I don't understand why. He abandoned you when you needed him the most. I was there, remember? I was the one who picked up your pieces after he destroyed you."

"So what?" she asked.

"*So what*?" I replied, flabbergasted. "That means you should at least trust my opinion over his."

She nodded slowly. "He said you'd say that."

"Excuse me?"

"He said you'd play the cancer card on me, reminding me that you were there for me when no one else was. Parker made a mistake, okay? And based on the past few months of your life, you know what it's like to make a mistake."

"That's not fair, Mari."

"No, you know what's not fair? Holding it over my head every day that you stayed. Reminding me whenever I have any kind of feelings that you were the one who stuck around to help me during the cancer. So what, am I now forever indebted to you? I can't move on and live my life?"

"You think working under Lyric is going to be you living your life? All this is happening because of Lyric's need to control everything."

"No, all this is happening because you slept with your sister's husband."

"What?" I whispered, shocked by my sister's words, by the way they fell from her lips so effortlessly, and I stood there for a second, stunned, waiting for her to apologize, waiting for her cold stare to soften, waiting for my sister, my best friend, my Pea to come back to me. "Take it back," I said softly, but she wouldn't.

She'd been poisoned with love—the same love that had once destroyed her.

It amazed me how love could hurt so much.

"Look, Parker thinks…" She paused and swallowed hard. "Parker and I both think that Lyric helping take control wouldn't hurt things. She's a businesswoman. She knows the laws and how to help build up the shop. She wants the best for us. She's our sister."

"She's *your* sister," I corrected. "She's your sister, and this store now belongs to you and her. I want nothing to do with it. I want nothing to do with either of you. Don't even bother firing Chrissy. I quit."

I walked around to the back, gathered all my belongings, and tossed them into a cardboard box. When I walked to the front of the store, I took the shop's keys off my key chain and placed them on the front counter.

Mari's eyes were still cold, and I could tell she wasn't going to change her mind. I knew I wasn't going to change mine either, but before I could leave, I had to speak my final truths—even though she'd think they were lies.

"They're going to let you down, Mari. They are going to use your trust and let you down and hurt you. This time, though, it's your choice. You have the free will to deal with the devils or not, and just don't let them hurt you.

"I know what I'm doing, Lucy. I'm not stupid."

"No," I agreed. "You're not stupid. You're just too trusting, which is a million times worse." I swallowed hard and blinked back the tears that wanted to fall. "For the record, I never slept with him. I love him with every ounce of my heart. I love the way he loves me so quietly, but we never slept together, not once, because I could never get past the idea of doing something like that to my sister. Now, though, I see the truth—being a sister isn't just defined by blood. It's defined by unconditional love. Lyric was never my sister, and she never will be." I took the heart-shaped necklace from around my neck and placed it in Mari's hands. "But you are my heart, Mari, and I know I'm yours. So when they hurt you, find me. Find me, and I'll put your heart back together, and then maybe you can help me fix the cracks in my own."

"Hey, where have you been? I've been calling you, but your phone went straight to voicemail," Graham said as I stood on his front porch, exhausted. His eyes were filled with concern and a heavy dose of guilt as he held Talon in his arms. "Are you okay?"

I nodded slowly and stepped into his foyer. "Yeah. I stopped by Monet's and got into another big fight with Mari. Then I went for a run to clear my head, and when my phone died, I realized my charger was here, so I just came to pick it up. I hope that's okay." I brushed past him and blinked my eyes a few times, trying to hide the emotion that was seeping from my spirit.

"Of course it's okay. I was just worried." His eyes stayed glued to me, his concern never easing up, but I tried my best not to notice as I walked into Talon's room to grab my charger.

My heart was beating uncontrollably as I tried my best not to fall apart. My mind was spinning, thinking about everything that had just unspun with Mari in the shop. It was as if my favorite person in the whole world had been drugged and was being controlled by the hands of hate and confusion yet was being told it was love driving her decisions.

It was heartbreaking to watch your best friend set herself up for heartache.

"Lucille," Graham said, following after me.

I blinked.

Oh, Graham...

The comfort of his smooth voice went right to my soul.

"I'm okay," I told him, walking past him with my charger. I avoided eye contact, because I knew eye contact would make me melt, and I couldn't melt into him. Maybe Mari was right. Maybe every feeling I had for the man before me was wrong.

If only love came with a timeline and instructions.

If it had, I would've fallen in love with him when our timing was right. If love came with a timeline, Graham Russell would've always held my heart.

"I think I'm going to just stay at a hotel for a few nights. I think it's too messy to stay here knowing Lyric is back. I'm going to grab some of my things."

"That's ridiculous," he told me. "You're staying here. This is your home."

Home.

If he knew me, he'd know that all my life, home was always shift-ing. I never planted my roots anywhere, and when it was time to move, it was time to move.

Even if going meant leaving my heartbeat behind.

"No, really, it's okay," I said, still avoiding eye contact. I didn't want to fall apart, not in front of Graham. I'd wait until I got to the hotel to lose myself. *Feel less, Lucy. Feel less.*

That was almost impossible when I felt a tiny hand reach out to me and tug on my shirt. "LuLu," Talon said, making me turn toward her. She had the brightest smile and the widest beautiful eyes, which were staring my way. Oh, how her smile made my heart beat. "LuLu," she repeated, reaching out for me to lift her up.

It cracked my heart, which I was trying so hard to keep intact.

"Hey, honey," I said, taking her from Graham's arms. I knew it wasn't right, knew she wasn't mine to have, but that little girl had changed me in more ways than I could've ever imagined. She never looked at me with judgment for my mistakes. She never turned her back on me. She only loved unconditionally, fully, honestly.

As I held her so tight in my arms, my body started to shake. The idea that I wouldn't wake up to her sounds every day was weighing on my soul. The idea that the past year with Talon and Graham would be the last year we all spent together was soul-crushing.

Yes, Talon wasn't mine, but I was hers. All of me loved that child. All of me would give my world for her and her father.

I couldn't stop shaking, couldn't fight the tears that started flood-ing my eyes. I couldn't change the person I'd always been.

I was the girl who felt everything, and in that moment, my whole world began to crumble.

I held Talon against me and cried into her shirt as she kept speaking her random words. My eyes shut tight as I sobbed against the beautiful soul.

This was where I had felt it for the first time.

What it felt like to be happy.

What it felt like to be loved.

What it felt like to be part of something bigger than myself.

And now, I was being forced to leave.

A hand fell against my lower back, and I curved into Graham's touch. He stood behind me, tall like the oak trees in the forest, and lowered his lips against my ear. As the words danced from his mouth and into my spirit, I remembered exactly why he was the man I chose to love fully.

When he spoke, his words forever marked my soul as his. "If you need to fall, fall into me."

CHAPTER 29
Graham

Jane came back the following day, as if she had a right to stop by whenever she pleased. I hated the fact that I didn't know what she had up her sleeve. I hated the unease I felt about the idea of her being back in town.

I knew she was capable of anything, but my biggest fear was that she'd try to take Talon away from me. If I knew anything about Jane, it was that she was intelligent—and sneaky. One never really knew what she was up to, and that made my skin crawl.

"Is she here?" Jane asked, stepping into the foyer of the house. Her eyes darted around the space, and I rolled my eyes in response.

"She's not."

"Good." She nodded.

"She's taking Talon for a walk."

"What?!" Jane exclaimed, shocked. "I told you I didn't want her around my child."

"And I told you that you didn't have a say in the matter. What exactly are you doing back here, Jane? What do you want?"

There was a moment when her eyes locked with mine. She looked nothing like her sister. There was no light in her eyes, only her dark irises, which didn't contain much heart within them, but her voice contained more gentleness than I'd ever witnessed before. "I want my family back," she whispered. "I want you and Talon in my life."

I couldn't believe the nerve of her—to think she could just walk back into our lives as if she hadn't taken a yearlong vacation.

"That's not happening," I told her.

She tightened her fists. "Yes, it is. I know I made a mistake leaving, but I want to make it right. I want to be here for the rest of her years. I deserve that right."

"You deserve nothing. *Nothing*. I was hoping we wouldn't have to go to court, but if that's the way it's going to be, that's the way it's going to be. I'm not afraid to fight for my daughter."

"Don't do this, Graham. You really don't want to," she warned, but I didn't care. "I'm a lawyer."

"I'll fight you."

"I'll win," she told me. "And I'll take her from you. I'll take her away from this place if it means Lucy won't be anywhere near her."

"Why do you hate her so much?" I blurted out. "She's the best person I've ever met."

"Then you need to meet more people."

My chest was on fire at the idea of this monster taking my child from me. "You cannot come back and just decide you're ready to be a mother. That's not how it works, and I would never in my life let you do that. You have no right to her, Jane. You are nothing to that child. You mean nothing to her. You're merely a human who abandoned a child because of your own selfish needs. You are not equipped to take my child away from me, even if you are a lawyer."

"I can do it," she said confidently, but I noticed the vein popping out of her head from her anger building. "I won't stand around and see my daughter be transformed into the person Lucy is."

Her words made my skin crawl. I hated the way she spoke as if Lucy was the monster in our lives. As if Lucy hadn't saved me from myself. As if Lucy was anything less than a miracle.

"And who are you to say who Talon can and cannot be around?" I asked, my chest aching as my heart beat rapidly.

"I'm her mother!"

"And I'm her father!"

"*No, you're not!*" she screamed, the back of her throat burning from anger as her words bounced off the walls and slammed into my soul.

It was as if a bomb went off in the living room and shook the entire foundation of my life. "What?" I asked, my eyes narrow and low. "What did you just say to me?"

"*What?*" a voice questioned from behind us. Lucy stood there with Talon in the stroller, stunned.

Jane's body was still, except for her shaky hands. When her eyes met Talon's, her shoulders rounded, and I saw it happen—her heart started to break, but I didn't care. Not for a moment did I care about her pained expression. All I cared about was the fact that she was trying to tear my family away from me.

"I said, you're…" She swallowed hard, looking at the floor.

"Look at me," I ordered, my voice stern and loud.

Her head rose, and she blinked once before releasing a heavy sigh.

"Now repeat yourself."

"You're not her father."

She was lying.

She was evil.

She was dirty.

She was the monster I always thought I would be.

"How dare you walk in here with your lies to try to take her," I whispered low, trying my best not to let them overtake me—my shadows, my ghosts, my fears.

"It's not…" She grimaced and shook her head. "I…um…"

"It's time for you to leave," I said, sounding strong, hiding my fear. A part of me believed her. A part of me felt as if there was always that feeling somewhere deep in the back of my mind and I just did my best to hide it, but a bigger part of me looked at Talon and saw pieces of me in her stare. I saw myself in her smile. I saw the best parts of me in her soul. She was mine, and I was hers.

"You were on a book tour," she whispered, her voice shaky. "I… um…I was sick for weeks around that time, and I remember being annoyed that you went a week without even checking on me while you were on the road."

My mind started racing back to that time period, trying to grasp any memories, trying to pick up any kind of clues. Talon had been early. When I'd thought she was thirty-one weeks, she was twenty-eight, but I hadn't let that idea simmer. Talon was my daughter. My baby. My heart. I couldn't imagine that being anything less than true. "You had the flu, and you kept calling me."

"I just wanted…" She paused, unsure what else to say. "He stopped by to check on me."

Lucy's voice was low. "Who's *he*?" she asked.

Jane didn't reply, but I knew exactly who Jane was speaking of. She'd told me the story many times. How caring he was, while I was cold. How he was gentle to all people. How he was always there for strangers and truly there for those he loved.

"My father," I said, my voice cracking. Kent Theodore Russell, a man, a father, a hero.

My personal hell.

There *were* parts of me that I saw in Talon's eyes, but a bigger part of me looked at Talon and saw pieces of him in her stare. I saw him in her smile. I saw parts of him in her soul, yet she was not his, and he was not hers.

Even so, it was enough to break my soul.

"You should go," Lucy told Jane.

Jane stood up straight and shook her head. "If anyone should go, it's you."

"No," I scolded, uncertain how my heart was still beating. "If anyone should go, it is you. Right now."

Jane went to argue, but she saw it—the fire inside me. She knew if she got one step closer, I would burn her to the ground. She gathered her things and left after stating that she'd be back.

When she was gone, I hurried over to Talon and lifted her in my arms. How could she not be my world?

She was mine, and I was hers.

I was hers, and she was mine.

She'd saved me.

She'd given me something worth living for, and now Jane had come back to try to rip that away from me.

"Can you watch her?" I asked Lucy, feeling the world crashing against me.

She walked over and took Talon from my hold. Lucy's hand landed on my arm, and I pulled away slightly.

"Talk to me," she said.

I shook my head and walked away, not speaking a word. I went to my office, closed the door behind me, and sat staring at the blinking cursor on my computer screen.

I hated him. I hated how he controlled me. I hated that even after death, he had still somehow destroyed my life.

CHAPTER 30
Thanksgiving

*Y*ou must be the woman who's inspiring my son's writing," Kent said, walking into Graham's home seconds before he was about to leave with Jane to go introduce her to Professor Oliver for the first time.

"What are you doing here?" Graham asked his father, coldness in his voice, harshness in his stare.

"It's Thanksgiving, son. I was hoping we could catch up. I saw your last book hit number one, and we haven't celebrated the success of it yet." Kent smiled over at Jane, who was staring his way with wide eyes, as if it were a legend standing before her instead of a monster. "He takes after his father."

"I'm nothing like you," Graham barked.

Kent snickered. "No, you're a bit grumpier."

Jane giggled, and the sound upset Graham. He despised how everyone laughed when they were around Kent.

"We're leaving for a dinner," Graham told Kent, wanting nothing more than for him to leave.

"Then I'll be quick. Listen, my publicist was wondering if you'd do *an interview for ABC News with me. He thinks it will be great for both of our careers."*

"I don't do interviews, especially with you."

Kent bit his lip, and his mouth slightly twitched. It was a warning sign that he was growing upset, but over the years, he'd learned how to control it around strangers. Graham, however, knew the look well, and he knew the anger that simmered under his father's surface.

"Just think about it," he said, a bit of bark in his tone that Jane missed. Kent turned to her and gave her the smile that made all people fall for him. "What's your name, sweetheart?"

"Jane, and I have to say I am your biggest fan," she gushed.

Kent smiled wider. "Bigger fan than you are of my son?"

Graham grimaced. "We're leaving."

"Okay, okay. Just email me if you change your mind, and, Jane," Kent said, taking her hand and kissing it, "it was a pleasure to meet such a beauty. My son is a lucky man."

Jane's cheeks reddened, and she thanked him for his kind words.

As he turned to leave, he allowed his eyes to dance across Jane's figure one last time before he spoke to Graham. "I know we've had some tough times, Graham. I know things haven't always been easy for us, but I want to fix that. I think this interview is a step in that direction. Hopefully soon you'll let me back into your life. Happy Thanksgiving, son."

Kent drove off, leaving Graham and Jane standing on the porch. Jane shifted her feet around. "He seems lovely," she commented.

Graham lowered his brows and stuffed his hands into his slacks, walking toward his car. "You do not know anything about the monster you speak of. You're merely falling into his trap."

She hurried behind him, trying to keep up in her high heels. "But still," she argued. "He was kind."

She didn't say anything else, but Graham knew what she was thinking—that Kent was kind, funny, charming, and the opposite of the man Graham presented himself to be.

Kent radiated light while Graham lived in the shadows.

CHAPTER 31
Lucy

Lyric had set him up. She had given him no real choice in his future by controlling his heart.

Graham didn't settle into the idea of not being Talon's father. He fought it the best he could, and when he took the paternity test, I believed his heart hoped Lyric was wrong. When the results came in, I saw the light inside him die away.

Lyric presented him with the biggest choice of his life, which wasn't even a choice, really: invite her back into his life so he could keep his daughter, or stay with me and she'd take Talon.

The day she told him, I was there. I stood by his side as she threatened to rip his world apart. She had all the control over every part of Graham, and I knew there was only one thing for me to do.

I had to pack my bags and go. I was certain I had to do it before he came back too. He'd been speaking with a lawyer all afternoon, and I knew if I didn't leave now, I'd only make things harder for him. He couldn't lose his daughter; he couldn't lose his soul.

So I began to pack my bags.

"What are you doing?" he asked, his voice dripping with confusion.

"Graham." I sighed when I saw him standing in the doorway of the bathroom. His heavy-lidded mocha eyes stared at me as I reached for a towel and wrapped it around my body. "I didn't know you were home."

"I saw your things in the front lobby."

"Yes."

"You're leaving," he said breathlessly. He had shaved the day before, yet his five-o'clock shadow was already back. His lips were tight, and I knew for a fact he was clenching his teeth. His chiseled square jawline was always more evident when he clenched his teeth.

"I think it's for the best."

"You really think so?" He stepped into the bathroom, shutting the door behind him. The sound of the running water was the only noise for a few seconds as we stared at each other.

"Yes, I do," I replied as the pit of my stomach fell and my heart drummed. I followed his hand as he reached for the doorknob and locked it. His steps toward me were slow as heat curled down my spine. "Graham, please," I begged, although I didn't know if I was begging for him to stay or go.

"I need you," he whispered. He was in front of me, his stare locked with mine, and even though he hadn't touched me yet, I felt his entire being. "Please," he begged back, his thumb tilting my chin up as he bit his bottom lip. "Don't leave me."

His hands grasped my behind through the towel, and my breath hitched. His mouth grazed down my neck, and he whispered between kisses as he lifted me up, forcing me to drop my towel to the floor.

"Stay with me. Please, Lucille, just stay."

I knew how hard that was for him—to ask for someone to stay—but I also knew the reasons why I couldn't.

My mind sizzled as he held my body against his and stepped over the edge of the tub, forcing the shower to rain over us. His lips bit against my breast before he took my nipple into his mouth, sucking it hard. My mind fogged as he shoved my back against the shower wall, his clothes getting soaked and clinging to his skin.

"Gra—" I felt dizzy, faint, happy, high. *So high...*

His fingers moved down my chest, down my stomach, and he slid them inside me with need, with want, with ache. "Don't leave me, Lucille, please. I can't lose you," he whispered against my lips before discovering my mouth with his tongue. "I need you more than you know. *I need you.*"

Everything quickened—his motions, his grip, his fingers, his tongue. I hurriedly unbuckled his jeans, sending them to the bottom of the tub, and stroked his hardness through his soaked boxers. When those were removed, he pulled his fingers from my core and locked eyes with me.

We made a choice that we added to our list of mistakes. We used each other's bodies to get high. We soared as we touched, moaned, and begged. I ascended as he lifted my butt cheeks and slammed me against the tiled wall. I cried out as he slid his hardness into me, inch by inch, filling me with indescribable warmth. He kissed like heaven and made love like sin. As the water fell around us, I silently prayed for this to be mine, Graham and me, forever and always. My heart told me I'd love him for all time. My brain told me I only had a few more moments and that I should enjoy each one, but my gut...

My gut told me I had to let go.

As he continued making love to every inch of my body, he moved his lips to the edge of my ear. His warm breaths brushed against me as he spoke. "Air above me…" He grasped one of my breasts in his hand and lightly pinched my nipple. "Earth below me…"

"Graham," I muttered, dazed, confused, guilty, in love.

He wrapped his fingers in my hair and slightly pulled it, putting a curve in my neck. A spark shot down my spine as he began sucking my skin. "Fire within me…" He continued sliding his hardness deeper and harder into me, taking control of his speed, taking control of his desires, taking control of our love. He moved me to the other wall, and the steaming water slapped against us as I moaned his name and he moaned his words against my neck. "Water surround me…"

"Please," I begged, floating on the edge of make-believe, feeling the final buildup of our final mistake as he placed one hand against the wall and one hand around my waist. His arms were tight, each muscle defined with tight, sharp lines. We locked eyes, and my body began to shake. I was so close…so close to pure ecstasy, so close to our final goodbye. "Please, Graham," I muttered, unsure if I was begging for him to let me go or to hold me forever.

His mouth slammed against mine, kissing me harder than we'd ever kissed before, and I could tell as his tongue danced with mine, as he sucked me with his hurts and his love, that he also knew how close we were to goodbye. He too was trying to hold on to the high that was already slipping to the ground.

He kissed me to say goodbye, and I kissed him to pray for more seconds. He kissed me to give me his love, and I kissed him to give him mine. He kissed me with his always, and I kissed him with my forever.

Right after we soared to our highest heights, we descended and crashed to our lowest lows, but not before his air became my breaths, not before his earth became my ground. His flames were my fire, his thirst was my water, and his spirit?

His spirit became my soul.

Then we prepared ourselves for goodbye.

"I didn't think it would be this hard," I whispered, hearing Graham's footsteps behind me as I stood in Talon's bedroom, where she slept peacefully. The idea that I wouldn't be there to watch her grow up made my chest ache more than ever.

"You can wake her," Graham told me as he leaned against the doorframe.

"No." I shook my head. "If I see those eyes of hers, I'll never be able to leave." I wiped away the tears that fell from my eyes and took a deep breath, trying to face Graham. As we looked at each other, we both wanted nothing more than to stay together, to be a family, to be one.

But sometimes what one wanted wasn't what one received.

"Your taxi is here, but I can still take you to the airport," he offered.

I had finally taken the leap and cashed in all the coins from the negative thoughts jars I'd collected over the years. I was taking the trip to Europe that Mari and I had always dreamed of. I had to get away, as far away as I could, because I knew if my heart was still on the same continent as Graham, I'd find my way back to him.

"No, it's okay, really. It's easier this way." I placed my fingers against my lips, kissed them, and then placed them on Talon's forehead. "I love you more than the wind loves the trees, sweet girl, and I'm always here for you, even when you don't see me."

As I took steps toward Graham, he moved in closer as if he were going to hug me, to try to take away my grief, but I wouldn't allow it.

I knew if I fell into his arms again, I'd beg him to never let me go. He helped me carry my luggage out of the house and loaded it into the car.

"I won't say goodbye," he told me, taking my hands in his. He brought the palms of my hands to his lips and kissed them gently. "I refuse to say goodbye to you." He released his grasp and walked back to the porch, and right as I went to open the door to the taxi, he called out to me. When his lips parted, he said, "What's the secret, Lucille?"

"The secret?"

"To your tea. What's the secret ingredient?"

I narrowed my eyebrows and bit my bottom lip. My feet started walking in his direction. The closer I got, the more steps he took toward me. When we stood in front of each other, I studied the caramel color of his eyes, a color I might never see again, and I held that sight close to my heart. I'd remember those eyes as long as I could.

"Tell me what ingredients you think are in it, and then I'll tell you the final one."

"Promise me?"

"Promise you."

He shut his eyes and began to speak. "Cinnamon, ginger, fresh lemons."

"Yes, yes, yes."

"Hot red peppers, sugar, black pepper."

"Uh-huh." I breathed out, chills running up and down my spine.

"And peppermint extract." When his eyes opened, he stared at me as if he could see a part of me that I'd yet to discover.

"That's all correct," I said.

He smiled, and I almost cried, because when he smiled, I always felt at home.

"So what is it?" he asked.

I glanced around the area, making sure no one was within earshot, and I leaned in closer to him, my lips slightly grazing his ear. "Thyme," I told him. I stepped backward and gave him the kind of smile that forced him to frown. "Just give it a bit of thyme."

"Thyme." He nodded slowly, stepping farther away from me.

"Sorry, ma'am, but I can't wait here all day," the taxi driver called after me.

I turned to him and nodded before looking back at Graham, who was still staring at me. "Any final words?" I joked, nerves rocking my stomach.

He narrowed his eyes at me and combed my hair behind my ears. "You're the best human being of all human beings."

I swallowed hard. I missed him. I missed him so much, even though he was standing right there in front of me. I could still reach out and touch him, but for some reason, he felt farther and farther away. "One day, you'll be happy we didn't work out," I promised him. "One day, you'll wake with Talon on your left side and someone else on your right, and you'll realize how happy you are that you and I didn't work out."

"One day, I'm going to wake up," he replied, his mood somber, "and it will be you lying beside me."

My hand went to his cheek, and I placed my lips against his. "You're the best human being of all human beings." A tear rolled down my cheek, and I kissed him slowly, lingering against his lips for a moment before finally letting him go. "I love you, Graham Cracker."

"I love you, Lucille."

As I opened the taxi door and stepped inside, Graham called out to me one last time.

"Yes?"

"Time," he softly said.

"Time?"

He shrugged his left shoulder and allowed it to drop quickly. "Just give it a bit of time."

CHAPTER 32
Graham

That night, I awoke from a dream only to find myself in a waking nightmare.

The left side of my bed was empty, and Lucy was on a flight, traveling far away from me. It had taken everything inside me to not beg her to stay when that taxi pulled up in front of the house. It had taken every ounce of me to not allow gravity to force me to my knees. If she'd stayed, I would've never let her go again. If she'd stayed, I would've started all over from day one, learning how to love her even more than I already had. If she'd stayed, I would've always flown, but I knew she wouldn't—she couldn't. With my current situation, there was no way I could've kept her and given her the love she deserved.

She was my freedom, yet I was her cage.

I lay in bed, my chest tight from the longing my heart felt, and I almost fell apart right then and there. I almost let my heart harden back to the way it was before Lucy walked into my life, but then a beautiful little girl started crying in the nursery, and I hurried to go get her. When I arrived, she reached for me and instantly stopped her crying.

"Hey, love," I whispered as she curled in against me, laying her head on my chest.

We headed back to my bedroom and lay down, and within minutes, she was sleeping. Her breaths rose and fell, and she lightly snored as she curled up against me.

It was in that moment I remembered why falling apart wasn't an option. I remembered why I couldn't allow myself to fall into a pit of loneliness—because I wasn't alone. I had the most beautiful reason to keep moving forward.

Talon was my savior, and I'd promised myself to be a dad to her, not merely a father. Any person could be a father. It took a real man to step up to the role of being a dad. And I owed that to her. She deserved to have me fully.

As she clung to my shirt and found dreams that brought her comfort, I allowed myself to rest too.

It amazed me how love worked.

It amazed me how my heart could be so broken and yet so full all at once.

That night, my greatest nightmares and most beautiful dreams intermixed, and I held my daughter closer as a reminder of why I'd have to rise in the morning, just like the sun.

Jane moved her things into the house the following week. She made herself comfortable in a home that held no love for her. She went about doing things as if she knew what she was doing, and every time she picked Talon up, I cringed.

"I was hoping the three of us could go out to dinner, Graham," she told me as she unpacked her suitcases in my bedroom. I didn't care enough to tell her not to sleep in my room. I'd sleep in the nursery with my daughter. "It might be good for us to start reconnecting."

"No."

She looked up, bewildered. "What?"

"I said no."

"Graham—"

"I just want to make something really clear to you, Jane. I didn't choose you. I want nothing to do with you. You can live in my house, you can hold my daughter, but you need to understand that there's not an ounce of me that wants *you*." My hands formed fists, and my brow knitted. "I chose her. I chose my daughter. I'll choose her every second of every day for the rest of my life because she is my everything. So let's stop pretending that we are ever going to live happily ever after. You are not my final sentence. You are not my last word. You are simply a chapter I wish I could delete."

I turned and walked away from her, leaving her standing stunned, but I didn't care. Every moment I could I would spend with my daughter in my arms.

One day, somehow, Lucy would come back to us both.

Because she was always meant to be my last word.

"You shouldn't be here," Mari told me as I walked into Monet's Gardens.

I took off my hat and nodded. "I know."

She stood tall and shifted her feet around. "You really should go. I don't feel comfortable with you being here."

I nodded once more. "I know." But I stayed, because sometimes the bravest thing a person can do is stay. "Does he love you?"

"Excuse me?"

I held my hat against my chest. "I said does he love you? Do you love him?"

"Listen—"

"Does he make you laugh so hard you have to toss your head backward? How many inside jokes do you share? Does he try to change you or inspire you? Are you good enough for him? Does he make you feel worthy? Is he good enough for you? Do you sometimes lie in bed beside him and wonder why you're still there?" I paused. "Do you miss her? Did she make you laugh so hard you had to toss your head backward? How many inside jokes did you share? Did she try to change you or inspire you? Were you good enough for her? Did she make you feel worthy? Was she good enough for you? Do you sometimes lie in bed and wonder why she's gone?"

Mari's small frame started to shake as I asked the questions. She parted her lips, but no words left her tongue.

So I continued speaking. "Being with someone you aren't meant to be with out of fear of being alone isn't worth it. I promise you, you'll spend your life being lonelier with him than you would being without him. Love doesn't push things away. Love doesn't suffocate. It makes the world bloom. She taught me that. She taught me how love works, and I'm certain she taught you the same."

"Graham," Mari said softly, tears falling down her cheeks.

"I never loved your oldest sister. I've been numb for years, and Jane was just another form of numbness. She never loved me either, but Lucille…she's my world. She's everything I needed and so much more than I deserve. I know you might not understand that, but I'd go to war for her heart for the rest of my life if it meant she'd find her smile again. So I'm standing in your shop right now, Mari, asking if you love him. If he is everything you know love to be, stay. If he is your Lucille, then don't for a second leave his side. But if he isn't…if there is even a sliver of your soul that doubts that he's the one—*run*. I need you to run to your sister. I need you to go to war with me for the one person who always stayed, even when she owed us nothing. I can't be there for her right now, and her heart is broken halfway across the world. So this is me going to war for her by coming to you. This is me begging you to choose her. She needs you, Mari, and I am going to assume that your heart needs her too."

"I…" She started to fall apart, shaking as she covered her mouth with her hands. "The things I've said to her…the way I've treated her…"

"It's okay."

"It's not," she said, her head shaking. "She was my best friend, and I tossed her and her feelings to the side. I chose them over her."

"It was a mistake."

"It was a choice, and she'd never forgive me."

I grimaced and narrowed my eyes. "Mari, we're talking about Lucille here. Forgiveness is all she knows. I know where she is right now. I'll help you get there so you can do whatever you need to do to get your best friend back. I'll handle all the details. All you have to do is run."

CHAPTER 33
Lucy

Monet's gardens at Giverny were everything and more. I spent time walking around the land, breathing in the flowers, taking in the sights day after day. In those gardens, I almost felt like myself. Being surrounded by that much beauty reminded me of Talon's eyes, of Graham's crooked smile, of home.

As I walked a stone path, I smiled at all the passersby who were taking in the experience of the gardens. Oftentimes, I wondered where they came from. What had brought them to the point they were at in that very moment? What was their story? Had they ever loved? Did it consume them? Had they left?

"Pod."

My chest tightened at the word and the recognition of the voice that produced it. I turned around, and my heart landed in my throat when I saw Mari standing there. I wanted to step closer, but my feet wouldn't move. My body wouldn't budge. I stood still, as she had.

"I…" she started as her voice cracked. She held an envelope tight to her chest and tried again. "He told me you'd be here. He said you visit every day. I just didn't know what time."

No words from me.

Tears formed in Mari's eyes, and she tried her best to keep it together. "I'm so sorry, Lucy. I'm sorry for losing my way. I'm sorry for settling. I'm sorry for pushing you away. I just want you to know, I left Parker. The other night, I was lying beside him in bed, and his arms were wrapped tightly around me. He was holding me so close, but I felt as if I was falling apart. Every time he told me he loved me, I felt less and less like myself. I've been so blind to the truth that I let my fear of being alone drive me back into the arms of a man who didn't deserve me. I was so worried about being loved that I didn't even care if I loved back. And then I pushed you away. You've been the only constant in my life, and I can't believe I hurt you the way I did. You're my best friend, Lucy. You're my heartbeat, and I'm sorry, I'm sorry, I'm—"

She didn't have time to say anything else before my arms wrapped around her body and I pulled her closer to me. She sobbed into my shoulder, and I held her tighter.

"I'm so sorry, Lucy. I'm so sorry for everything."

"Shh," I whispered, pulling her closer to me. "You have no clue how good it is to see you, Pea."

She sighed, relief racing through her. "You have no clue how good it is to see you, Pod."

After some time of settling down, we walked across one of the many bridges in the gardens and sat down, cross-legged.

She handed me the envelope and shrugged. "He told me to give this to you, and he told me not to let you leave the gardens until each page is read."

"What is it?"

"I don't know," she said, standing up. "But I was instructed to give you time to read it by yourself. I'll be exploring, and I'll meet you here when you're done."

"Okay. Sounds good." I opened the package, and there was a manuscript titled *The Story of G.M. Russell*. I inhaled hard—his autobiography.

"Oh, and, Lucy?" Mari called out, making me turn to look her way. "I was wrong about him. The way he loves you is inspiring. The way you love him is breathtaking. If I am ever lucky enough to feel even a fourth of what you two have, then I'll die happy."

As she walked away, I took a deep breath and started chapter one.

Each chapter flowed effortlessly. Each sentence was important. Each word was required.

I read the story about a boy who became a monster who slowly learned to love again.

And then I reached the final chapter.

THE WEDDING

His palms were sweaty as his sister, Karla, straightened his tie. He hadn't known he could be so nervous about making the best decision of his life. Throughout his whole life, he'd never imagined falling in love with her.

A woman who felt everything.

A woman who showed him what it meant to live, to breathe, to love.

A woman who became his strength during the dark days.

There was something romantic about the way she moved throughout the world, the way she danced on her tiptoes and laughed without any regard for appearing ridiculous. There was something so true about how she held one's eye contact and the way she smiled.

Those eyes.

Oh, how he could've stared into those eyes for the rest of his life.

Those lips.

Oh, how he could've kissed those lips for the rest of his days.

"Are you happy, Graham?" asked Mary, his mother, as she walked into the room to see her son's eyes glowing with excitement.

For the first time in forever, the answer came so effortlessly. "Yes."

"Are you ready?" she questioned.

"Yes."

She linked her arm with his, and Karla took his other. "Then let's go get the girl."

He stood at the end of the aisle, waiting for his forever to join him— but first, his daughter.

Talon walked down the aisle, dropping flower petals and twirling in her beautiful white gown. His angel, his light, his savior. When she reached the end of the aisle, she ran to her father and hugged him tight. He lifted her up into his arms, and the two of them waited. They waited for her to join them. They waited for those eyes to meet their stare, and when they did, Graham's breath was stolen from his soul.

She was beautiful, but that wasn't a surprise. Everything about her was stunning and real and strong and kind. Seeing her walking toward him, toward their new life, changed him in that moment. In that moment, he promised her all of him, even the cracks. They were, after all, where the light shone through.

When they stood together, they locked their hands as one. His lips parted when it was time, and he spoke words he'd dreamed of speaking. "I, Graham Michael Russell, take you, Lucille Hope Palmer, to be my wife. I promise it all to you—my broken past, my scarred present, and my complete future. I am yours before I am my own. You are my light, my love, my destiny. Air above me, earth below me, fire within me, water surround me. I give you all of my soul. I give you all of me."

Then, in every cliché way possible, in every facet of their lives, they lived happily ever after.

The End

I stared at his words, my hands shaking as tears rolled down my cheeks. "It has a happily ever after," I whispered to myself, stunned. Graham had never in his life written a happily ever after ending.

Until me.

Until us.

Until now.

I stood up from the bridge and hurriedly found my sister. "Mari, we have to go back."

She smiled wide and nodded knowingly. "I was hoping you would say that." She took off the heart-shaped necklace Mama gave to me and placed it back around my neck. "Now come on," she said softly. "Let's go home."

CHAPTER 34
Lucy

I stood on Graham's porch, my heart pounding in my chest. I wasn't certain what was on the other side of that door, but I knew whatever it was wouldn't make me run. I was going to stay. Forever and always, I was staying.

I knocked a few times and rang the doorbell, and then I waited.

And waited.

And waited some more.

When I turned the doorknob, I was surprised to find it open. "Hello?" I called.

The room was dark, and it was clear that Graham wasn't home. When I heard footsteps, I tensed up. Lyric came from the bedroom hurriedly, two suitcases in her hands. She didn't see me right away, and when she looked up, there was a look of panic in her eyes.

"Lucy," she said breathlessly. Her hair was wild, like how Mama's had always looked, and her eyes were bloodshot.

I knew I owed her nothing. I knew I didn't have a word to say to her or comfort to give her way.

But the way her eyes looked, the heaviness of her shoulders…

Sometimes the ugliest people were the ones who were the most broken.

"Are you okay?" I asked.

She snickered, and a few tears fell from her eyes. "As if you care."

"Why do you think I hate you?" I blurted out. "Why in the world do you hate me?"

She shifted her feet and stood tall. "I don't know what you're talking about."

"Sure you do, Lyric. I don't know why, but it seems you've always had a problem with me, especially after Mama passed away. I just never understood why. I always looked up to you."

She huffed, not believing me.

"Seriously."

She parted her lips, and at first, no words came out, but then she tried again. "She loved you more, okay? She always loved you more."

"What? That's ridiculous. She loved all three of us girls the same."

"No, that's just not true. You were her heart. She was always talking about you, how free you were, how smart you were, how amazing you were. You were her light."

"Lyric, she loved you."

"I resented you. I resented how she loved you, and then I come back here, and he loves you too. Everyone has always loved you, Lucy, and I was left unlovable."

"I always loved you, Lyric," I said, my chest hurting from the pain in her voice.

She snickered in disbelief as her body shook and tears rolled down her cheeks. "You know the last thing Mama said to me as she was lying on her deathbed and I was holding her hand?"

"What's that?"

"'*Go get your sister*,'" she said, her voice cracking. "'*I want Lucy.*'"

I felt it too, the way those words cracked my sister's heart, how ever since, she hadn't been able to put the pieces back together.

"Lyric…" I started, but she shook her head.

"No. I'm done. I'm just done. Don't worry. You can have your life. I don't belong here. Nothing about this house is home to me."

"You're leaving?" I asked, confused. "Does Graham know you're leaving?"

"No."

"Lyric, you can't just walk out on them, not again."

"Why? I did it before. Besides, he doesn't want me here, and I don't want to be here."

"But you could've at least left a note like you did last time," Graham said, making us turn to face him.

When his eyes locked with mine, I felt my heart remember how to beat.

"I didn't think it was necessary," Lyric said, grabbing the handles on her suitcases.

"Okay, but before you go, wait here," Graham said, walking over to me with Talon in his arms. "Lucille," he whispered, his voice low, his eyes filled with that same gentleness I'd seen a few months back.

"Graham Cracker," I replied.

"Can you hold her?" he asked.

"Always," I replied.

He wandered off to his office, and when he came back, he was holding paperwork and a pen.

"What is this?" Lyric asked as he held the sheets of paper out to her.

"Divorce papers and legal paperwork granting me full custody of

Talon. You don't get to run again without making this right, Jane. You don't get to walk away and then leave the possibility of you taking my daughter away hanging over my head."

His voice was stern but not mean, straightforward yet not cold.

She parted her lips as if she were going to argue, but when she looked at Graham, she probably took strong note of his stare. His eyes always told a person all they ever needed to know. It was clear that he'd never be hers, and it finally clicked in Lyric's head that she'd never truly wanted him. She slowly nodded in agreement. "I'll sign them at your desk," she said, walking into his office.

When she was out of view, I watched the heavy sigh leave Graham's body.

"Are you okay?" I asked him.

He kissed me to say yes.

"You came back to me," he whispered, his lips against mine.

"I'll always come back."

"No," he said sternly. "Just never leave again."

When Lyric walked back into the room, she told us the paperwork was signed and she'd be no more trouble. As she stepped out the front door, I called after her.

"Mama's last words to me were 'Take care of Lyric and Mari. Take care of your sisters. Take care of my Lyric. Take care of my favorite song.' You were her final thought. You were her final breath, her final word."

Tears rolled down her cheeks, and she nodded, thanking me for a level of peace only I could give her soul. If I had known how heavily it weighed on her heart, I would've told her years ago.

"I left Talon a gift," she said. "I figured it was better for her than it was for me. It's sitting on her nightstand." Without another word, Lyric disappeared.

As we headed to the nursery, my hand fell to my chest as I saw the gift Lyric had left for her daughter—the small music box with a dancing ballerina that Mama had given her. It sat there with a note on top, and tears fell down my cheeks as I read the words on the paper.

Always dance, Talon

CHAPTER 35
Lucy

When Christmas came around, Graham, Talon, and I had three celebrations. The day started with us being bundled up and drinking coffee in the backyard with Ollie's tree. Each day, Graham visited that tree, and he'd sit and talk to his best friend, his father, telling him every story of Talon's growth, of his growth, of us. I was glad he had that connection. It was almost as if Ollie would live on forever in a way.

It was beautiful to see his tree standing tall every morning and night.

That afternoon, we headed to Mary's home to celebrate the day with their family. Mari joined us, and we spent all our time laughing, crying, and remembering. The first Christmas without a loved one is always the toughest one, but when you are surrounded by love, the hurts hurt a little less.

That evening, Graham, Talon, and I packed up the car to go spend the remainder of the holiday with Mama's tree. Mari told us she'd meet us up there a few hours later. On the whole trip to the cabin, I stared at my hand that was linked with Graham's. My air, my fire, my water, my earth, my soul.

I hadn't known a love could be so true.

"We're doing this, aren't we?" I whispered, glancing back at Talon, who was sleeping in the back seat. "Staying forever in love?"

"Forever," he promised, kissing my palm. "Forever."

As we pulled up to the cabin, everything was lightly dusted with snow. Graham climbed out of the car and hurried over to the tree, carrying Talon's car seat in his hand.

"Graham, we should head inside. It's cold."

"We should at least say hi," he told me, looking at the tree. "Can you plug in the lights? I worry if I put Talon's car seat down, she'll cry."

"Of course," I said, hurrying over in the chilly air. When I plugged them in, I turned to Mama's tree, and my chest tightened as I saw the lights spelling out words that forever changed my life.

Will you marry us?

"Graham," I whispered, shaking as I slowly turned around to face him. When I did, he was down on one knee, holding a ring in his hand.

"I love you, Lucy," he said, not calling me Lucille for the first time ever. "I love the way you give, the way you care, the way you laugh, the way you smile. I love your heart and how it beats for the world. Before you, I was lost, and because of you, I found my way home. You're the reason I believe in tomorrow. You're the reason I believe in love, and I plan to never let you go. Marry me. Marry Talon. Marry us."

Tears formed in my eyes as I stood in front of them. I lowered myself down so I was kneeling beside him. I wrapped my body around his, and he held me close as I whispered yes repeatedly, the word traveling from my lips and straight into his soul.

He slid the ring onto my finger, and my heart pounded more and more, knowing that my greatest hope had finally come true.

I was finally planting my roots in a home so warm.

"So this is our happily ever after?" I asked softly against his lips.

"No, my love, this is merely our chapter one."

When he kissed me, I swore, in the darkness of the night, I felt the warmth of the sun.

EPILOGUE
Graham

SIX YEARS LATER

And he was your best friend, Daddy?" Talon asked as she helped me dig around in the garden. The summer sun touched our faces as we picked green peppers and tomatoes for dinner that night.

"My very best friend," I told her, knee deep in dirt. The sunflowers we planted a few months ago were as tall as Talon. Whenever the wind blew past us, the flowers Lucy picked out lit up our senses.

"Can you tell me his story again?" Talon asked, placing her shovel into the ground. She then picked up a green pepper and bit into it as if it were an apple—just like her mama. If I were inside and couldn't find the two, they were normally in the backyard eating cucumbers, peppers, and rhubarb.

"The dirt is good for the soul," Lucy always joked.

"Again?" I asked, arching an eyebrow. "Didn't I just tell the story last night before bed?"

"Maktub," Talon replied with a sly grin. "It means *it is written*, which means you were supposed to tell the story again."

I laughed. "Is that so?" I asked, walking over to her and scooping her into my arms.

She giggled. "Yes!"

"Well, okay, since it is written after all," I joked. I walked her over to Professor Oliver's tree, where three chairs were lined up, two full-size chairs and one child's plastic chair. I placed Talon in her chair, and I took mine beside her. "So it all began when I was in college and failed my first paper."

I told her the story of how Professor Oliver came into my life and how he planted a seed in my heart that grew into love. He was my best friend, my father, my family. Talon always loved the story too. The way she smiled as she listened closely always filled me up with love. She listened like Lucy—wholeheartedly with a sparkle in her eyes.

When I finished the story, Talon stood up as she did every time, walked over to the tree, and hugged it tight. "I love you, Grandpa Ollie," she whispered, giving the bark a kiss.

"Again?" Lucy asked, speaking of Professor Oliver's story as she walked outside. She waddled over to Talon and me, with her full-grown pregnant stomach, and when she lowered herself to her chair, she sighed heavily as if she'd just run a full 5K.

"Again." I smiled before I bent over to her and kissed her lips and then her stomach.

"How was your nap, Mama?" Talon asked, filled to the brim with energy. It was amazing to watch her run around and grow excited. Years ago, she fit in the palm of my hand. Years ago, it wasn't certain that she'd survive, and today, she was the definition of life.

"Nap was good," Lucy replied, yawning, still tired.

Any day now, we'd be losing even more sleep each night.

I'd never been more excited and ready in my life.

"You need anything?" I asked. "Water? Juice? Five pizzas?"

She grinned and closed her eyes. "Just the sun for a little bit."

The three of us sat outside for hours, soaking in the sunlight. It felt amazing, being surrounded by my family.

Family.

I somehow ended up with a family. Never in my life had I thought I would end up like this—happy. The two girls who sat beside me were my world, and the little boy who would be here soon was already controlling my heartbeat.

When it was time to go prepare dinner, I helped Lucy out of her chair, and the minute she stood, we both paused for a moment.

"Mama, why did you pee your pants?" Talon asked, looking over at Lucy.

I cocked an eyebrow, realizing what had just happened. "Hospital?" I asked.

"Hospital," she replied.

Everything was different from when Talon was born. My son was welcomed into the world at eight pounds and three ounces. He came into the world screaming, allowing us all to be aware of his strong lungs.

I often looked back on the happiest seconds of my life and wondered how a man like me became so blessed. There was the moment Talon was released from the NICU. The first time Professor Oliver called me son. The time Lucy first told me she loved me. The second when the adoption papers went through for Talon to officially become Lucy's and my daughter. My wedding day. And now, as I held my handsome son for the first time in my arms.

Oliver James Russell.

Ollie for short.

We headed home one day after Ollie was born, and before Talon was off to bed that night, she walked over to her brother, who was sleeping in Lucy's arms, and kissed his forehead. "I love you, baby Ollie," she whispered, and my heart expanded more. It grew each day, being surrounded by my loves.

I carried Talon to her bed, knowing in the middle of the night, she'd find herself sleeping between her mother and me. I welcomed her each night with a hug and a kiss, because I knew there would come a day when she wouldn't be lying beside Lucy and me. I knew there would come a day when she was too old and too cool to be near her parents. So whenever she wandered into our room, I held her tight and thanked the universe for having my daughter to show me what true love looked like.

After Talon was tucked in, I headed back to the nursery where Lucy was falling asleep in the gliding chair with Ollie still resting. I took him from her arms and laid him in his crib, gently kissing his forehead.

"Bedtime," I whispered to my wife, kissing her cheek and helping her stand.

"Bedtime," she muttered back, yawning as I helped her to our room.

After I pulled back the covers on the bed and laid her down, I crawled into bed beside her and held her close to me.

Her lips brushed against my neck as she moved in closer. "Happy?" she yawned.

I kissed her forehead. "Happy," I replied.

"I love you, my Graham Cracker," she said softly seconds before she fell asleep.

"I love you, my Lucille," I said, kissing her forehead.

As we lay there that night, I thought about our story. How she found me when I was lost. How she saved me when I needed her the most. How she forced me to stop pushing people away and proved to me that real love wasn't something from fairy-tale books. She taught me that real love took time. Real love took work. Real love took communication. Real love only grew if those involved took the time to nurture it, to water it, to give it light.

Lucille Hope Russell was my love story, and I promised myself I'd spend the rest of my life being hers.

After all, maktub—it was already written.

We were destined to live happily ever after as our hearts floated near the stars and our feet remained on solid ground.

Enjoy this brand-new annotated chapter as Brittainy Cherry takes you on a tour of the world of The Gravity of Us

CHAPTER 1
Graham

2017

Two days before, I'd bought flowers for someone who wasn't my wife. Since the purchase, I hadn't left my office. Papers were scattered all around—note cards, Post-it notes, crumpled pieces of paper with pointless scribbles and words crossed out. On my desk sat five bottles of whisky and an unopened box of cigars.

My eyes burned from exhaustion, but I couldn't shut them as I stared blankly in front of me at my computer screen, typing words I'd later delete.

I never bought my wife flowers.

I never gave her chocolates on Valentine's, I found stuffed animals ridiculous, and I didn't have a clue what her favorite color was.

She didn't have a clue what mine was either, but I knew her favorite politician. I knew her views on global warming, she knew my views on religion, and we both knew our views on children: we never wanted them. *no babies!*

Those things were what we agreed mattered the most; those things were our glue. We were both driven by career and had little time for each other, let alone family.

I wasn't romantic, and Jane didn't mind because she wasn't either. We weren't often seen holding hands or exchanging kisses in public. We weren't into snuggling or social media expressions of love, but that didn't mean our love wasn't real. We cared in our own way. We were a logical couple who understood what it meant to be in love, to be committed to each other, yet we never truly dived into the romantic aspects of a relationship.

Our love was driven by a mutual respect, by structure. Each big decision we made was always thoroughly thought out and often involved diagrams and charts. The day I asked her to be my wife, we made fifteen pie and flow charts to make sure we were making the right decision.

Romantic?

Maybe not.

Logical?

Absolutely.

he will be romantic later on...

Which was why her current invasion of my deadline was concerning. She never interrupted me while I was working, and for her to barge in while I was on a deadline was beyond bizarre.

I had ninety-five thousand more to go.

Ninety-five thousand words to go before the manuscript went to the editor in two weeks. Ninety-five thousand words equated to an average of six thousand seven hundred eighty-six words a day. That meant the next two weeks of my life would be spent in front of my computer, hardly pulling myself away for a breath of fresh air.

My fingers were on speed, typing and typing as fast as they could.

The purplish bags under my eyes displayed my exhaustion, and my back ached from not leaving my chair for hours. Yet when I sat in front of my computer with my drugged-up fingers and zombie eyes, I felt more like myself than any other time in my life.

"Graham," Jane said, breaking me from my world of horror and bringing me into hers. "We should get going."

She stood in the doorway of my office. Her hair was curly, which was bizarre seeing as how her hair was always straight. Each day, she awoke hours before me to tame the curly blond mop on her head. I could count on my right hand the number of times I'd seen her with her natural curls. Along with the wild hair, her makeup was smudged, left on from the night before.

I'd only seen my wife cry two times since we'd been together: one time when she learned she was pregnant seven months ago, and another when some bad news came in four days ago.

"Shouldn't you straighten your hair?" I asked.

"I'm not straightening my hair today."

"You always straighten your hair."

"I haven't straightened my hair in four days." She frowned, but I didn't make a comment about her disappointment. I didn't want to deal with her emotions that afternoon. For the past four days, she'd been a wreck, the opposite of the woman I married, and I wasn't one to deal with people's emotions.

What Jane needed to do was pull herself together.

I went back to staring at my computer screen, and my fingers started moving quickly once more.

"Graham," she grumbled, waddling over to me with her very pregnant stomach. "We have to get going."

"I have to finish my manuscript."

"You haven't stopped writing for the past four days. You hardly make it to bed before three in the morning, and then you're up by six. You need a break. Plus, we can't be late."

I cleared my throat and kept typing. "I decided I'm going to have to miss out on this silly engagement. Sorry, Jane."

Out of the corner of my eye, I saw her jaw slacken. "Silly engagement? Graham…it's your father's funeral."

"You say that as if it should mean something to me."

"It does mean something to you."

"Don't tell me what does and doesn't mean something to me. It's belittling."

"You're tired," she said.

There you go again, telling me about myself. "I'll sleep when I'm eighty, or when I'm my father. I'm sure he's sleeping well tonight."

She cringed. I didn't care.

"You've been drinking?" she asked, concerned.

"In all the years of us being together, when have you ever known me to drink?"

She studied the bottles of alcohol surrounding me and let out a small breath. "I know, sorry. It's just…you added more bottles to your desk."

"It's a tribute to my dear father. May he rot in hell."

"Don't speak so ill of the dead," Jane said before hiccupping and placing her hands on her stomach. "God, I hate that feeling." She took my hands away from my keyboard and placed them on her stomach. "It's like she's kicking me in every internal organ I have. I cannot stand it."

"How motherly of you," I mocked, my hands still on her.

"I never wanted children." She breathed out, hiccupping once more. "*Ever.*"

"Yet here we are," I replied. I wasn't certain Jane had fully come to terms with the fact that in two short months, she'd be giving birth to an actual human being who would need her love and attention twenty-four hours a day.

If there was anyone who gave love less than I did, it was my wife.

"God," she murmured, closing her eyes. "It just feels weird today."

"Maybe we should go to the hospital," I offered.

"Nice try. You're going to your father's funeral."

Damn. he really doesn't want you

"We still need to find a nanny," she said. "The firm gave me a few weeks off for maternity leave, but I won't need all the time if we find a decent nanny. I'd love a little old Mexican lady, preferably one with a green card."

My eyebrows furrowed, disturbed. "You do know saying that is not only disgusting and racist, but saying it to your half-Mexican husband is also pretty distasteful, right?"

"You're hardly Mexican, Graham. You don't even speak a lick of Spanish."

"Which makes me non-Mexican. Duly noted, thank you," I said coldly. At times, my wife was the person I hated the most. While we agreed on many things, sometimes the words that left her mouth made me rethink every flowchart we'd ever made.

How could someone so beautiful be so ugly at times?

Kick. Graham will love

Kick. this kid...

My chest tightened, my hands still resting around Jane's stomach.

Those kicks terrified me. If there was anything I knew for certain, it was that I was not father material. My family history led me to believe anything that came from my line of ancestry couldn't be good.

I just prayed to God that the baby wouldn't inherit any of my traits—or worse, my father's.

Jane leaned against my desk, shifting my perfectly neat paperwork as my fingers lay still against her stomach. "It's time to hop in the shower and get dressed. I hung your suit in the bathroom."

"I told you, I cannot make this engagement. I have a deadline to meet."

"While you have a deadline to meet, your father has already met his deadline, and now it's time to send off his manuscript."

"His manuscript being his casket?"

Jane's brows furrowed. "No. Don't be silly. His body is the manuscript; his casket is the book cover."

"A freaking expensive book cover too. I can't believe he picked one that is lined with gold." I paused and bit my lip. "On second thought, I easily believe that. You know my father."

"So many people will be there today. His readers, his colleagues."

Hundreds would show up to celebrate the life of Kent Russell. "It's going to be a circus," I groaned. "They'll mourn for him, in complete and utter sadness, and they'll sit in disbelief. They'll start pouring in with their stories, with their pain. 'Not Kent, it can't be. He's the reason I even gave this writing thing a chance. Five years sober because of that man. I cannot believe he's gone. Kent Theodore Russell, a man, a father, a hero. Nobel Prize winner. Dead.' The world will mourn."

"And you?" Jane asked. "What will you do?"

"Me?" I leaned back in my chair and crossed my arms. "I'll finish my manuscript."

"Are you sad he's gone?" Jane asked, rubbing her stomach.

Her question swam in my mind for a beat before I answered. "No." I wanted to miss him. → so sad! 7

I wanted to love him.

I wanted to hate him.

I wanted to forget him.

mixed emotions[8]

But instead, I felt nothing. It had taken me years to teach myself to feel nothing toward my father, to erase all the pain he'd inflicted on me, on the ones I loved the most. The only way I knew how to shut off the hurt was to lock it away and forget everything he'd ever done to me, to forget everything I'd ever wished him to be.

Once I locked the hurt away, I almost forgot how to feel completely. Jane didn't mind my locked-away soul, because she didn't feel much either.

"You answered too quickly," she told me.

"The fastest answer is always the truest."

facts[9]

"I miss him," she said, her voice lowering, communicating her pain over the loss of my father. In many ways, Kent Russell was a best friend to millions through his storybooks, his inspirational speeches, and the persona and brand he sold to the world. I would've missed him too if I didn't know the man he truly was in the privacy of his home.

"You miss him because you never actually knew him. Stop moping over a man who's not worth your time."

"No," she said sharply, her voice heightened with pain. Her eyes started to water over as they'd been doing for the past few days. "You don't get to do that, Graham. You don't get to undermine my hurt. Your father was a good man to me. He was good to me when you were cold, and he stood up for you every time I wanted to leave, so you don't get to tell me to stop moping. You don't get to define the kind of sadness I feel," she said, full-blown emotion taking over her body as she shook with a flood of tears falling from her eyes.

I tilted my head toward her, confused by her sudden outburst, but then my eyes fell to her stomach.

Hormonal mess.

"Whoa," I muttered, a bit stunned.

She sat up straight. "What was that?" she asked, a bit frightened.

"I think you just had an emotional breakdown over the death of my father."

She took a breath and groaned. "Oh my God, what's wrong with me? These hormones are making me a mess. I hate everything about being pregnant. I swear I'm getting my tubes tied after this." She stood up, trying to pull herself together, and wiped away her tears as she took more deep breaths. "Can you at least do me one favor today?"

"What's that?"

"Can you pretend you're sad at the funeral? People will talk if they see you smiling."

I gave her a tight fake frown.

She rolled her eyes. "Good, now repeat after me: my father was truly loved, and he will be missed dearly."

"My father was truly a dick, and he won't be missed at all."

She patted my chest. "Close enough. Now go get dressed."

Standing up, I grumbled the whole way.

"Oh! Did you order the flowers for the service?" Jane hollered my way as I slid my white T-shirt over my head and tossed it onto the bathroom floor.

"All five thousand dollars' worth of useless plants for a funeral that will be over in a few hours."

"People will love them," she told me.

"People are stupid," I replied, stepping into the burning water falling from the showerhead. In the water, I tried my best to think of what type of eulogy I'd deliver for the man who was a hero to many but a devil to me. I tried to dig up memories of love, moments of care, seconds of pride he'd delivered me, but I came up blank. Nothing. No real feelings could be found.

The heart inside my chest—the one he'd helped harden— remained completely numb.

Annotated Chapter Guide

Images and words on page 294: Thought bubble surrounding chapter title. Square surrounding dateline. A row of flowers midway down the page.

    1. *No babies!*

Images and words on page 295: A heart at the top and the bottom of the page, connected by a squiggle line.

    2. *He will be romantic later on...*

Images and words on page 296: Squiggle lines at the top of the page. A heart midway down the page.

    3. *Underlined text:* "'I have to finish my manuscript.'" *Work, work, work...*

Images and words on page 297: Drawing of hearts at the top, bottom-left, and bottom right of the page, connected with squiggle lines and dots. A frowny face.

    4. *So grumpy...*

Images and words on page 298: A design of inverting Vs across the side and bottom of the page.

> 5. *He really doesn't want to.*
> 6. *Graham will love this kid...*

Images and words on page 299: Drawing of hearts at the top and bottom-left of the page, connected with squiggle lines.

> 7. Underlined text: "I wanted to miss him." *So sad!*

Images and words on page 300: A design of alternating Vs and ls down the side of the page. A squiggle line bracketed by dots along the bottom of the page.

> 8. Boxed text: "I wanted to love him. I wanted to hate him. I wanted to forget him." *Mixed emotions.*
> 9. *Facts.*

Images and words on page 301: Drawing of hearts down the edge of the page. Drawing of a squiggle along the bottom of the page.

> Boxed text: "My father was truly a dick, and he won't be missed at all."
> Boxed text: "'People will love them,' she told me. 'People are stupid.'"

Images and words on page 302: Drawing of three large broken hearts.

Acknowledgments

Writing this novel was so hard for me, and so many people came through to help me get to those final words, *The End*. Yet there was one lady who truly listened to me fall apart and then helped piece me back together with this book. She spent hours on the phone with me talking me through it, and when I deleted seventy thousand words, she held my hand and told me I could start over and make it even better. Staci Brillhart—you were my rock with this book. You kept me grounded when I wanted to float away, and you were nothing more than a concrete angel for me. I have no clue how I've been lucky enough to meet someone like you, who is patient and caring and always there for me. But I thank you from the bottom of my heart for holding my hand and listening to my tears. I'm always here for you if you need me, day or night, my friend. You are the reason I believe in the good of this world.

To Kandi Steiner and Danielle Allen—two women who make my heart soar. You two are the definitions of strength, charm, and loyalty. Thank you for reading parts of this book, listening to my panics, and still loving me the same. You both are two of the best things to come from this book world. I adore you both more than words could ever say, my loves!

To my tribe of women who lift each other up and cheer for one another's success: How lucky am I to know such beauty?

To Samantha Crockett: You're my best friend. Thank you for the encouraging memes to get me through this book. Thank you for the trips to Chicago to get my mind off the book. And thank you for being my very best friend. I'm blessed to know you, and I love you wildly. Even if you like peas.

To Talon, Maria, Allison, Tera, Alison, Christy, Tammy, and Beverly, my favorite group of betas in the world: Thank you for challenging me and not letting my words settle with just being decent. You all make my stories stronger, and because of your voices, I'm learning to find my own. *Thank you* isn't enough, but since you aren't beta reading this part, you can't tell me how to make it better. Haha!

A big, big thank-you to my copy editors, Ellie at Love N Books and Caitlin at Editing by C. Marie. Thanks for giving your all to my messy words and polishing them until they shine. Oh, and thanks for dealing with me going, "Wait! Let me add this!"

Virginia, Emily, and Alison—the best proofreaders in the world. Those small details and those annoying commas that I overdose on: thanks for helping fix those weird mistakes. I'd say I'll do better next time, but I fear that's a lie.

To my amazing editing team at Sourcebooks Casablanca. Thank you for cleaning up my messes. I'd be nowhere without your help!

To my family and friends who somehow still like me even though I mostly live in a writing cave for a good amount of my life. Thank you for understanding that sometimes I stop midconversation and go to my notepad to write down random words. Thank you for understanding that sometimes I play the same songs on repeat when writing certain scenes. And thank you for loving me even on the days (okay, weeks) when I don't make my bed or put on makeup. Living with a writing zombie must be awkward, but still, you all love me.

And finally: To you. And you. And you. Thank you for reading this book. Thank you for giving me a chance. Without you all, the readers and bloggers, I would just be a girl with a dream and a novel that's unread. You changed my life. Thank you for pushing me to be better with each novel. Thank you for showing up when I need you the most. Thank you for the messages that sometimes take me weeks to reply to (but I promise I read them all). Thank you for loving the written word and taking the time to open my books. I'm going to love you all forever and always. You're my Lucilles of the world. You're my heart. You're my favorite human beings of all human beings.

Maktub.

About the Author

Brittainy Cherry is an Amazon bestselling author who has always been in love with words. She graduated from Carroll University with a bachelor's degree in theatre arts and a minor in creative writing. Brittainy lives in Milwaukee, Wisconsin, with her family. When she's not running a million errands and crafting stories, she's probably playing with her adorable pets.

Website: bcherrybooks.com
Facebook: BrittainyCherryAuthor
Instagram: @bcherryauthor